BELOVED

Little
DOZEN
press

Beloved

Published by Little Dozen Press
Stevensville, Ontario, Canada
www.littledozen.com

Cover design by Mercy Hope
Copyright 2015

ISBN: 978-1-927658-43-7

BELOVED

BOOK 3 OF THE PROPHET TRILOGY

by Rachel Starr Thomson

Little Dozen Press
2015

In memory of Kathy Vanzandt,
Friend, prayer warrior, true believer.
When revival comes to my generation,
it will be the result of your prayers.
Thank you for believing in us.

PROLOGUE

The wiry, hairy figure crossed the desert slowly, as though he were a drifting tumbleweed and not a man. Hawks and hoopoes that flew overhead eyed him as he ambled from one place to another, digging here, rooting there, wandering in caves and shadows through the days and the nights.

At night he sat, awake, and gazed at the stars.

His name was Kohan, and he was not drifting, not aimless. No, rather, he was searching for something.

The stars above told a story. The constellation Isha, the Beloved, ran toward the Dragon with its jaws open to devour her.

For more than four decades Kohan had waited to see that story play out on the desert mountains of the Sacred Land. In that time he had lost himself, lost his name, lost his humanity. They had called him Kol Abaddon, the Voice of Destruction.

But now he searched. To find the missing piece of the story in the stars.

And, perhaps, to find himself.

His wandering led him into a narrow valley overshadowed by

towering sandstone pillars that gazed silently down on him. His pulse quickened at the sight of a dark recess in the base of the tallest of the red giants. Wordless, adrenaline surging, he reached the recess and knelt at its mouth, digging in the sand until he had carved away the dirt from an opening much wider and deeper than initially met the eye.

When his hand touched it, tears filled his eyes. He paused a moment, breath caught in his throat, hovering in the space between the desert and the cool object still half-buried in the dark.

He found his breath again and kept digging until there could be no doubt. The contours of the object appeared beneath his dust-coated hands, and then, farther back in the recess, the second one. Two tablets of stone, as tall as a small man and easily as heavy as one.

Kohan wrestled the tablets out of the tomb where they had been buried since a time long ago, a time before the Sacred Land forgot its God and began its rush toward the Dragon.

The covenant stones. It was time for them to go home.

CHAPTER 1

Rechab went through her morning oblations woodenly. Sleeves rolled to her elbows, she dipped her hands in the bowl of cold water and brought it to her face, washing away the sweat and dust of the night. She knew she dressed and readied herself too slowly. Aaron and the others were waiting for her.

When she had ruled over her desert caravan, Flora had always started every day with prayer. So now, queen in Flora's stead, Rechab was expected to do the same. It was important, Aaron insisted. It would draw them together, unite them.

Unite them with the newcomers, who saw Aaron and Rechab and their outpost as some sort of restoration of the Sacred Land's true leadership and purpose.

Rechab suspected what they were building was treason, and she trembled. But she did not have the courage or the clarity to stop Aaron, in his growing passion and strength, or to question those who came so ardently to his side, to sacrifice, worship, mine, and even fight alongside him.

Not for the first time, she wondered what Flora would think of all this. Rechab had come with Flora's caravan, impersonating her friend with Flora's approval in order to remain hidden and protected. When beggars in the village of Nachush had pleaded with them to intervene on their behalf with the local elders, who were unjust, oppressive taskmasters, Aaron had urged Rechab to use Flora's money and power to make a difference. Things had spun out of control from there, until the elders were deposed—most killed—and Rechab had become the face of a movement to cast off oppression. As much as Aaron assured her she was doing right, that the governor's sister would wholeheartedly approve, Rechab wondered if she wasn't just heaping up more damning substance to Flora's long-time appellate, "Unlucky."

That was the one bright side to their growing notoriety. Word would carry to wherever Flora was, and then, if she felt the way Rechab suspected she would, the mistress herself would come sweeping in and put everything right.

Rechab just had to hold on until then. Hold on, and try to do right by the Great God.

Drying her face on a linen towel, Rechab finished dressing and faced the cave entrance. Light was streaming through, sparkling on her wash water. She could of course have taken up residence in the village, but she did not want to. She and Aaron and the other leaders had all opted to stay in the caves on the mountainside, facing the sunrise, hidden in the rock, above the village and its recent, still-raw memories.

She stepped out onto the limestone ledge and soaked up the brilliant morning sun as it warmed her arms and legs and dried the last of the water from her face.

Below, the village streets filled with people like a conduit bringing water in a single direction: toward the entrance to the mines, where Aaron had erected an altar.

Rechab descended the mountainside to join the flow. She was aware of the bodyguards who fell into step behind her and the eyes

 RACHEL STARR THOMSON

that turned to watch her come down. The people altered their paths to clear a space for Rechab to walk in their midst.

Some of those who joined the parade on its way to the altar were long-time residents of Nachush. Others—many others—were not. Warriors, seekers, pilgrims. They had been arriving in the city by the dozens. The villagers saw their chance to regain their fortunes and turned their homes into inns, mostly keeping a wary distance from the newcomers but happy enough to give them a roof and collect their coin. Even in the streets, they divided like sheep from goats on their way to the altar.

By the time they arrived at the clearing at the head of the street, Rechab's stomach was churning. She had done this now every day for weeks, and every day her misgivings grew worse.

Aaron stood by the altar, wearing a green silk shirt and a matching turban. A gold ring glinted in his ear. His jaw taut, golden eyes scanning the gathering crowd, he was beautiful.

And she loved him.

Didn't she?

She chided herself for asking that question as her feet carried her over the sandy ground to the rise where the altar stood. Her bodyguards closed in more tightly behind her, and others fell into the ritual procession they'd done now daily for weeks, arraying themselves to either side and behind her as she reached the altar.

Of course she loved him.

And anyway, they were in this together now. Bound together. They could not change this. They'd made fate when they took this city for the Great God. Made it and now were under its control.

The altar, beaten out of local bronze by a smith who had come to them shortly after the takeover, glimmered dully in the sunlight. It had replaced the rough stone altar Aaron originally built for them here.

Rechab took a deep breath as she peered down at its inlaid surface. *You know what to do.*

She picked up a small pouch of incense from the side of the altar and ceremoniously poured it over the surface. A servant on her right—one of Flora's retinue—handed her a lit torch, and she touched it to the incense and watched it spark and flare, catching with a rush of spiced, heady scent that began to rise in curling tendrils of smoke to the heavens.

Covering her face and rocking on her feet, Rechab spoke-sang a prayer. "Our Great God, see us here before you. We offer our worship and ask your protection. Purify us, O Lord, in this your valley of the Sacred Land. Amen."

The voices of the worshipers—some two or three hundred, spread through the valley and up the sides of the hills, chanted the "Amen" after her.

Rechab lifted her hands and her voice. "Let the sacred fire burn throughout the day and bring the Great God's eyes upon us always!"

"Amen!" the crowd sang.

"Let the sacred fire purify our hearts!"

"Amen!"

"Let the . . ."

Unexpectedly, her voice faltered. She swallowed. "Let justice come upon our land and purge all our unrighteousness."

"Amen."

She closed her eyes for a moment as she held out her hands. Another servant, this one from her right, placed a bird into her palms. Her fingers closed around its warmth, its soft feathers, its still-beating heart.

 RACHEL STARR THOMSON

She hated this part.

She held the bird aloft.

"Let the Great God see our offering and cover our sins."

Lowering it, she waited while Aaron took a dagger and cut the bird's throat. Carefully, she spilled the blood over the surface of the altar, not extinguishing the still-burning incense.

The last "Amen" carried through the air. She felt as though a weight had lifted off her chest.

The deed was done for the day.

But it had not been the only weight pressing on her, and her heart was still heavy.

Aaron offered his arm as the crowd began to disperse. "May I walk you back?" he asked.

She nodded. He already knew where she wanted to go—back to her cave. It had become her ritual. Emerge, too slowly, for the morning rites at the altar. Go back and remain cloistered until evening, when she would join Aaron and the elders and all who were notable among the newcomers for a feast.

Her pulse quickened a little as she rested her hand in the crook of Aaron's strong arm. They were to be wed in a fortnight.

He had wanted the deed done days ago, but she had asked for more time.

More time to . . . she didn't know what.

Perhaps to mourn Alack, her childhood friend and first love, who had disappeared into the desert to become a prophet. Or to remember her old life with her father, to honor those who had raised her—the household of servants she called "family" in the absence of a mother or of sisters who truly cared for her. Or to think of Flora.

She wondered again where Flora was.

Why she had not yet come to end this charade.

Maybe Aaron was right, and Flora approved of their work so strongly that she had decided to leave them alone in perpetuity, giving up her name and fortune forever. Rechab understood now why Flora had always seen both as a burden.

Aaron covered her hand with his. The gesture was gentle, reassuring. His unspoken words had not changed: *You are doing the right thing. This is right, Rechab. It is what Flora would want. We are helping these people. We are serving the Great God. This is what you wanted, what we wanted.*

But she looked away from him, and her hand beneath his was stiff. Her eyes swept the valley with its village, the mines in the distance, the crowds. She still shuddered at every memory of the takeover. Of the blood Aaron had shed. Why, if this was right, did she need so much reassurance?

She no longer believed that Flora would approve of this, nor that her use of Flora's name and money was justified. She was stealing from the woman who had given so much from her. She only wished Flora would hurry back to stop her.

She surely did not have the courage to stop herself.

"The birds are such a small thing, Rechab," Aaron said abruptly. They were still fifty paces from her refuge—her cavern where no one else could come, not him, not anyone. "I know it pains you to shed blood, but the sacrifice means so much to the people—"

"It's not the birds," she said.

He tightened his grip on her hand. Trapping her against his arm. Her weakness against his strength.

All at once it was too much. Her eyes filled with tears, and she

     RACHEL STARR THOMSON

wrested away from him and rushed for her cave.

"Rechab!" he called after her. "I—"

But she only curled up in the darkness, shaking, leaving the oil lamp unlit and her prayers unprayed. She wanted to weep but could not.

She stayed there, unmoving, until he headed uncertainly away.

Flora, she thought. *Where are you?*

———◆———

Flora rode in darkness with her hands bound in front of her. Amon, the Southern Trader who had taken her captive, did not want her visible to anyone they might encounter on the road, so she sat within a covered wagon drawn by oxen. Guards, silent, sat at either end of the cart. Whether they had no wish to speak to her or simply did not dare to do so, she didn't know.

The deaths of the men who had befriended her, the guards she had spoken to so freely, played out before her eyes again and again. She would not open her mouth even if these, their replacements, wanted her to. If the blood of those men was on Amon's head, not on hers, it was still far too connected to her. Like so many other deaths.

Flora Laurentii Infortunatia—Flora the Unlucky—had always been followed by death. The tragedy was that it only seemed to take those whose orbit brought them close to her and never so much as nipped at her own heels.

That, at least, was likely to change.

The cart bumped over rocks and pits in the rutted desert roads. Beneath the cover the air grew stifling hot.

Flora just concentrated on breathing.

Her first two husbands had died of disease and old age while she remained young and as healthy as an especially healthy horse. The guards had died for befriending her while she remained Amon's prized possession. The grief was overwhelming; the guilt was worse.

Of course, Flora was no stranger to guilt.

Without warning, she stood, kicked aside the heavy wagon covering, and jumped down to the dirt road, narrowly avoiding twisting an ankle. Ignoring the surprised yelps of the guards and the flurry of consternation that arose from the caravan as soon as anyone spotted her, she tossed her head and marched toward the head of the line where she knew Amon was riding. Her injured shoulder throbbed from the jump, but she ignored that too.

As she walked, Flora yanked at the ropes around her wrists, but they held—as they had done every time she tried, rubbing her wrists raw in the process. She bit her lip against the pain.

Amon, riding in state on camelback at the head of the procession, turned at the sound of the shouts behind her. His kohl-lined eyes widened as she reached his camel, then immediately looked behind her. "Where are your guards?"

"Coming, I have no doubt." The sound of pounding feet behind her confirmed that. She wondered what had taken them so long.

"What do you think you're doing?"

"Breathing. It's stifling hot in there."

"Flora, you do not seem to understand that you are a prisoner here."

She almost laughed at that. "Oh, I understand. Believe me."

"Then I suggest you return to the cart and comport yourself like one."

The guards had arrived and were maintaining a respectful difference while she spoke to their leader—or owner, more likely.

 RACHEL STARR THOMSON

"It's dizzying, Amon, keeping up with your requirements. You didn't like me to comport myself as a prisoner when I first got here."

"That was before you interfered with my business. I suggest you remember what happens when you cross me."

Her eyes glinted. "You don't have anyone left to threaten me with, Amon. No one dares even speak to me now."

His gaze was pointed. "I'm not above threatening you with innocents."

She glared daggers at him but didn't say another word. The guards hesitantly took her arms, and when she didn't fight and Amon just nodded, they led her back to the cart.

Nevertheless, they left the covering open at the back and front so air could get through. Flora breathed a little easier and silently blessed the Great God, who allowed her to dare gods and devils over and over again and never die.

She did not understand his ways.

The gaps that let in air also let in light, so Flora knew when the sun set and dusk fell. The caravan did not slow, continuing forward in torch-lit shadows. She wondered at the urgency that drove Amon. His caravan was large and well-armed, not at great risk from bandits or wild animals, but even so the desert held dangers in its wild night. Strange that he did not simply camp and begin again in the morning. The Holy City could not be more than another day's travel ahead; if they moved quickly up the road, they would make it before sunrise.

Her stomach sank deeper at the thought.

The night passed painstakingly slowly, but she did not feel tired. Her life lay before her in crystalline clarity, still and sharp. Her days spun out from childhood in a tapestry of escape: trying to run from the gods of the Hill People, trying to run to the Great God, trying to run to a higher way, a better way, and now ending here. Tangled in the ill-fated threads of her own flight.

The deep stab wound in Flora's shoulder ached dully, the ache growing into a throb that worsened as the night passed. She bit her tongue to keep from shouting against the pain. In her weakness she could wish for infection: for raging fever that would carry her off the way it had carried off her first husband before she could ever reach Shalem and the exchange that awaited her there: Amon's exchange of her life in return for favor with the new queen and the new queen's horrendous deity.

But her good health remained. Amon prized her too much. His physicians had cleaned the wound and kept it well tended. The pain she felt now was the pain of healing, of tissue knitting itself back together.

It was remarkable, really. Even with the attendance of the doctors, one would have expected such an attack to put her in a more precarious position. Mashi, she thought ruefully, must have stabbed her with an exceedingly clean and short knife.

The caravan rolled forward in near silence. Only the sounds of the camels and oxen lowing, of wheels rumbling over hard-packed earth, and of the occasional direction from a driver disturbed the calm before the storm.

She shifted to keep her balance as the road grew steeper and the oxen strained at the cart. The guards exchanged glances, barely visible in the scant light from torches lighting the caravan's way.

The Holy Mountain. The ascent to Shalem had begun.

Flora took a deep breath and offered a prayer. *You are with me. Be with me now.*

She did not expect an answer, and yet she heard one.

I am with you, Beloved.

 Rachel Starr Thomson

Her eyes filled with tears, and she shook her head in the darkness. Part of her recognized her own stubborn perversity: arguing with the Great God in the moment she needed him most!

But . . . Beloved?

Flora was many things, but not that.

Yet the terrible conversation with Amon, just before he killed the guards who had befriended her along with her faithful servant, Joachim, came back to her mind, and she remembered how he had claimed that she and others like her—people whose faith was in the Great God—were at the center of the Adversary's will because he hated them so much.

And she knew that to be true. She had felt the hatred of the god she now ascended toward, Kimash of the Hill People, the Dragon. She had felt it all her life and fled from it, taking refuge in the Great God of the Sacred Land even though, as a half-blood Hill Woman, she knew she did not belong.

If Kimash could hate her, could the Great God not love her?

She dismissed the question.

Foolish to try to discern the thoughts of the Divine, much less his emotions.

The road took them through Bethabara.

The town on the slopes of the Holy Mountain slept. She thought of Aurelius, her brother, and Marah, his wife, no doubt asleep with the people they governed. She would never again spring an unwanted visit on Aurelius, never again plead with him to save his soul by turning to the Great God as she had done. The thought made her cry and laugh at the same time, and the guards watched her, stoic and silent, as she dashed away mixed tears and let out a single sound of frustration.

She'd always known she was mortal, but she hadn't expected the end to come so soon, or to leave so much unfinished.

She prayed for Rechab. Chances that she would ever get word to the girl were slim to none, so she prayed that Rechab would have wisdom and would know what to do, and that Amon would never find her, and that she would continue to wear Flora's name and to manage all her wealth and possessions as Flora would have done. They had known one another for only a very short time, but Flora had no one else she would rather leave everything to. Rechab was a gentle, generous soul. She loved the Great God. She would care for Flora's servants and use the wealth well.

At least, Flora hoped she would.

The ascent grew steeper. As though day had dawned, the caravan became a dust storm of noise and activity as Amon's servants rearranged loads and rehitched the animals to enable them to pull more efficiently. Servants put their shoulders to the heavier loads, aiding from behind. Flora braced herself in the cart and clenched her teeth against the pain in her shoulder as every muscle strained to keep herself in place.

The sharp ascent would end quickly, and they would have reached Shalem. The gates of the city, with their high towers and watchmen, were not far ahead.

Through the noise of the caravan, other sounds began to fill the air. The noise of life in Shalem never entirely died away.

Flora felt the black cloud the moment they entered the city walls. It was the same darkness that had hovered here for some time now. Long ago, in her youth when she first fled Kimash, the Holy City was the place where the Great God's presence still dwelt. The city and its sacred temple had represented his presence at the heart of the Sacred Land, and with his presence and his priests were justice, and refuge, and hope.

　RACHEL STARR THOMSON

But that had changed. Even in those days the Holy People had not been faithful to the Great God, worshiping idols at shrines in the streets and in their homes. Even then, they had welcomed the influence of Kimash of the Hills and Amon-Heth of the Southern Plains, and the heavenly bodies and too many other little gods to mention. But things had grown far worse. The gods had moved into the temple itself, leaving only the inner sanctum—the Holy Place—consecrated to the Great God. Amon had hinted to her that even that sanctuary had been desecrated, though she refused to believe it.

On principle alone, she would not believe that.

And as the People had left the worship of the Great God, a shadow had spread over the city. Flora could feel it whenever she visited, growing in power and influence with every year and month that passed, until she had finally stopped going altogether, unable to bear the weight of darkness and the sorrow of watching the People in decline.

It pushed down on her now, oppressive as tar, sharpening the throbbing in her shoulder and threatening to drown her in fear and dread.

But a word cut through it.

Beloved.

The road leveled and changed to the clatter of paving stones. The air grew thick with incense and the oily smoke of lamps and braziers. City lights flashed through the cart, drawing slow stripes of illumination across the interior until Flora's guards exchanged glances once more and then drew the gaps in the covering closed.

She was plunged into darkness and totally alone. Footsteps and voices outside told her that other guards had come to surround the cart, guarding Amon's gift to the god Kimash.

Flora drew her knees up and hooked her arms around them. She didn't know exactly where they were headed, but it could not be much further now.

CHAPTER 2

On the balcony of his villa outside Shalem, Aurelius Florus Laurentinus stared down through the night at the city lights. Palm fronds whispered above him as a breeze passed through. The stars above shone peacefully.

Aurelius's soul was in turmoil.

The movements at the borders of his property were not hidden from him. The soldiers stationed there to prevent him from leaving. He was a prisoner in his own home, though the king, Beniah, denied it vehemently. The soldiers were there to protect him, Beniah said, in these troubled times.

Aurelius snorted. Beniah himself was the trouble. Beniah and his cursed wife and her cursed uncle and his cursed assassins.

But even as curses spilled through his mind, agitating him into pacing the length of the balcony, he cursed himself too. Always smooth-tongued, always in control of every situation, he had opened his mouth in the presence of Beniah and his allies and destroyed more with every word than any ruthless conqueror could have done.

Because of him, Bethabara was betrayed. The little city he had so carefully governed for so many years would be turned over to someone else, because Aurelius had protested the slaughter of a household by the high priest of Kimash.

Because of him, the high priest would find Rechab and force her into marriage.

Because of him, Izevel would send soldiers to destroy Essea, the religious community where Flora had lived most of her adult life.

Because of him, Flora herself would be brought here—for what ends Aurelius could not imagine, but he had not missed the glances exchanged between Izevel and her uncle, and the uncanny resemblance between the queen and Aurelius's sister had to mean something.

Nothing good, of that he was certain.

The breeze picked up, sending the palms into a manic dance even as Aurelius paced harder, faster, the turmoil in his soul pounding itself out on the smooth marble floor.

At first the king and his allies had not indicated any intention to hobble Aurelius himself. They had assured him they would handle everything in Bethabara and sent him on his way. But before he could reach the villa to collect Marah and begin preparations to go home, soldiers had overtaken him with a letter from Beniah ordering him—diplomatically—to stay in Shalem.

For his own good. His own protection. To make sure things went "smoothly" in Bethabara.

Aurelius cursed aloud and smashed his hand against the railing of the balcony, not caring if the soldiers heard. They knew what kind of game they were playing. Let them hear their prisoner vent his frustration and anger.

"Are you going to pace and roar like a lion all night?" Marah asked, startling him. He hadn't realized she was there.

     RACHEL STARR THOMSON

He turned. Marah was leaning against the doorpost, wrapped in a scarlet shawl. Her hair was disheveled from sleep—or from tossing in the attempt to sleep. Her eyes were weary.

"We are hemmed in on every side," Aurelius said.

"Yes."

"Beniah is going to let them destroy everything."

The corner of Marah's mouth quirked. "Not *everything*."

"Everything that matters."

She pushed herself off the door frame and laid a soft hand on Aurelius's arm. "Bethabara?"

"And Flora. And Essea."

"Your definition of what matters has changed."

He met her eyes. They stood in one another's gaze for a long time, searching.

In the end he nodded. Yes, it had changed for him. And for her too. He saw that in her eyes.

Aurelius was descended from the people of the Westland. His was a family of foreigners who had managed to gain influence with the royal family of the Sacred Land two generations back. Marah's forebears were Holy People through and through: hers was an old family, old and landed aristocracy, descended in a pure line from those whom the Great God had first called his chosen and set apart. Her forefathers had built the temple and consecrated it. They had been the priests who offered sacrifices according to the Great God's dictates and taught his laws and justice to the People, before the books of the law had been ignored and forgotten, and many of the most important scrolls lost. In her features, in her blood, was a past that no longer seemed connected to the present.

And for the first time, that mattered to her.

"You can feel it, can't you?" she whispered. "The darkness here?"

He nodded. He and Marah had never spoken of spiritual things. Politics and power, governance and riches, fair policy and shrewd dealing: those were the ground on which they had forged their marriage alliance.

It seemed the ground was shifting beneath them both.

"All these years," Marah continued, her voice so soft he could hardly hear it and yet clear, "Kol Abaddon's warnings, judgment—it all seemed like so much rattling tin. Just noise. But I hear it all now. This place has changed. It has become something I do not recognize. Something broken and twisted."

"It has," Aurelius said.

She shuddered.

In twenty years of marriage, he had never seen her show fear. He laid his hand over hers, wished to comfort her.

"We have done our part," she said. "In bringing it here. In opening the gates to this . . . this evil."

"It's too late now," Aurelius said. "Too late to change it."

She met his gaze. "But is it too late to fight it?"

Out beyond the balcony, through the palm trees, a small cluster of soldiers gathered, their voices drifting over.

"We are hemmed in," Aurelius said.

She gripped his arm tighter, looking out toward the soldiers, her fingernails digging into his skin. He watched as her jaw set with determination.

She turned her eyes back to his. "It is not a sealed trap. A door will open."

He nodded. "When it does, we will walk through it."

"Promise me," she whispered.

He swallowed a lump in his throat. "I promise you."

They both knew he was promising more than escape. Yes, they would flee the villa. But they would not seek safety for themselves without also looking for some way to fight.

———◆———

In the shadows beneath the balcony, Shem listened to his master and his wife.

He should not have been able to hear them. They whispered. But the breeze blew the words straight to him. His ears were sharper than they had ever been. He was like a jackal: a prince of the night.

Silently he blessed Amon-Heth for his preternatural senses, for allowing him to hear what he needed to hear.

Shem too, servant in Aurelius's household all his life, had found new purpose. He too had found new ground beneath his feet.

He waited until Aurelius and Marah had left the balcony before continuing the ceremony they had interrupted.

Carefully, he sprinkled incense on the ground in the shape of an eye, surrounding the rabbit he had trapped and cut into pieces earlier that evening. Then, closing his hand over the amulet of Amon-Heth that he constantly wore, he waved his other over the sacrifice and chanted words under his breath.

Words that came to him from another world.

His pulse quickened as the strange language spoke itself through him. Fire danced in his veins. He took a flint, struck up a spark, and lit the incense and the little bundle of kindling beneath the rabbit and let the sacrifice burn.

In the smoke that rose from it, images took form.

He saw a woman with her eyes blindfolded and her hands outstretched, running. Before her a great, dark mouth opened up. Long, pointed teeth took shape. Wings stretched out from either side, rising into the night sky and stretching over Shem and the courtyard and the villa, over Shalem itself.

Glory, he thought; *glory, glory to the Dragon. Glory to the fire.*

The flames of the sacrifice leapt. Heat seared across his face. The Dragon breathed its breath of flame.

Shem awoke on his back, blinking against the light.

Sunlight in his eyes.

Sunrise.

He was still, sore, and confused. Where was . . .

Sitting up with a groan, he saw the remnants of the fire. His sacrifice.

He remembered the woman. The Dragon. And the teeth.

What he could not remember was what had happened after he saw those things in the thin, wavering smoke of the fire. What had happened to *him.*

An unreasonable fear gripped him: that Aurelius or his wife would have seen, would have found him lying there by the remnants of his sacrifice, and would know. But it was unreasonable because they hadn't seen; that much was obvious. If they had they would not have left him to lie there all night and awaken, stiff, in the dew.

His senses were all coming back to him now, in a confused rush, and he scrambled to his feet and kicked dirt over the fire, spreading the ashes and the charred remains of the rabbit so it would not be immediately obvious what had happened here or why. Aurelius, his human

 Rachel Starr Thomson

master, would not be pleased to know what Shem had been up to. He never had approved of dabbling in occult things.

But Shem grew indignant as he thought back to the conversation on the balcony that he had overheard. Neither of them had come right out and said it, but there was a shift in both the master and the mistress toward the religion of Shem's ancestors. Toward the so-called Great God, whom Shem did not worship.

He had chosen his god. He fingered the amulet of Amon-Heth and tucked it beneath his shirt. All his life he'd heard that he was one of the Holy People—one of the Great God's chosen race. Yet the Great God had never done anything for him, and Amon-Heth, god of the Southern Plains, had seen him in his obscurity and chosen him as a messenger.

Shem's chest swelled with pride as he wandered into the villa.

"There you are." Aurelius's voice, sharp and aimed straight at him from a corner of the veranda, startled Shem so he jumped.

Aurelius looked him over, displeasure twitching in the corners of his mouth. "Where have you been so early?"

"Tending the garden," Shem said.

"You look more like you were sleeping there." Aurelius stepped forward and looked Shem over one more time before turning away and saying over his shoulder, "Attend your mistress; she's looking for you. Marah is your responsibility, not the roses."

Shem bit back a protestation, nodded, and headed toward the lady's wing.

"And Shem," Aurelius said, stopping him in his tracks.

Shem turned slowly to face his master and lifted his chin, carefully masking his gaze so as not to betray anything he was thinking or feeling.

"Be careful," Aurelius said. "These days it seems everyone is choosing sides. It behooves a man to watch whose side he takes."

Shem nodded and hurried away.

CHAPTER 3

Jonah bar Kebna, the Teacher of Essea, stood and watched as the men of the community finished digging a hole in the soft earth between two white boulders in a hill above the river. They dug down till they reached the buried cave mouth and the cool, dry space within it: long Essea's secret, a hiding place for the books where they would be safe when destruction and judgment came.

Jonah had been there when the cave was first buried. It had been partly his idea, his and his brother's. His brother was long dead. Most who lived in Essea now had no memory of this place. The few who did watched or dug with grim expressions. They had never truly believed they would come to this pass.

Beside Jonah, Nadab the Trader also watched. He stood on unsteady legs, still recovering from the attack that had left him all but dead in the desert, before the brothers found him and brought him here as a sign that the Great God would give them a second chance. The sun was beginning to set over the dig, casting long shadows. The work had taken hours.

Nadab spoke through a throat that sounded perpetually parched. Since being drawn out of the wilderness, he had never ceased sounding thirsty. "It is treasure you will bury here?"

"In truth," Jonah said. "The greatest treasure Essea possesses."

"I knew of you in Bethabara," Nadab said, "but not that you had wealth to hide. All we ever heard was that you were simple and poor."

Jonah smiled to himself. Weeks ago, he would have taken Nadab's words as an attempt to finagle an estimate of the community's worth so that he could try to advantage himself in some way through it. Weeks ago Nadab had been a calculating, greedy man, no more treacherous than your average merchant but no less treacherous either. But he had changed. Death, loss, contrition, and the Great God's grace had changed him. His questions now were simple and honest observations. No angle to play. No gain to be had.

"You were not wrong," Jonah said. "What we have, no one in Bethabara would likely consider valuable. But it is valuable to us, and we would protect it with our lives. As we scatter, we will set the Sacred Land itself to watch over it."

Wonder and curiosity filled Nadab's face, sharpening the ever-present sadness that was there as well. "What treasure can be so precious to you and yet so without value to others?"

Jonah watched the digging and wondered whether to tell this man the whole truth. But after all, there was no real reason to hide it.

"What makes the Holy People holy?" he asked Nadab.

The merchant thought a moment, reddening as he said, "I do not know that answer as well as I should, but I was always told it was that the Great God chose us for himself."

"He did," Jonah said, his tone reassuring, as though he spoke to a young student. "And he made a covenant with us, one etched in stones. They are lost—the covenant stones. Hidden at the entrance to the Sacred Land, no one knows where. Buried in order to preserve them. But part and parcel with that covenant, he gave us also a law. Teachings. The way of righteousness, of justice."

 RACHEL STARR THOMSON

"They say that is lost too," Nadab observed.

"But that is only partly true," Jonah said. "The priests know a great deal of it by memory even now. The oral law was passed down for generations; the older of them still know it. But they ceased to teach it. Ceased to treat it as a treasure, ceased to pass it along to the People or to enforce it when called upon to judge. Instead they made deals with other gods and their priests, and deals with rulers and those who could give bribes, and justice was lost to us. The original scrolls on which the law was written, however . . ."

"Lost too," Nadab said. "That much I learned as a boy."

Here Jonah smiled. "But that too is only partly true."

Nadab gaped at him for a moment. "Here? You have the law here?"

Jonah nodded slowly. "Some of it. In the beginning the law was written on seven scrolls; we have four. The other three are truly lost. But we also studied under priests, and we learned all we could from them and wrote our own scrolls to recover the rest. We cannot know for certain. But we think we have a close approximation of the law in its entirety here. We have tried to teach and live it faithfully now for a generation." And his voice grew sad, heavy with the knowledge that they prepared to leave it all behind: the scrolls, the community, the hall where they prayed together, the way of life they had built.

They had no choice. Their enemies were coming for them. He was absolutely convinced of it.

Nadab was mulling over what he had been told. "To think," he said, shaking his head. "All this time. You have had the scrolls—some of the original books of the law—here!"

Jonah smiled wryly. "True believers have always said there was treasure here, if only others would seek it. So few ever did."

"I should have known," Nadab said. He reddened even more deeply. "Fool that I am . . . asking about your treasure. I should have known it would not be money. You saved my life, not for money, but because of this greater treasure of yours."

The big man's eyes filled with tears as though he were a child. "I think I have learned at long last what really matters. I only grieve that I learned it so late. Now, when everything is nearly lost, and because of me."

He fought to gain control of his voice. Jonah simply laid a hand on Nadab's shoulder and let him grieve. The man's simple tears reflected the pain in his own heart.

The diggers finished their work and emerged from the hole covered in grime, dust, and sweat. The clatter of wheels announced that the cart had arrived. Jonah turned to see it, pulled by a single ox, a simple two-wheeled cart filled with clay vessels containing three scrolls each. There were over twelve of the pots, holding the greatest treasure not only of Essea but also of the Sacred Land: the very word of the Great God entrusted to them. The four original scrolls were there, invisible to the eye but wrapped in protective skins and treated muslin to keep them supple and waterproof. The other scrolls were collected wisdom, the oral recollections of so many, the gathered precepts and principles of decades of Essea's most important work. They were full of repetition, it was true, as many men had attempted to catalog what many other men knew and remembered. Jonah himself had spent cumulative years of his life gathering, recording, editing, and guarding the information on those scrolls.

It was imperative the scrolls remain. If every man and woman among them were martyred as enemies of Kimash, the words of God had to outlast them.

"It is a good thing," Nadab said, tears now running unabashedly down his face as the Essean brothers carefully lifted the clay pots from the cart, two men to a vessel, maneuvering them with utmost care toward the black spot in the ground where they would go to rest. "Such a good thing that you love these words, that you guard them. Without them, I know it now, you would not have cared for me. Only the words of a true God could make men love their enemies."

The brothers were lowering the first of the vessels into the hole in the red sunlight of the waning day when Nadab finished speaking, and suddenly the world tilted around Jonah Bar Kebna and he saw clearly, for the first time in his life, that this was all wrong.

"Stop!" he yelled, startling himself, startling Nadab the Trader, startling the brothers and sisters surrounding the hole.

Micah, Jonah's trusted acolyte, ran toward him. "Teacher, what is it? What is wrong?"

"Stop, stop," Jonah said, waving his arms, tears blurring his vision so he could not see. He staggered forward, older than his age, and felt Micah's strong young hands steadying him.

"Stop," Jonah wheezed. He fell to his knees. His people were gathering around him, whispering with shocked, fearful voices.

And then Jonah looked up at them and smiled. He shook his white head. "This," he said, gesturing at the hole. "Can't you see? We've been wrong. Wrong. We've dug a hole to contain the word of God."

He got carefully to his feet and turned so he could see Essea behind him, on the other side of the hill from the river. The compound with its white walls stood where it had been since he and his brother laid the first stones so many years ago. Faithful and sterile as a tomb.

He shuddered. Was that what they had meant to do, so many years ago? Build a grave for the people of God? Was that the object of their youthful zeal, or had they somehow, along the years, lost their way?

"We built walls around the people of God," Jonah announced. "And all the time . . ." His voice cracked. He turned and looked for Nadab. The man stood close by, and Jonah beckoned for him to come closer.

The merchant did, looking uncertain, tears still running down his face. The attack had changed Nadab, made a child of him—in his heart, perhaps even in his mind. The eyes he turned on Jonah now were full of questions, yet trusting that the Teacher would have answers.

Jonah laid his hand on Nadab's shoulder and squeezed it. He looked at him for a moment, leaving his sentence unfinished. Looked at him as though he could see the mystery of his life solved in the tears in this man's eyes.

Yes. Yes, he saw clearly now. He saw the truth. He understood where they had gone wrong.

"All the time," he said, raising his voice so everyone could hear—as he had done so many times in the hall of Essea, teaching a small group of cloistered men and women the words of the scrolls and the prophecies of Kol Abaddon—"All the time, the People have needed the words of God brought to them. This man: he is the People. He is the chosen of the Great God. Can we bury the Great God's commands where he will never read them? Never hear them taught? Can we place a barrier of earth and rock between our God and the wounded People whom he loves?"

Decades of his own sermons came back to him in a rush. He heard himself denouncing the people: denouncing their idolatry, their sin, their love of money, their unfaithfulness. Declaring the Great God's anger with them. They were guilty, yes, just as Nadab had been. When this man came to them, he had been guilty of betraying his own daughter to a life worse than death, guilty of loving money more than kin, guilty of caring nothing whatever about the Great God. Yet he had come to them wounded, next to death, and what else could Essea do but care for him?

After all—and now Jonah's guilt poured back, his torment over his own betrayal of Rechab, of driving out Flora Laurentii, and of causing the Great God to abandon them—after all, were they not guilty too?

 Rachel Starr Thomson

If there was grace for one such as Nadab—as clearly there was—and grace for one such as Jonah Bar Kebna—as there evidently was also—could there not be grace for the People, for the whole Sacred Land?

But they would never know if they did not hear the words. If the scrolls went into the ground. If the Esseans simply moved to some new cloister.

They were all staring at him. Jonah's hand still lay on Nadab's shoulder. His challenge still hung in the air. They were waiting for him to say more. To explain.

Micah asked, in a faltering tone, "But . . . the scrolls. They are a thousand years old, they . . ."

"We must risk them," Jonah said.

Micah stopped, startled. "What did you say?"

"We must risk them. They were never meant to be buried. Better they are lost in battle with the Adversary than rotted away in a crypt."

The whispers among the brothers and sisters grew in intensity, a wave of chatter, of questions, of reaction. Jonah waited for it to die down without quieting it. It had never been so important that they hear him out. But for once, it had to be their choice to listen, not his to command.

They quieted. Fixed their eyes on him again. Waited.

"We . . I stand here now, and I look on the community my brother and I built. We built it because our hearts desired to be faithful to the Great God. Because we saw that Shalem was growing corrupt and that the priests no longer cared for their office. We determined to learn all we could from them, to bring our knowledge here, to salvage the faith of our fathers and guard it from attack. And we drew others here who share the same heart. You, my friends . . . you have come here out of a good heart. It is I who have led you astray."

"No, Teacher," Micah protested. "You have never . . ."

"I have. I have taught you to cover your light and to hoard food in the midst of a hungry people. I have taught you that in battle, it is best to embalm one's strength, to bury one's sword. How could I have been so misguided?"

His voice nearly broke then, and Micah placed a hand on his shoulder and said, quietly, "Your heart was also good."

"I don't know," Jonah said. "I don't know if it was. But I know what I see now. We cannot bury these scrolls. These words. Ourselves. We must go out from this place, yes. The enemy is at our heels. But perhaps that is the Great God's way of driving us out of our own cemetery and forcing us to do what we should have been doing all along."

Fire leaped from his heart into his eyes, and in that moment he felt as though thirty years had rolled off his back. "The People need us. They need to know what we know. They need to be called home."

"But . . ." someone said. "Their idols. Their blood guilt."

Jonah nodded at him solemnly. "Terrible things. Judgment is coming upon them. So we must make our voices heard and call for repentance."

Once again the exchanged glances, the whispers, the shock.

Micah ventured the question. "Will the Great God allow them to repent, do you think? At this late hour?"

A face filled Jonah's mind. A woman's face. Beautiful, angry with him, passionate and honest enough to call out his hypocrisy as no one had dared do in all his years in Essea. He thought of her, and he knew.

"He will allow them to repent," he said. "He wants them to repent."

"But why?" Micah asked.

Jonah's eyes filled with tears as he answered, "Because they are beloved."

 Rachel Starr Thomson

CHAPTER 4

Flora the Unlucky did not see the sun when it rose on Shem in the garden, nor did she see it set as Jonah Bar Kebna awoke from his slumber to face into the night as a man on fire with light. She was moved from darkness to darkness without explanation: from the darkness of the cart to the darkness of a blindfold, through the darkness of the streets, to find herself confined in a room without windows, only a few feet square. She did not know where in the city she was. She used her bound hands to worry the blindfold until she was able to pull it off, but there was no light, and having her eyes free told her nothing about where she was or how long she was liable to be here. She tried a few ways to measure the passage of time and gave up when all of them gave way to a jumble of thoughts and memories that battered her.

She had heard that when a man or woman faced death, they might sometimes see their whole life pass before their eyes. She was fairly certain that death lay close before her, and it seemed her mind was determined to dredge up the whole of her existence and play it out before her in careful, analytical detail. But in the darkness it was hard even to hold on to thought, and so her attempts to process the life that had led her to this point failed, spinning away into incoherence every time.

Flora was driving herself crazy. She found herself wishing the confrontation would come so that it could be over with, and living or dead, she would at least be allowed to embrace her fate instead of hanging in this limbo.

Her wish came when the door opened and let in a stream of blinding light, jolting her awake.

She had no idea when she'd fallen asleep.

Figures stood in the light, but after being in darkness so long she couldn't make them out. Two took her arms—the guards?—and hauled her out, stopping before a smooth-skinned silhouette she thought was Amon. She tried to glare at him but couldn't keep her eyes open and trained on his face in the brilliant light.

The silhouette motioned with his head. "Over there," he said. There was no mistaking her enemy's voice.

The guards cut her hands free and then shoved her into another room, the motion sending shooting pains through her back and shoulder. She muffled a cry. She would not give Amon the satisfaction.

Spots still danced in her vision, but her eyes were adjusting to the light, and she saw that she was in a small lady's chamber with a wash basin and a pitcher of water, oils and brushes, and a clean dress laid out, simple but beautiful. The fabric was a rich, deep green.

Not my best color, Flora thought ruefully. Peevishly, she wished for the red dress Amon had forced on her when he first took her captive, the one she had nearly driven him mad by refusing to wear.

Moving slowly and carefully to protect her wound, Flora washed her face, brushed her hair, and applied oil to her skin. It was foolish for a woman who was already dead to relish such material comforts. But relish them she did. As the water washed away the grime of the road and the oil softened her skin and revitalized it, she fingered the soft fabric of the dress and smiled to herself. And she did something,

    RACHEL STARR THOMSON

there, that she had never done before.

She raised her smile toward the ceiling and said to the Great God, not "I'm sorry," but "Thank you."

In Essea they taught that true servants of the Great God lived an ascetic, flesh-denying life. Flora's beauty and her need to straddle the fence between the world and the cloister had always made her something of a second-class pilgrim, always indulging herself too much and always apologizing for it.

But *this* morning—she thought it was morning—here was water, here was oil, here was cleanliness and beauty, and she knew deep in her soul that she would be an ingrate not to simply thank the Creator for it all.

She felt as though he was reaching down and touching her head, like a father a child he feels tenderly toward. Caring for her in a way she could feel.

As she combed out her thick black hair, releasing tangles and letting the pull of the brush wake her up to being alive, she wondered fleetingly if all those years in Essea had been misguided somehow. If she should have been saying thank-you all along.

But here, on the doorstep of the end of her life, there was no time to think about that question.

Her captors were waiting. She could hear Amon clearing his throat and picture him crossing his arms impatiently. She didn't hurry.

When she had finished luxuriating, she slowly dressed and emerged from the chamber.

Amon looked her over without a word, then turned on his heel and said, "Follow."

The guards stood to either side of her as though they would take her arms and force her along again, but this time she strode after Amon on her own, and they trailed along behind. She did not offer her hands to be bound again, and they did not demand them.

Flora Laurentii had been making her own way in life since she was a girl, always forcing others to follow along. She had walked in no one's favor but her own, and so she had made her own favor strong enough, imperious enough to bring the world into line behind her, allowing her to seek the Great God and protect herself from the evil that lay tangled in the roots of her childhood, always waiting to snatch her up again. But this was different. This time, as she walked behind Amon not like a captive but like a queen, she felt that she walked in the favor of the Great God himself.

They were on the ground floor of a house, decorated in simple but ornate fashion, with tiled floors and bronze filigree running through murals on the whitewashed walls. Like most wealthy homes in the city, the rooms were tall but narrow, without the sprawling openness of the countryside villas. In years past Flora had visited most of the wealthier homes in Shalem, but this one was foreign to her. It likely belonged to one of the old landed families, then: Flora's dealings had been with the merchant class, the men whose wealth and power had come not through blood but through their own usually less-than-honest maneuvering. It was an open secret that the rich held all the real power in Shalem. Even the king, Beniah, was little more than a puppet. When the merchants had opened the doors wide to the gods of the foreigners with whom they dealt, Beniah's great-grandfather five generations back had protested only weakly before embracing the change himself. The kings since then had followed suit.

The house was a honeycomb that extended back a distance from the street. Flora followed Amon through chamber after chamber before they emerged into the sunlight of a cobbled road. Almost directly above them, the temple spires towered, golden roofs gleaming in the sun.

The temple, built to honor the Great God.

     RACHEL STARR THOMSON

The temple, long since adulterated.

The temple, where a Hill Woman was forbidden ever to enter.

Flora shivered at the sight of it.

But Amon's march did not take them to the temple gates. Instead he met two chariots waiting for them just outside the house. He climbed into one and took the reins; Flora climbed into the second when her guards indicated she should do so, and they crowded in after her. One of them snapped the reins, and they followed Amon through the streets.

Shalem's paths and marketplaces were packed. Slaves and free men, rich men and poor, baker wives and prostitutes, temple priests and idol hawkers, all mingled in an ever-churning, noisy crowd. Donkeys brayed as their owners tugged them through the press of people. Chariots crawled up and down the narrow streets, their drivers shouting for pedestrians to clear the way.

Flora sat in the back of her chariot, pressed between the guard and the vehicle's wooden side, and breathed her last few breaths of free air. The air was hot from the rising sun, stifling from the pack of people, rife and rich with every smell of the city. Yet she thanked the Great God for these moments too.

The chariot bumped and jolted beneath her, making the pain in her shoulder throb again. She bit her lip and closed her eyes, hoping to somehow concentrate it away. When that only made it worse, she opened her eyes again and tried to distract herself with the sights and sounds of the roiling city.

She opened her eyes to the sight of a shrine, crammed in on the side of the road between a tentmaker's stall and a stable. An idol of Amon-Heth stood prominently in the back, surrounded by purple curtains, and rows of incense candles burned in front of it.

She had not been here in over a year. The last time, the blatant paganism of the Holy City had sickened her so badly she swore she would not return. She had felt a threat here, a darkness that oppressed her with physical force.

She hadn't imagined that she would return as a gift to that very force, that very darkness.

She tore her eyes away from the shrine and looked up at the golden spires of the temple instead, the distance from them growing as the chariot bumped up the road toward the king's palace.

In spite of everything, was the Great God still here?

Here with you, a voice whispered in her soul.

So she said it again:

Thank you.

They continued through the crush of people right up to the palace gates. Flora peered over the top of the chariot and past the guard standing at the reins to its marble heights, stretching up as grand and intimidating as the temple itself though not to nearly the same height. Balconies and verandas on multiple levels overlooked the plaza and the streets. Pillared porticos and gates led to grand doors and garden pathways. It gleamed in regal beauty, and yet something about it still looked like a real home.

Ahead of them, Amon said a few sharp words to the palace guards, and the gates swung open. They passed through.

The change was immediate and almost startling as the crowds disappeared and they drove over the rattling stones of the plaza. Palm trees and flowers wafted in a slight breeze, blowing lavender fragrance over the cobbles. The music of nearby fountains flowed, hushing the sound of the crowds so nearby.

The chariots jerked to a halt, and the guard hemming Flora in jumped down. She stretched her legs tentatively and accepted his hand in descending. Her shoulder ached after the ride with blinding inten-

     RACHEL STARR THOMSON

sity, but as soon as her feet touched the ground it lessened. She was grateful. She needed her wits about her.

Palace guards stood at ease all around, keeping loose formations and watching them carefully. A steward approached Amon and bowed low, and they exchanged words in the Southern tongue. After a moment, the steward bowed again and motioned for them to follow him.

They passed through the golden doors of the palace, and the transformation was complete: the noise of the crowds fell away completely. The air felt clean and tinged with lavender and hints of cassia; the room was open and airy like an inner courtyard. Floor, walls, and high arched ceiling were all white marble. The arches rose to meet in the center, letting in sunlight from outside. Palm fronds graced the corners in bronze pots; a fountain flowed in the center of the open room, filling the air with the sound of tranquility. Birds in a cage tweeted and flapped their wings. Flora smiled at them. She pitied their captivity—but surely there were worse places to be imprisoned.

"Amon!" a genial voice called out.

They turned as one. The steward seemed surprised. Amon did not. The slightest of smiles graced his face as he bowed his head to the newcomer.

"King Beniah."

The king of the Sacred Land was not a young man, but his ruddy face and broad shoulders still gave the impression of youth. He greeted Amon with a hand on each shoulder and a kiss on each cheek, a gesture Amon returned but not—Flora noted—warmly.

Then the king turned to Flora, and his bushy eyebrows rose.

"By the stars," he said. "She does resemble my Izevel, doesn't she?"

Flora stiffened at the mention of the new queen's name. The new queen, a Hill Woman, a devotee of Kimash.

And, if Amon was correct, Flora's younger sister.

"We have heard much of this Flora Laurentii," the king went on, smiling as though she were not a prisoner and there were no threat at all to her here. "I am pleased to meet her."

To Flora's surprise, he turned to her, took her hand, and kissed it. "Welcome," he said.

"I thank you, my lord," she said, wondering at the ease with which the words slipped off her tongue. Deceptive ease, for she could not have been taken more off guard at this reception.

Amon's eyes narrowed. To Flora it seemed that he was not pleased by the greeting or the welcoming tone of the king in general. But he said nothing about it. Instead, he said, "Your home is more magnificent than I remembered it, your majesty. And you are looking very well. Allow me to congratulate you on your marriage."

Beniah beamed. "Best thing I ever did," he said. "I recommend it, Amon, recommend it highly. You find a beautiful woman, you marry her."

He seemed about to turn to Flora again, but Amon interrupted him. "And I hear great things about the alliance with the Hill Country also. How the fortunes of the world do change."

"Yes, that is so, that is so. When I was a younger man we would not have bothered to ally with them. But they are on the rise again."

"As their god is on the rise again," Amon said.

The comment seemed to make Beniah uncomfortable. He shifted and turned a little redder and said, "Yes, that is so." He cleared his throat. "But I am not one for talk of gods. I leave that to our priests and to men like you, eh, Amon?"

Amon smiled again—the same thin, warmthless smile. "To men like me, yes."

 RACHEL STARR THOMSON

"Well," Beniah said, looking to his steward as though he wanted help. When none was forthcoming he said "Well" again, and then, "We shall feast to celebrate your arrival. And to continue celebrating my marriage, of course. It has been a feast every day. I welcome you all to join us."

"I shall do so with pleasure," Amon said quickly, "but the lady needs her rest. She was unfortunately injured on the journey."

Beniah turned solicitous eyes on Flora and caught sight of the bandaging beneath her dress. "I am sorry to hear it! Yes, of course you must rest. Thoughtless of me. I will have my servants take you to your chamber until Izevel and the high priest of Kimash are ready to receive you. They are eager to meet you, most eager."

"I will be a part of that meeting, of course," Amon said hurriedly. Then that smile. "I would not wish to miss it."

"Of course, of course." Beniah's eyes flicked from Flora to Amon and back again as though he were trying to discern something beyond his ken. Failing, he nodded to his steward. "See to it that they are all made comfortable," he said, "and send a servant to usher our Southern friend to the feast. Make sure the lady is especially comfortable."

"And tended well," Amon cut in. "I will have my own guards attend her. But if you would be so good as to post others outside her chambers." He met Flora's eyes coldly. "The queen's double has enemies."

She smiled back at him. Enemies indeed.

— ◆ —

By the time she reached the luxurious chambers that were to be her prison for the next while, Flora had halfway formulated a plan and all the way lost her intention to surrender without a fight.

In the desert when he had threatened her servant and the guards who had befriended her, Amon had left her with little choice but to try to save them at any cost. For their sake and for Rechab's, she had offered herself to him as a gift to the god whose favor he so badly wanted to curry. He had accepted the gift—and then slaughtered her friends anyway.

She'd been too deeply in mourning to go back on her decision at the time, but now, here, with the temple spires gleaming in the distance and a new day offering itself to her in the riches of the king's palace, she decided that if Amon was going to break the agreement, then it was broken. She would not go willingly into the hands of her enemies.

And it was there that hope lay. Because it was clear that Beniah, whose house she and her enemies alike dwelt in, did not know she was an enemy. He did not even know she was a prisoner. As far as he was concerned she was his guest.

And he was king of all the Sacred Land.

A patsy, yes. A puppet, yes. And, judging from the slight waver in his stance when he'd met them, something of a drunk. But still a king, and that counted for something no matter how poorly Beniah himself made use of it.

If Flora wanted to avoid death or worse, all she needed was to remain in the king's house and in his favor. You could not simply kill someone in such a position without repercussions. Even Amon had to know that. Even Izevel and her uncle—Flora's uncle—had to know that.

So as she glided over the threshold of the expansive apartments Beniah had set aside for her, noting with approval the gleaming marble floors, the golden basins and jars for washing, the elegant bed stretched out in the midst of rich cushions and silk hangings, Flora determined that nothing on earth would move her out of the king's favor. If she played it right, she could keep herself out of Amon's clutches and make

     RACHEL STARR THOMSON

it impossible for him to do what he wanted with her.

She could hear Amon's guards pacing outside her door. She dashed aside purple curtains to let in the streaming sunlight and stepped out onto the balcony. More guards paced in the gardens below. A handful of children dashed through the flower beds, giggling and bickering with each other, while harried household servants followed behind. The scent of flowers wafted up, a welcome change from the stink of the city streets.

Flora smiled at a guard who happened to look her way. Amon was a fool. He'd had triple guards posted to keep her here, when "here" was exactly where she wanted to be. Safe in the eye of the storm.

She turned to reenter her apartments and felt the barest twinge of regret. She had intended to martyr herself. To die for the Great God's sake. To give that up was a loss.

But she heard his voice thrumming in her spirit, and his voice did not say "Die."

His voice said "Live."

CHAPTER 5

Rechab saw the stranger at the edge of the crowd even as she let the blood drain from the bird—a young man, dressed in dusty white, carrying a traveler's staff and a bundle on his back.

Though he stood at a distance, she recognized the expression on his face as one of deep sorrow, and unlike so many who had come here to Nachush because of loss and anger and desire for revenge, she thought he was sorry for her.

It shook her. Her hands trembled even harder than usual as she finished the sacrifice and rushed through the prayers.

Aaron turned to speak to her as the crowds began to disperse, but she was already hurrying away to find the stranger and speak to him. To her relief, he was not wandering away with the others. He still stood where he'd been during the sacrifice, in the broad sunlight on the hillside. A white turban wrapped his head and shielded him from the heat.

Aaron followed her. She could hear his footsteps close behind and did not know if she was glad he was there or unhappy about it.

The thought struck her, and caused a hitch in her step, that she could not go through with the marriage while such feelings still wrestled within her.

She cleared her throat and raised her voice as she approached the stranger, who was watching her come with calm expectation.

"Welcome, stranger!" she said. "You are new in our midst."

"I am," he answered as she drew closer. He was tall, not as youthful as she'd thought from a distance but not at all old. He bowed respectfully.

When he raised his head again, she froze. She recognized him.

So did Aaron—if not personally, then at least from his clothing. Aaron's tone was vaguely hostile as he said, "You are Essean."

The man inclined his head again. "I am one of the brothers of Essea, yes."

Rechab couldn't stop herself. "Then you know that . . ."

"That you are not Flora Laurentii? Yes, of course." A smile lurked in the young man's mouth, but still he seemed sorrowful. "I am sorry not to find her here, for I had much to tell her. Yet I am pleased to find you, for I know how much your welfare lay on her heart when last she was with us."

Rechab laid her hand over her heart. Her breath was coming too rapidly as she tried to process what this man's presence here meant. And what he meant by his strange words.

"Isn't Flora with you?" she asked. "In Essea, I mean. I thought she . . ."

"Flora left us some time ago," he said. "We have not heard from her. When I heard of this settlement I thought Flora must have relocated here."

There was a story here he was not telling, and Rechab thought it

   RACHEL STARR THOMSON

had something to do with the sadness in his face. But she couldn't ask in front of Aaron.

The man spared her the need to do so. "My name is Micah," he said. "I came seeking Flora, but I find you, and I believe that must be the Great God's will."

Aaron cut in, angling between Rechab and Micah. "The Great God's will is being done here," he said.

Micah's eyes flared a little. Rechab sensed there was more to this man than his placid exterior indicated—enough to him that he might be a match for Aaron. And that pleased her. No one had been a match for Aaron in all this time, no one had been able to stand up to him. Least of all her.

"I don't think it is," Micah said, then quickly followed with, "That is, I believe you could use my help to discern the will of the Great God. I come bearing—"

"We need no help from Essea," Aaron said. He folded his arms.

"We should hear him out," Rechab said, but Aaron did not listen.

"The Great God is at work here," Aaron said. He spread his arms out to take in the hillside, the altar, the crowds wandering back to work in the mines. "We have brought justice to this place and freed these people, and we have established worship of the Great God."

"Against his own laws. Proper worship can be established only in the temple," Micah rejoined. He cleared his throat and visibly took a step back. "I apologize. I'm a poor guest who attacks his hosts without establishing first that he respects them."

Micah fixed his eyes not on Aaron as he spoke, but on Rechab. "I believe you want to honor the Great God, as do I. But I have learned—we of Essea have lately learned—that we have been wrong in our attempts, wrong for some time and to great damage. I only come to tell you what I have learned. To confess it. And perhaps to show you another way."

Rechab gaped at him. She remembered now where she'd seen him before: he was one of the Teacher's acolytes. She'd seen him in the hall of Essea, standing at his master's side. The Teacher had towered above all those gathered to pray and to learn. His voice had been the voice of God. All those who bowed to the presence of the Great God, prostrate before their leader, had aspired to be like him.

Micah's tone now was different. Very different. Something had changed.

The young man in white addressed Aaron now. "I do not blame you for your feelings toward me," he said. "Essea has not offered the kind of help our people have needed. You have tried to do so, and I honor—"

"We have done so," Aaron said.

Rechab reached for him. "Aaron . . ."

He shook her hand off and planted his feet, facing off with Micah as though they stood in a sparring ring. "You in Essea have talked for decades. We have been here a matter of weeks, and we have acted. You come here and want to tell us how to carry out the Great God's will?"

Rechab's alarm grew with every word from Aaron's mouth. When had he become so entrenched—so certain of everything they were doing? It was a certainty she didn't share, had never shared. But Aaron seemed absolutely convinced of the rightness of their cause.

To his credit, Micah did not flare up again. Instead, he stepped back, seemed to deliberately make himself smaller, humbler. "I honor what you have done," he said again. "And I accept your rebuke. As I said: Essea has not acted as we should. But I bring you a gift . . . a valuable gift. Will you receive it?"

Rechab dared reach for Aaron again, laying her fingers lightly on his arm. He didn't shrug her away this time. His jaw was set, his stance still defensive. But there was no way to reject Micah's offer without sounding like a stubborn fool.

A crowd was starting to gather—staring and listening. Aaron was not free to act without censure.

"Very well," he said finally. "Let us see this gift you offer."

Micah smiled faintly. He reached behind him and took the pack from his shoulder, laying it gently on the ground and drawing out a long, cylindrical form wrapped in white cloth. Slowly and tenderly, he unwrapped layer after layer until leather casing appeared, enclosing what could only be a scroll.

The leather was old—even ancient. Rechab wondered about the age of the scroll within.

Micah held it out carefully, an end in each of his palms, extending it to Aaron as though he held a life in his hands.

"This is the greatest treasure of the Sacred Land," he announced, loudly enough that the closest of the crowds could hear. "I bring you one of the lost scrolls of the law."

Gasps attended the announcement. Aaron stared hard at Micah for a moment before reaching out to accept the scroll. Micah laid it in his palms, and Aaron seemed lost—standing there holding something ancient and precious, but without knowledge of what to do now.

"I will read it to you," Micah said softly. "If that is what you wish."

"We do," Rechab said, raising her voice. She wanted the crowds to hear her accept the gift on Aaron's behalf. She could not take the chance that he would turn it away.

She said it again, more softly. "We do."

———•◆•———

That night, late in the hours between twilight and sleep, Aaron, Rechab, and a handful of their chief officers sat cross-legged on the floor of Aaron's cave. Oil lamps burned, casting golden shadows around the room. Stillness hung in the air, a silence still filled with the memory of Micah's words.

Or rather, of the Great God's words, read out into the stillness.

There was no doubt now. No question as to the rightness or wrongness of what they did here. Micah had not accused, had not vilified. He had simply and humbly read the words of the scroll.

No altar was to be built to the Great God outside of the temple in Shalem. No sacrifice was to be offered by any other than his priests. No incense was to be burnt except that given by his law and consecrated by appropriate sacrifice. All of the Great God's people were to come to Shalem, to the temple, every year for a Gathering. All of the people were to offer sacrifices there as he had commanded, to free their slaves, and to dedicate their firstborn sons.

And Rechab let tears run down her face at another command, one Micah had read first. "You shall not steal."

And another: "You shall not kill, lest you bring a curse upon the Sacred Land."

She said nothing. Made no sound. Just sat and cried silently for all the wrong they had done. Aaron, who had killed. She, who had stolen. And they both, setting up an altar and making a sham out of worship.

"It is our fault," Micah said into the silence.

They all looked up at him, still wordless. Rechab alone was crying; she did not know if the others were silent for grief or some other reason. She trembled beside Aaron, not knowing whether he might erupt in anger, in stubbornness, or if the inarguable words had pierced his heart like they had hers.

 Rachel Starr Thomson

"It is our fault," Micah repeated. "We in Essea have had these words for years. We've oiled the scrolls, wrapped them, sometimes read them. But we have not shared them. We kept them behind our walls where they could do you no good. If you have incurred wrath, it is our fault as much as it is yours."

Rechab shook her head and found her voice. "But I knew. I knew it was wrong to use Flora's wealth this way. I knew."

She felt Aaron's sharp displeasure but refused to meet his gaze. She held her hands still from trembling and met Micah's eyes. "I knew we should not sacrifice here. That is . . . the People know that."

"Rumors," one of the men said. "We have heard that the law said something of the kind. But who can trust what the law says when it only comes to you in hearsay? In old wives' stories?"

"Even so," Micah said, nodding. "Thus it is our fault. We could have shown you plainly what the law said."

"So why now?" Aaron demanded. His voice was taut, as though he held his spirit like a bowstring. Prepared to let go and pierce his adversary. "Why come here now and tell us this? Why not wait as you have always done for others to come to Essea and seek out the truth?"

"Essea is no more," Micah said.

"What?" Rechab blurted, sitting forward. "What—"

"It is a long story," Micah said, "and of special interest to you, my sister. But the short version is this: we recognized our wrong and tended to a man in great need, and that man has powerful enemies. We have chosen to disband and leave our walled city to the jackals before our enemies can come to destroy us."

"And yet you trust in the Great God," Aaron said, faintly mocking. "But you will not take up arms to defend yourselves."

"No," Micah said, searching Aaron's face. "No, we will not. There would be no good in bloodshed. And we have seen our error. We should, all along, have taken the law to the people. You should have heard the Great God's words before you could transgress against them."

At that, Aaron's bowstring snapped. He leaped to his feet and paced. Rechab wanted to tug at his clothing, to pull him back down beside her. But she knew better than to shame him that way. She feared how he might react if she tried.

"And now you have a right!" Aaron said. "Now you have a right to come here and tell us, who have enjoyed the Great God's great favor, that we are in the wrong. That he does not smile on us. You admit you have been hiding his words for decades, but now that you have seen your error, you are the voice we should listen to. We should accept you as the sages that you are."

Micah looked pained. "It is the Great God's words themselves you should accept," he said. "The messengers are fools, and rightly rebuked."

"But fools we're to trust. How do we know that is a lost scroll? How do we know you haven't written it yourself to bring us all into bondage?"

"You can see for yourself the scroll is old," one of the other men said. "Ancient. What else could it be?"

Aaron turned on him with eyes flaring. "Because of course, there can be no other ancient book. Because this one is old, we should bow down before it like Hill Men before their idols!"

Rechab gasped. Aaron turned on her. "And you! Crying and fearful before this . . . this imposter!"

She didn't know where she found the courage to say the words, only that she said them. "We are the imposters, Aaron. We have always been imposters here."

For a moment she thought he would strike her—he was that angry. From the corner of her eye she saw Micah tense to come to her aid.

But they were interrupted. A trembling, breathless servant appeared in the entrance of the cave.

"What is it?" Aaron barked.

"Please, my lord," the servant said. "The watchmen send word."

"Out with it," one of the men ordered.

The servant nodded, trying to catch his breath. He trembled and sweat like one who had run a long way. "There is . . . there is an army. On its way."

Aaron went white. "What?"

"It is nearly here. My lord, we are under siege."

The guard around the villa increased rather than lessening day by day. There was nothing said, no announcement to tell Aurelius that he and his wife were becoming increasingly imprisoned hour by hour. But he observed, and he understood what he was observing.

He sat on an ornate stool, watching the movement in the garden. Three men pacing where yesterday there had been one. Evening was falling with a golden blush, heightening the greens of the garden and the fragrance of the roses and delicate irises, Marah's pride.

His wife laid a hand on his shoulder. She had come up behind him silently, unheard as he was deep in thought, but he did not startle at her presence. It felt right.

He covered her hand with his own but did not take his eyes from the guard.

"Tripled," she murmured.

"Yes."

"How many people does Beniah think he is guarding?"

"I don't believe Beniah knows about this," Aurelius said. "He's trusted the wrong people with power, and they are misusing it."

"I am not sure the guards themselves like to be misused," Marah said. Her voice low, calm, a steady current in Aurelius's otherwise tumultuous world.

She waited a beat and then said, "Our letter got through. And a reply has already come."

Aurelius nodded, just barely, keeping his own voice almost imperceptible. "Is it arranged, then?"

"Indeed. My cousin is most eager to help us."

That was no surprise. They would not have revealed their plight, much less dared ask for help, from anyone they did not already trust to be on their side. Asking for help to thwart the official will of the king was, after all, a form of treason.

"When?" Aurelius asked.

"Tomorrow."

He nodded. The guards in the garden switched places as the shadows deepened, and the gentle golden light turned deep amber before it began to disappear altogether.

"I want to take Shem," Marah said.

He tightened his grasp on her hand, and she pulled away immediately. A wordless rebuke for hurting her—for opposing her.

"There is no need for him to come," Aurelius said.

"There is no need for him to stay."

"We need the household servants here to cover for us."

 RACHEL STARR THOMSON

"There are enough without him."

Aurelius sighed deeply. The plan was risky. They were assuming no one would try to visit them, from the palace or otherwise, and raise the alarm when it was discovered they were not there. Their servants had been instructed to run the household in all respects as if he and Marah were at home; the guards, who kept a respectful distance, should never know the difference. They would be out and gone with tomorrow's visitors, and if the palace called for them, they would send their regrets that they were ill. Aurelius did not expect that, with Beniah's continued feasting over his marriage and the high priest's more important people to attend to, anyone would bother to check in on one small-town governor and his wife under unofficial house arrest.

Not until they were well away. By the time they were discovered, it was possible things would have blown over and it would not matter. Of course, it was also possible that it would matter—but Aurelius and Marah had decided that come what may, they could not make a deal with the devil Kimash. They had to return to Bethabara and try to intervene in some way to protect the people they had long governed. After that, perhaps it was time to visit the homeland of Aurelius's ancestors. Rumor had long reached them that the Westland thrived in every way. Alliances in the old country might be wise, and there could be no better time to forge them.

But Shem . . .

Aurelius stood and patted his wife's shoulder apologetically. She didn't look at him.

She was right, there was no reason to leave Shem behind. He wasn't necessary to maintain the appearance of a busy household. And he had always remained a close part of their personal retinue before. But lately Aurelius was unhappy with the boy. Ever since he'd sent him out to find Rechab, Shem had seemed changed. Lately he seemed like a stranger, and Aurelius didn't like what he saw in the boy's eyes.

But Marah had been close to the lad's mother and had always favored him. He was one of those servants who stood to benefit greatly from the prosperity of the house and would probably receive his freedom one day, along with rewards and a home of his own. Aurelius had always intended to do right by him—more than right by him.

Maybe that was the answer, he thought suddenly. Perhaps it was time to manumit Shem. Now, while he was still young. He could give the boy money and holdings and let him make whatever he would of himself, without Aurelius being responsible any longer for exactly what that might be.

He opened his mouth to suggest as much to Marah, but she took a few steps away from him. "I will pack for you," she said.

He nodded.

The servants could do that, but Marah had never allowed them to. Some women served their husbands. Marah watched over hers. Watched over him, managed him, partnered with him.

He'd always been grateful. Yes, he would trust her with this: they would take Shem with them. And then he would give the boy freedom and send him away, while he and Marah went forward into whatever future awaited them.

CHAPTER 6

Lights dotted the hills around the valley like fireflies. It would have been beautiful had it not been accompanied by the sound of tramping feet and clanking armor: the sound of troops deploying around the valley.

Nachush and its people were surrounded.

Rechab watched from the outskirts of the town. They had abandoned their caves, gathering everyone into the city. Two hours later, the hillsides where the caves were located were overrun by enemy soldiers. The people of Nachush, accompanied by the many disenfranchised rebels and zealots who had joined them since Aaron began his little uprising, had gone to work immediately building barricades out of every piece of equipment and loose stone they could find, even tearing down some of the older houses to use their stones to build a wall.

But Rechab knew it would do no good.

They all knew that.

They expected the attack to launch at dawn. There had been no offer of parley, no extension of peace. It seemed the army from Shalem simply intended to make war, and the end could only be death for them all.

Rechab stood in the street, watching the torches as they bobbed on the dark hills like insects. She could hear women weeping and wailing, their children crying in confusion.

This was her fault.

It was all her fault.

Aaron had been storming around all night. Issuing orders. Tearing stone from stone and mortar with his bare hands and heaving every muscle into the work of building the wall. He had not spoken to her since the confrontation in the cave.

We are the imposters here, Aaron. We have always been the imposters here.

She wandered in the street, feeling useless. Men ran past her, shouting to each other. Empty, dark doorways stared like lifeless eyes. She recognized the house where, what seemed like so long ago, she had descended into this town in disguise and listened to the people curse the Great God, curse Flora Laurentii, curse her, and curse their fate.

How much worse their fate now. How much more deserved the curses.

But not on the Great God. Not on Flora. Only on her.

She had seen Aaron multiple times. Rushing here and there. Every time she saw his face in the torchlight, she saw the haunting in its lines. He was still pale. Still white as a ghost. That had not changed from the moment he heard the news.

"I'm sorry," she said to the air.

Then she said it again, but this time to the Great God, whose eye was always on her. "I'm sorry. I did not mean for this to happen. I went against your laws, and it was wrong. I did it because I was afraid. I have been afraid from the first day I stepped out, and I am afraid now."

 RACHEL STARR THOMSON

She swallowed hard. Her eyes were dry—completely dry for the first time in weeks. She had run out of tears. Run out of strength to cry.

"I am still afraid, and I do not want to die tomorrow. But more than that, I don't want these people to die. I don't want Aaron to die. I led him into this. I did."

A voice in the back of her head said that wasn't true. Aaron had done this to himself. Aaron had pushed her, manipulated her, *used* her even as he declared he loved her, in his zeal to accomplish his revenge against the world for robbing him of his family so many years ago.

She was finally willing to admit the truth of all that. But she saw her own complicity too. It was true what she confessed to the night, and to the God of her fathers. This was her fault, because she had been afraid.

She looked out toward the altar, where a thick cluster of lights had gathered. She thought she could see the shape of some other object: a catapult perhaps, or some kind of battering ram. Not that the king's army would need it to get over the hastily erected walls of Nachush.

The men circled back around, still shouting, and this time they were pushing a wagon toward the walls. It would be turned on its side, used to fortify some small part of the city. In the morning soldiers would reduce it to splinters, perhaps burn it. What had been the livelihood of some man, pulled by an ox or a donkey that was his joy, would become one more piece of wreckage in this ruin of lives.

Behind her, a crash of falling stonework alerted her that another house had come down. Clouds of dust filled the air, and she covered her mouth and nose to keep from choking. A child began to cry out, over and over again, a name Rechab couldn't quite make out.

She had no more tears, but inside she wept.

She didn't know where Aaron was. She'd lost track of him.

She lifted her eyes to the lights in the hills again. The cluster by the altar was growing larger. Perhaps that was where the commander of this force was.

All of a sudden Rechab found courage.

Still covering her mouth and nose with her headscarf, she picked up her skirts and hastened her steps toward the hillside.

The shadows were deep and the streets busy. No one noticed her go.

Halfway between Nachush and the gathering of lights on the hillside, Rechab found a pocket of air that was totally still and totally silent.

She let her scarf drop away from her face and breathed clean, quiet air. Above her, stars shone. They told a story, but she did not know it. Still, she gazed up and wished she could understand what it was she saw. The lights of heaven shone earnestly, as though willing her to read them and to act because of what they said.

Instead she raised a tentative hand to salute them and passed on.

The pocket of silence was gone in an instant. Now the sounds of the troops gathered on the hillside replaced the sounds of the village completely. Jingling, clashing, tramping, even snoring. The air filled with the smell of horses and footmen, and of the sulfur and pitch of torches.

"Who's there?" a sentry called as she approached. Lights thrust themselves at her. She raised her hands, letting her veil hang away from her face so they could clearly see that a young woman approached.

The sentry and a fellow soldier exchanged glances she did not like, but before they could greet her, she said, "I want to see your leader."

 Rachel Starr Thomson

"Look here, little lady," the first sentry began.

She cut him off, holding her voice steady. "Do not mistake me. I am the priestess and governess of this village, and I want to see your leader. I must see him. Take me to him, now if you please."

Rechab had imitated Flora Laurentii before—had taken on her bravado and her imperious tone. But it had always been an act.

This time she was not imitating Flora, and it was not an act.

The sentry peered sideways at her as though he expected to catch her in a trick. "And who should I say wants to see him?"

"Tell him that Rechab, Nadab's daughter, wishes to speak with him," she said. "On behalf of this village, whose people I have lately led."

They stared at her as though she had two heads, but after a minute's hushed conference, the second of the men motioned for her to follow him.

"I can't promise you an audience," the man said. He barked a short laugh. "But I don't think he'd forgive me if I didn't at least tell him you wanted to see him."

Rechab's face burned a little, but she followed him and kept her head high. She knew he mocked her, though exactly why or how she wasn't sure. One thing she knew: not one of these men would respect her for Flora's wealth, Aaron's sword, or the Great God's supposed blessing. They would respect her for herself alone: for how she carried herself, for the words she spoke, and for the true favor of the Great God upon her.

If indeed she carried that favor at all anymore.

Somehow, the stars above told her she did.

The man led her into a hastily erected encampment. Some of the men slept, but it was clear they did not intend to be here long: their shelter was limited to rolls on the ground, laid out in squares four men by four men, with a fire in the center. There was little to be seen in the way of provision or even of extra weaponry. Every man had a sword strapped to his side and a spear in his hand, and with that they intended to lay quick waste to Nachush.

They reached a tent—the only such shelter in sight—and the man leveled a harsh glare at Rechab. "Stay here," he said, "while I see about getting you an entrance. You move a muscle, and I'm not responsible for what happens to you."

She nodded and tried not to feel vulnerable when he disappeared into the tent's lit interior. Many men wandered or patrolled the encampment, and every one of them set eyes on her for too long a minute, a lamb in a camp of wolves.

She kept her head up. Prayed silently. Trusted in the Great God's watching eye.

She stiffened as a man turned and came toward her, walking with a confident, threatening gait that said he knew exactly why he approached her. But before he reached her, her escort reappeared and held open the tent door.

"Enter," he said, warning the other man off with a glare.

She did, breathing out her relief.

The interior of the tent was sparse, as different as possible from a merchant's tent. No carpet lay over the dirt floor; no ornate furnishings made it a home. The tent was large enough for a group of five or even ten men to gather and strategize, but it was mostly empty. The far corner held a cot, a chair, and a simple washbasin. Blocks held spears and swords. In the center of the tent, another chair sat, backless and low to the ground, with a man brooding upon it.

This man looked up when Rechab entered. Thick, swarthy features spoke of his heritage among the Hill People. He narrowed his eyes at the sight of her.

   Rachel Starr Thomson

"Priestess, eh?" He snorted. "Governess? Of this miserable rabble? Why do you waste my time?"

The greeting caught her off guard. She hadn't immediately recognized the man as the commander, much less expected to be addressed with so little ceremony. But she gathered her wits about her and dropped a bow.

"My lord," she said. "Commander of these troops . . ."

"I know who I am," he said, folding his arms over his chest. But she didn't miss the gleam in his eyes. He was pleased by her respect.

"You have come some way to be here," she said, hoping it was true. They must have come from Shalem, the Holy City—where else would the troops have been mustered? A three-day march, then, at least. "And without much in the way of comforts. A pity we could not greet you and make your way more comfortable."

He looked incredulously at the soldier who had escorted her here. "What are you talking about, woman? We've come to destroy you."

Her stomach sank, even though it was not news, to her or to anyone else. "And there is the pity," she said. "To destroy us—with no offer to surrender? No talk of peace?"

"We have our orders," the commander said. "They didn't say 'make peace.' They said 'wipe them out.'"

Rechab itched to ask who "they" were. This attack didn't seem typical of Beniah, even if Aaron's uprising had been characterized to him as treason . . . as, in a way, it was. But she didn't dare come out and demand an answer to that question.

"The king has heard grave things against us, then," Rechab said.

This time the commander did not meet her eyes. Instead, he waved impatiently for a servant to attend him. One quickly did, emerging from the shadows in the back of the tent to serve him a chalice of what

Rechab assumed was wine. The commander took a sip and wiped his mouth.

"It's not my business what the king has heard," he said. "Nor what the queen has heard, nor what the high priest of Kimash has heard. It is my business to carry out orders. And those orders are to wipe you out."

He eyed her carefully. "Not you personally, you understand. The village."

"They are my people. I have led them for some months now."

"So my soldier tells me. What I don't understand is how a girl like you became a leader of anything. Nadab's Daughter . . . that is your name?"

She nodded. Before she could go on, the commander did. "I knew Nadab. The merchantman, richest bastard in this desert at times. Known for shrewd dealing, not for leading uprisings."

Rechab had intended to go on flattering, go on wheedling details out of the man. But these words knocked her off course.

"You speak . . ." she hesitated. "You speak as if my father is dead."

The commander's thick eyebrows rose. "As he is, Miss, unless he's simply spirited himself away from his house and his riches forever. Fallen afoul to bandits, they say, or to the same devils who murdered his household."

At that, Rechab's world spun around her. She wanted to reach out to steady herself, but she stood on a bare floor in a bare tent, without friend or staff or tent pole to reach for.

The commander took another sip from his goblet, watching her. "I see I bring you news. Well, I ask your pardon for breaking it so roughly. But mind, woman, this is a battlefield, on the eve of a slaughter. You should be running away from here, not standing in the tent of your enemy hearing gossip straight from his lips."

　　　　RACHEL STARR THOMSON

He stood abruptly and waved his arm, calling more servants over. "Get the lady a chair, some way to sit down. She's going to faint. And wine, bring her wine."

A moment later Rechab found herself mercifully seated, wrapped in a cloak and holding a goblet of red wine. She didn't know whether to feel hopeful that her enemy was so kind or hopeless that she would ever manage to make the plea she'd come to make. Her head was still spinning over the news she'd just received.

Nadab was dead?

And his household . . . murdered? By whom? And why?

The commander watched her sharply as she took a sip of the wine and then set it aside, forcing herself to focus again. She decided not to stand—not to cast the cloak aside. She was about to throw herself on this man's mercy—herself and everyone else. Better that she appear to be in need of it.

"I would hear more of what you say," Rechab said, "but that is not why I came here tonight. I have come to plead with you—to beg you—for mercy."

The commander let out a barely perceptible groan, and she latched on to it as to hope. "You tell me I ought to be running away from here. That I ought to flee. Would you allow it? If we fled, would you allow us through your lines? That is all I ask. Not that you withdraw your troops; not that you give clemency to those who would fight you. But there are innocents in that village. Women and children. Men who had nothing to do with . . . with the reasons you have come here. Would you let them through? Will you give us the chance to flee?"

She thought of the families whose homes were being torn down to build the barricades. It was Aaron's warriors who were doing the tearing, the ripping down of generations and years of lives. While the people of the village, whose only real crime had been being victimized by their former governor and his ilk, and then refusing to trust that Aaron and Rechab wanted to help, were subjected to the end of that "help" without any way to save all they held dear.

Rechab held her breath as she awaited the commander's answer. She knew the army had not intended to give the people a way out. Had that been the intent, their approach would have been very different. And she knew that even if this man said yes, if he promised the villagers safe passage if they would run, she would still have to convince them to trust her enough to try it. And to trust that there could be a life for them beyond this place—that running would not simply mean a miserable death in the wilderness.

She had not even begun to ask herself how she would prevent that. One thing at a time.

The commander was visibly disturbed. He dashed his wine goblet aside and began to pace, his short cloak hanging over one shoulder. He turned on her and growled. "I have my orders."

"Of course," she said. "But children? Women? Are your orders . . ."

"I am not to show mercy."

"Not to anyone?" She pleaded with her eyes, considered getting down on her knees in the dirt and begging. She didn't know if so degrading herself would make him more or less likely to accept her plea, so she stayed where she was.

And then tried a new tack. That of complete honesty.

"It is my fault," she said, letting her eyes fill with the tears that were suddenly back somehow. "Whatever folly you have been sent to put down, it is mine alone. If you must kill for it, then I beg you to kill me, but let these people slip past you in the morning and find a new life. They are not responsible for what has happened here."

The commander did not sit back down, but he ceased his pacing

 RACHEL STARR THOMSON

and stared hard at her—at her disheveled hair, her face streaked with dust and tears, the soldier's cloak wrapped around her.

"I was told there is a rebellion here," he said. "That they have started a religion in defiance of the king and the ancient laws."

"The fault is mine," she answered. "Did I not tell you I serve as priestess here? I have led them daily in unlawful sacrifice and prayers."

"A governor was killed, murdered in cold blood, along with the elders of the town."

"For my sake," she said, trembling. It was true. Her mouth had not cast the spell that killed Azeda nor her hand wielded the sword that killed the elders: all of that had been Aaron's doing. But he had done it to protect her. To get her out of a situation she should never have been in to begin with. It was her fault.

"Brigands and cutthroats have gathered here from across the nation," the commander continued. "Amassing a force that looks as though it intends to rise against Shalem itself."

"I lead them." She raised her chin. It was partially true. "But I would not have led them against the Holy City."

That was wholly true—she hoped. Who knew what she might have eventually done had things continued the way they were? Who knew what sins she might have been convinced to carry out? In a way this attack was a mercy. It would stop her from damning herself.

The commander stared down at her. "You heap grave sins on your head."

"They are mine and mine alone," she said. "I will remain and bear the punishment, along with any who wish to take a stand against you and thus against the Holy City. All I ask is that you do not offend justice, nor the Great God whose character is justice, by refusing to let the wholly innocent go free."

He stepped closer and peered down at her as though she were a child and he a stern father. "I do not believe that anyone is wholly innocent," he said.

"But some are guilty only of being in the wrong place at the wrong time," she said. She let the tears stand on her face, afraid to break eye contact with him to wipe them away. "Did . . . the king . . . send you here to carry out justice? Or did he truly tell you to come here and destroy without pity, without compassion, without sense?"

She drew back even as those words escaped her mouth and his body went rigid. She had gone too far, and she knew it.

But he did not strike her, nor raise his voice, nor order her thrown out of his presence. Instead he resumed his pacing, slowly, half-turning every time he stepped in front of her to look at her again. She did not dare to move. She hardly dared to breathe.

At last he said, "I cannot kill you for the sake of these people. For one thing, I do not believe your claims. You are not responsible for the sins of an entire village, and certainly not for those who have gathered here in recent days. Yes, we heard rumors of a woman at the head of the goings-on here, a wealthy merchantwoman who acted as priestess and ruler. You are not what I expected. But you are a woman. And I do not believe you are the mastermind you claim to be. Even if rumor did not also say it, plainly, even if they were not already naming his name across the countryside, I would know there was a man behind you."

Rechab kept her eyes locked on his and did not answer.

"But you don't plead for his life," the commander continued. "Why not?"

She licked her lips. "Because . . . because I cannot ask you to release him. Because you are under orders, and you are responsible to the king. The man of whom you speak is as guilty as I. So I cannot ask you to incriminate yourself by letting him go."

     RACHEL STARR THOMSON

He nodded, half to himself, as though he'd expected to hear those words.

"I have seen and done many things in my life, young mistress," he said. "I, Callum of the Hills, have served the Holy People since I was a lad, in matters holy and in matters as far from holy as you can imagine."

Suddenly he drew up his chair and sat down so that he sat almost nose to nose with Rechab. He gazed into her eyes and she squirmed uncomfortably, but his gaze was searching—not threatening. Then he reached out and took her hand.

"This is what I agree to, little sister," he said. "You will stay here, under my arrest, to come back to the Holy City and stand trial. I will make the same offer to every man in the village. And the women and children I will let go free."

"But their fathers," Rechab began, imagining the women and their little ones trying to toil across the wilderness to some oasis alone, but Callum held a finger to her lips.

"It is all that I can do," he said. "You said it yourself. I have orders."

She nodded. He continued. "I already chance the displeasure of certain high officials by bringing some back for trial, but I think I can turn it to their advantage and please them in the end. I cannot promise anyone will be found innocent, but I can try to return those fathers to their families through the process of justice. In the end it will be up to the priests. I do not know how it will go."

"I understand," she said. The priests in Shalem were the official high court of the Holy People. If prisoners were brought back to stand trial, it would be before them. But it had been many years since the high court offered real hope to the innocent. They could only pray the priests who presided over them were both inclined to see real justice done and free enough of political control to carry it out.

He continued to search her face, still holding her hand. "I cannot let you go. You understand that."

"I never asked you to," she said.

He smiled. The warmth of his smile surprised her.

"You are a woman of courage," he said.

And for the first time in Rechab's life, it was true.

CHAPTER 7

Aaron did not sleep that night. He worked on building the barricades until the faint light before dawn, until every muscle ached with exhaustion, and yet adrenaline still pounded through him, kept him awake, sharp, alert. He peered out at the hills, dark and spotted with torches, then slowly lightening, becoming hazy and gray. The torchlight grew hazy as well as dawn approached. He could see figures stirring, then hear distant voices. The army was beginning to muster for the slaughter.

For so it must be. Unless the Great God smiled on them, unless he moved as he had moved in ancient days, they would all die here in Nachush.

But maybe, he thought, maybe a miracle would happen. Maybe the Great God would reveal his mighty arm as in days of old.

His altar was surrounded and cut off, but they should begin this day in prayer. Beseech their last and only Hope to come to their aid.

"Where is Rechab?" Aaron asked an aide. It occurred to him that he had not seen her all night. Knowing his betrothed, she was likely hiding in a house or a hole somewhere—some version of her cave where she could be alone.

Aaron would not admit, even to himself, that he was disappointed in her. He loved her. He needed her.

The aide ran off to find her, and Aaron stalked the line once again, examining it for breaches, for weak points. As if that would really make any difference against the force about to descend on them.

With their men, their arms, and their defensive position, Aaron estimated they would hold the city for an hour or two. Then it would be over, and they would go to their deaths in glory.

He heard others calling for Rechab, hunting the nearby houses and streets. He frowned.

The aide reappeared after a short time. "She is not to be found, my lord,"

"What do you mean?" Aaron asked. "She's hiding. She often hides . . . she likes to be alone. Rouse her!"

"But I am telling you, she is not be found. It is as though she vanished in the night."

It struck him that she might have run away.

It wasn't like he had been watching her. Why set guards around his beloved when every man was needed to secure the city around them? He had not even thought to ask if there might be any special threat to her. Or *from* her.

That she would run, leave him alone, abandon them all at a time like this—it made bile rise in his throat.

But just as quickly, he swallowed it. It was a lie. She had not run. Wherever she was now, he would never believe Rechab was a traitor. Not to these people, and not to him. Her heart was frail, but it was true.

And so worry replaced the fleeting anger that had shot through his heart. He spotted Micah, the acolyte from Essea, among the men

 RACHEL STARR THOMSON

of the village, sword in hand, and strode to his side. "Micah! Have you seen Rechab?"

"No, indeed," the soft-spoken pilgrim said. "Has she gone missing?"

"Vanished during the night," Aaron said. If possible, his adrenaline began to pound even harder. He was beginning to worry now. They had to find her. Yes, it was like Rechab to hide. But not to completely disappear at a time like this.

Aaron forgot about wanting Rechab to lead them in a ritual prayer. All he knew was that a battle was about to begin and the girl he loved was nowhere to be found. He wanted nothing more than to protect her, and he had already failed.

Trumpets blew from the hillside where the altar was.

Aaron spun and stared into the haze. He could see the mustered figures of troops and flags flying. The blast blew a second time. But this was not a command to attack. The flags were white.

It was an invitation to parley.

He stood and stared, and for a second all of his strength, all of the pounding energy and urgency of the night, drained from his body. He thought he would collapse there in the street. A parley meant the possibility of reprieve. The chance of mercy.

He had not expected this.

And he did not know what to do.

Oh, where was Rechab?

His men gathered around him. Micah lurked nearby, close enough to hear but not close enough to insert himself into the inner circle. Aaron knew he should beckon the man closer. He was the nearest thing they had to a priest, to a representative of the Great God's favor. But he didn't. He still stung from Micah's rebuke and the way Rechab had sided with the stranger against him.

"Gather my captains," Aaron told his aide. "We go to speak with our enemy."

———•◆•———

The enemy commander sat astride a dusty white horse. His captains, six of them, were arrayed behind him on horseback.

Aaron and his men came riding mules and asses. Surefooted on the hillside, but poor men's steeds.

The commander was a swarthy, thick-browed man wearing a short cloak over a bronze breastplate and arm bands that wrapped around bulging arms. A short but heavy sword hung strapped to his waist. His captains held spears.

The air here was clearer. The sunlight was already shining on the tops of the hills. Aaron and his men ascended up through the dawn mist of the valley into the clear light where their enemies waited for them.

Aaron dismounted upon approach. The enemy commander did not.

As a symbol of trust, Aaron drew his sword and drove its tip into the ground, to remain there until they finished speaking.

The commander nodded and drew his as well, handing it to an underling to likewise drive into the sandy earth.

"I greet you," the commander said. "Your reputation is heard throughout these parts. You are called Aaron, I believe?"

His tone was blunt, lacking ceremony or refinement. Aaron was glad for it. He had been Flora's mule driver, not one of her business managers. He did not have a gilded tongue to match one of the king's more garrulous representatives. This fellow suited him well.

"I am," he said loudly. "I greet you also."

"I have come to destroy you all," the commander said without

   RACHEL STARR THOMSON

preamble. He stopped and added belatedly, "I am Callum of the Hills, commander of the king's forces in Shalem." Before Aaron could think up an appropriate answer, Callum continued where he'd left off. "I have come to destroy you, but you have been effectively interceded for, and I take it upon myself to offer you different terms. You, Aaron of Nachush, are deemed a treasonous traitor to the king, and those who have gathered to you here are likewise deemed on the wrong side of the king's favor. But as your intercessor has pointed out, there are many among you who cannot be charged with any crime. So here are my terms: any man among you who agrees to return to Shalem as a prisoner to answer for his crimes will be given a trial. Whether it will be a fair one or not I cannot say. You throw yourself on my mercy, and I will be merciful. Throw yourself on the priests' mercy, and that is for them to decide. Any man among you who will not agree to return to Shalem to stand trial will be fought to the death on this day and will die here, today, gloriously or ingloriously as fate and his own conduct would have it. Your women and children are free to flee. We will attack when the sun breaks over those hills and kill without mercy any who remain within this valley. You have until then to surrender yourself, take your stand, or flee as the option is open to you. I trust you will pass the word on to your people in plenty of time for them to act."

Aaron's mind whirled. This was not the script he'd foreseen. Not the last stand he'd intended to make as he spent the long night tearing down walls to build new ones and shoring up his men with talk of miracles and the Great God's favor.

But this . . . was this offer of mercy not a miracle? Was this not the Great God's favor?

If it was, he did not want it. To be taken back to Shalem in chains like a dog, to throw himself on the doubtful integrity of the priests, to declare by his own surrender that his enterprise had been treasonous and a failure besides.

He could not. He would not.

"I deny your offer," he said. He heard murmurs behind him—his captains. The sound was not a happy one. But he ignored it. A leader had to be firm, confident. "You think to put us to shame. We will not grovel before you, grateful for the crumbs you throw us. No, we will not be paraded before the people of Shalem as traitors. What we do here is right. We have acted as the king should have acted years ago, to free his people from bondage and bring back the worship of the Great God."

At that one of his men exclaimed aloud. He didn't discern the words. He didn't try. He locked eyes with a clearly surprised Callum and said, "We will take our stand here when the sun hits the top of the hills. I look forward to meeting swords with you."

The big man shook his shaggy head slowly. An expression crept into his face, but it was neither the admiration nor the scorn Aaron expected to see. Rather, he looked like a father disappointed in his son.

"You are a fool, then," he said, "and a selfish one. I would rather take you back in chains to stand trial than kill you, for I think you might learn something valuable from it. But I have done all I can."

He reined his horse around to return to his camp, but Aaron called out after him, "Wait—wait, I wish an answer to a question."

Callum looked back over his shoulder. "Well?"

"You said someone had interceded for us. Tell me who."

He expected the answer to be Micah. Surely the tall, self-righteous hypocrite had snuck out of the village in the night, excusing himself from the labor of building the protective wall, and taken their enemy's side. When Aaron returned to the village, he would have the man publicly denounced and locked up until the battle was over.

"The woman," Callum said simply. "Rechab."

 RACHEL STARR THOMSON

Aaron's heart stopped, and he stared at the commander with uncomprehending eyes.

"She is my prisoner," Callum said. "I will take her to the Holy City to stand trial for her crimes when all of this is over. Crimes she was humble enough to confess. I wish you had half her wisdom, boy."

And he left. His captains reined their horses around after him and climbed the hill toward their camp, where fires dotted the hill and their troops waited for them.

Aaron stared after them, unmoving.

One of his own captains said, low by his elbow, "It is a worthy offer. We should . . ."

"No."

"But Aaron . . ."

"Do not address me by my first name."

"But sir," the man stressed, "the women. The children. Bad enough that the men of the village are entangled in this."

Aaron turned on him, eyes blazing. His spirit stung so he could hardly get the words out. "Would you take Rechab's side in this? Condemn the women and children to death in the wilderness? If we drive them from here that is all they will get."

"Let them make that choice," the captain said. Aaron couldn't even remember his name in the whirlwind of emotions that gripped his mind, his soul. The man was a relative newcomer, not one of Flora's old retinue. But he was milder than most. He had also been talking to Micah, Aaron recalled. Was there no end to this conspiracy against him?

"It is Micah who puts these thoughts in your head!" Aaron cried. He all but shoved the man away and strode toward his mule, snatching his sword from the ground as though he would take someone's head off with it.

Rechab!

This was Micah's fault. Micah and his scroll. Micah who had turned her against him.

His thoughts argued, wrestling with one another as he threw himself onto the mule's back and began to trot down the hill toward the valley. The mist was clearing, making the town more clearly visible. Dust clouds still rose from the demolition in the night. The barricade stretched around it, as high as a man in places.

It would not be enough. He'd had a glimpse of the troops waiting on the hillside. It was worse than it had looked in the night. They could not possibly hold.

Not without a miracle. Not without the Great God's help.

And without Rechab, Aaron was not sure the Great God would come.

———◆———

Rechab paced a rut in the floor of Callum's tent and prayed for Aaron.

She heard the soldiers returning and Callum giving orders. His voice was gruff, angry. Her heart sank. The parley had not gone well.

Callum stormed into the tent and threw his cloak aside as he busied himself about something, giving orders to the captains who followed him. He snatched up a spear from its block and scratched out orders in the earth. Halfway through he paused and looked up, his eyes catching Rechab's.

"I'm sorry," he said. "He's a fool."

He looked back down and continued his discussion with his captains.

Rechab tuned out the details of the coming attack and stood still in the midst of the tent. She felt the Great God's eyes upon her, his gaze strong and steady and not disapproving. She felt his gaze strengthening her. Here, literally surrounded by her enemies, she felt herself to be in the center of his will.

She cried out silently, *O God, change his heart!*

Turn it like the rivers of water.

Have mercy on the poor, the widows, the innocent.

Forgive us. Forgive me. Help us all.

Her legs weakened beneath her, and she sat on the small chair set there for her.

The captains cleared out. The air in the tent, cool after the night, was beginning to warm. Light washed up its edges as the sun rose outside. She swallowed hard. She'd heard Callum discussing his terms before he left the tent. The attack would begin in an hour, unless he decided to retaliate against Aaron's stubbornness and attack sooner.

But calm assurance flooded her heart. He would not. Her enemy was honorable, and he desired to have mercy. Her intercession had done what she desired. Only Aaron stood in the way now.

Callum left the tent, leaving her alone with her thoughts and fears. A few soldiers lingered outside, guarding her, but she did not think Callum was worried that she would run. His own heart was true, and so he recognized her intentions as pure and knew that she would not betray him. She prayed that his actions would not harm him, that those in Shalem who had sent him to destroy would not judge him a traitor for bringing her back.

The thought of returning to Shalem, to the darkness and the shadow there, threatened to bring fear back over her soul. Something in Shalem hunted her. She had fled from it, what seemed like so long ago now—fled with Flora and begun this strange chapter of her life.

And now she would return, of her own free will, to submit herself to the powers there. And it felt right. It felt inevitable.

She took comfort in the Great God's gaze. She did not go alone.

Questions about her father, about the murder Callum had alluded to, and about Flora filled her mind. With all her heart she wished she'd had a chance to speak more with Micah. He might have been able to tell her where Flora was, why she hadn't come to Nachush. He might have been able to explain more of what was happening in the world beyond this valley. And he might have been able to read to her from the lost scroll of the Great God and enlighten her soul.

She wished with all her heart for the chance for that to happen.

The train of thought made her heart sink again. The scroll. One of the lost scrolls—the most valuable treasure in the Sacred Land. A tangible assurance of the Great God's eye upon his people and a tangible way for them to return to him. Chances were it would be lost again, or even destroyed, in the attack. Micah would die, and without him, who would tell the People about the scroll and its contents?

She stood, new purpose flooding her. She had done all she could in interceding for the villagers. But she had not interceded for the word. Perhaps she could save it.

She went to the door of the tent and peered out, paling a little at the sight of the troops forming in battle lines. Hundreds of men, outnumbering the force in Nachush by three to one if she had to guess—and that was just from what she could see. She knew there were more men further back in the hills, waiting on Callum to call them into action. She searched the ranks for the commander and found him, astride his horse, giving orders not far from the tent. He was so close. But she couldn't interrupt him now.

One of the guards stationed near the tent was watching her. She turned to him and joined her hands in a plea.

 Rachel Starr Thomson

"What do you want?" he asked. It was clear he was not keen to listen to her. Perhaps he feared she would cast some kind of spell on him, as she had already done on the commander.

"I need to get a message to Callum," she said. "It's important. Please . . ."

"I'm not an errand boy," the soldier said. "You've said your piece. You'll get a chance to open your mouth again when you stand trial. I'll not hear naught until then."

"But this is important," she insisted. "You have to listen to me."

"I don't have to do anything," the soldier said, turning his back. "Best you remember who's a prisoner here and who's got the power."

"But it will be lost," she said. "It . . ." An idea came to her. She raised her voice. "There is a treasure. A great treasure, hidden. If Callum isn't told, it will be lost."

The soldier turned back, and she saw what she'd been hoping for: the light of avarice in his yellowed eyes. "A treasure, you say?"

She lowered her voice, drawing him closer, snaring him. "Some call it the greatest treasure of the Sacred Land."

"Here?" he asked, half-scoffing, but his eyes flicked to the hills and the mines. If he'd heard that she was Flora Laurentii—or at least rumored to be—it would only give credence to the deception. Yes, she'd told Callum who she really was, but these others didn't know. Flora was known across the land for her rich holdings and shrewd business dealings. The man was hooked as surely as a fish on a line, but how to turn his greed to her advantage?

She opened her mouth to tell him some lie—about how the scroll case was full of some precious silk, worth more than its weight in gold, or some magical incense the priests would pay for—when she changed her mind.

Lies had brought her here. She would not add to them.

"It is a scroll," she said.

The man jerked away. "Bah," he said. She reached out and grabbed his sleeve. He started to shake her off, but she rushed her words out. "One of the lost scrolls," she said, "the lost scrolls of the temple. Truly a treasure, don't you see? They are relics of the past. The temple is full of gold: the priests will pay well for them!"

That was not exactly a lie . . . but she knew it to be only a desperate hope.

The soldier knew it too. He did shake her off this time, with another "bah," though he was still listening. "They've been thought to be lost for generations," she said. "But all this time some of the scrolls were in Essea. An acolyte brought one here. I saw it with my own eyes."

"If the priests of the Great God had any real power in Shalem, what you say might matter," the soldier said. He folded his arms. "But the current powers aren't likely much to care. They might just as soon burn the lost scrolls."

"Who do you mean?" Rechab asked. "Who sent you here?"

Their conversation was interrupted by Callum, who glared down at them both with disapproval.

"Rechab, get back in the tent," he said. "I don't wish to see you out here again until I send for you. Shaul, return to your duties."

"My lord," Rechab said, dropping a curtsey and trying desperately to meet the commander's eye, "there is . . ."

"Not now. Not another word. I'm in deep enough because of you."

"But you don't under—"

"NOW," Callum roared.

Overhead, the sun was about to tip the mountains. Eyes filled with tears of frustration, Rechab ducked back inside the tent and dropped to her knees to pray feverishly.

The scroll could not be lost. Could not be destroyed. Could not be snatched away from the Holy People when they needed so badly to hear the Great God's voice.

In that moment Rechab knew that if she were to escape all of this with her life, and if the scroll too were to escape, she would learn its contents and proclaim them from every rooftop and high mountain. Lies had brought her here. Lies had brought all the Holy People to this place—to slaughter and treason and trouble. Truth, the Great God's truth written in scrolls and not lost any longer, would surely get them out.

A rustling at the door of the tent caused her to look up. It was the guard, Shaul, standing with his shoulder just inside. He did not turn his face toward her, but she heard his muffled words: "I will look for your treasure."

CHAPTER 8

Flora wasted no time putting her plan into action. There was little she could do with Amon's guards outside the door that led into the rest of the palace, so she began by making good use of the *other* door and positioning herself very publicly on the balcony. Her intention was to be seen by as many people as possible.

To her satisfaction, the gardens beneath her balcony were quite active with the coming and going of servants, and even more importantly, a flow of family members and important guests from within the palace. These would move through the garden in small waves, escorted by respectful guards a distance before and behind. Statesmen strolling side by side, engaged in conspiratorial whispers; Beniah's many children playing; his younger wives looking on as their nursemaids stayed on the little ones' mischievous heels. Stewards and gardeners, waiters and kitchen workers, all passed through the gardens at one time or another.

Flora was seen by all. She saw the slowed steps, the widening eyes; heard the whispers. More than once she startled someone and watched fear wash over their faces in a pale wave, replaced by relief and then confusion when they realized it wasn't her.

Izevel.

That was the name she heard whispered.

Izevel, the queen. Izevel, who had been here only a matter of months but had apparently given many cause to respond to her with fear. Izevel, worshiper of Kimash and niece of the pagan god's high priest. Izevel, Beniah's favorite new wife.

The servants, especially, cowered when they thought it was Izevel on the balcony.

It made Flora angry.

In Essea, the Teacher had spoken long and often about the kingship in Shalem. About how Beniah was a disgrace to it, and how his fathers before him had failed the office. But also of the ideal, set up by the Great God himself: of a line of kings set on the throne to represent God to the people and the people to God, to be their intercessor and judge, to be in the king's own sphere a kind of priest before them and thus a servant to them.

Not that the priests of the Great God were servants to these people any more than Beniah was. They all had long ago given up their callings in exchange for ill-gotten riches and abominable alliances.

Somehow knowing what they should have been made it all worse. Flora felt their wretched failing as if it were her own. She had always cared more deeply for these people than they did for themselves.

She made certain, as she stood on the balcony, to smile and nod at those individuals of any standing who caught sight of her, and to smile slightly and nod even more slightly at the individuals who were not of any standing, as though she were some benevolent goddess deigning to take notice of them. She caught the blushes and the surprised, fumbling curtseys and bows from those who realized she was looking at them, smiling at them. Eventually she started to hear her own name whispered: rumor was getting around.

Good. That was exactly what she wanted.

     RACHEL STARR THOMSON

When a clatter in the hall outside her room told her someone of importance was passing, she made certain to burst out and "accidentally" interrupt them before the guards could intercept her. She did this twice, once catching Beniah's youngest wife and an envoy of servants, the other time catching a senator. Both times, the results were good. She smiled at the wife and made her feel like a friend, and she winked at the senator.

She knew she shouldn't have done it. But she couldn't find it in herself to regret it.

The more people who saw her in the palace, the more people who felt they had some personal stake in her being there, the harder it would be for the high priest to do away with her. If she could manage it, she would install herself as firmly here as she had ever installed herself at Aurelius's home in Bethabara, just down the mountainside from here. He had always hated it when she showed up and took over, but he couldn't stop her. And Beniah was not so antagonistic as her brother had always been. There was a good chance she could make herself a very, very difficult woman to dislodge from the royal household.

After her second time bursting out of her chambers unannounced, she heard a key turn in her door. The guards were not taking any more chances. But she'd already accomplished much. That wink would take her far. She returned to the balcony to shine again upon the passersby below.

For a brief moment, as she stood there glimmering, she shook her head and laughed at herself. Flora Laurentii, on display before the world. She'd wondered sometimes if she would ever learn. It seemed she wouldn't. Chances were not good she would actually live through this, all her efforts notwithstanding. It figured she would go down as flamboyantly as ever she'd risen.

Fittingly, the summons came after dark.

Flora toyed with the idea of refusing to go. If she could manage it, if she could have a few more days to continue making herself a fixture here and bumping into various important people, she could win a greater chance at life.

But as she looked through the door of her chambers into the hall where guards stood three abreast on either side, forming two lines for her to walk down in the gleaming torchlight, she knew there was no point in stalling.

So she held her head high and walked out, letting them usher her away in silence.

The marble halls of the palace wavered eerily in the firelight.

The guards knew where to go. They took her to a large, dimly lit chamber, where besides the guards arrayed wordlessly on every side, three figures waited.

Amon, a distance to the left.

And on the low dais in the middle of the room, seated on small thrones, the high priest of Kimash and a woman Flora knew looked exactly like her.

They weren't just sisters, she realized with a start.

They were twins.

Her blood ran cold as Izevel looked her over from head to foot, slow and calculating as a snake. The high priest too was silent. He sat with his fingers resting lightly together, dressed in his long black cassock with a two-headed dragon embroidered down the back. On the small throne he looked like a king shrouded in shadows.

The real power in Shalem, Flora knew, was here.

She held her head as high as she could and broke the silence herself.

"Sister," she said. "Uncle."

The two on the dais exchanged glances, and the high priest slowly separated his fingers. "You know us?"

"Amon let me know who you are." She glared at the Southerner as though she could impale him with her eyes. "It seems he thought I should fear you."

"Fear your own family?" Izevel asked. Her voice was brittle. "This should be a joyous reunion."

"By all means, then," Flora answered. "Commence rejoicing."

The high priest slowly stood. A tall man, he towered above them all for a moment before taking a step down so he stood on level ground with Flora, below Izevel's watchful gaze.

"From the sarcasm dripping in your voice, I think you have gained a wrong impression of us. A wrong . . . expectation of us. We are your family."

"My expectations befit family who would keep me imprisoned and call for me only after dark," Flora answered. "Family who would reward the likes of Amon the Trader for dragging me here against my will."

"Reward?" the high priest asked, looking mildly surprised.

"That is the only reason he brought me here," Flora said. "I don't think you have disappointed him."

Amon looked away, refusing to meet her eyes.

"Let us dispense with games," Flora said. "I am here because I am your enemy. You worship a god I abhor. I worship a God you hate. In some form or another, that is why I am here. Beyond that I don't understand what you want with me. So I invite you to tell me."

Izevel stood, her white dress trailing behind her as she stepped down and took her uncle's arm. She continued to regard Flora with interest, the sort of interest a cat shows a mouse.

"'Enemy' is a harsh word," she said. "Most of the gods do not demand such division between their worshipers. Every man and woman may worship as they like or even take more than one deity to their heart."

"My God does not agree," Flora said.

"So we hear," the high priest answered, rubbing Izevel's hand where it rested high on his arm. "It is a sad and strange thing, my niece, when a people such as we rise in the world from contempt to honor and find, at the height of that honor, that one of our own still holds us in deep disdain. You should join our rise, not oppose it."

"It is not the Hill People I oppose," Flora said. "It is your filthy god."

"Listen to how she speaks of us, Uncle," Izevel said, turning her head to the high priest but keeping her eyes on Flora. "As though she is not even one of us." The queen's eyes flashed, and she turned to face Flora directly. "Tell me, sister: have you always been so ashamed of us?"

Flora met her gaze, and neither woman backed down.

Beloved, said the voice in Flora's soul.

"Just tell me what you want with me," she repeated.

Izevel spun and returned to her throne, petulant. Their smooth-tongued uncle, by contrast, lost none of his composure. He smiled, a red-lipped smile that revealed absolutely nothing of his soul.

"We only wish to welcome you to the family," he said. "You are to be congratulated: all these years separated from your kin, and now that you find us again, we are at the height of influence and power. We all have Amon to thank for reuniting us."

Flora's eyes flicked to Amon, who looked displeased. For a moment she wavered. Were they sincere? Could they possibly be sincere? She had expected some black-hearted treachery, not a welcome.

But then, her heart told her, from such as these a welcome could

    RACHEL STARR THOMSON

be the greatest treachery possible.

"Please, sit down," the high priest said. He gestured to a seat close to the dais. Nodding to servants who seemed to materialize out of the shadows, he directed them to move his own chair down so he could sit directly across from Flora, not above her. Reluctantly, she did as he requested.

The high priest raised his voice as he sat. "Leave us," he commanded. The soldiers and servants around the perimeter of the room exchanged glances but filed out without protest.

"You too, Amon," the high priest said. He kept his eyes trained on Flora as he spoke. She did not break his gaze, though she wanted to see the expression on Amon's face. She could feel his displeasure like a blast of heat across the space between them. It seemed things were truly not going as he had expected.

In a moment Amon was gone, leaving Flora alone with the high priest and the queen. Her family.

"Tell me," the priest said. "What do you know about yourself?"

She resisted the temptation to squirm. It was too open an invitation, too easy to slip into a vulnerable position answering it. But she couldn't just refuse to speak.

"I know a great deal about myself," she answered. "I have been a pilgrim for many years: I have spent more hours gazing into my own soul than most people will do in a lifetime."

He quirked a slight smile, but she couldn't tell if he was genuinely amused or just humoring her. The man's face was like a mask. No matter its expression, it hid the truth behind it. "I refer more to your origins than your present inner state," he said. "What do you know about where you come from?"

"I know that my mother was a woman of ill repute," Flora said. "A

Hill Woman. My father, Florus Laurentinus, a Westlander by descent who visited her . . . somewhat often, I am told. She raised me into young childhood in a modest home in the Hill Country, and then I ran away. After that my father took me in and finished raising me."

"You ran away," her uncle repeated. "Not *to* your father, specifically?"

"No."

"Then I assume you came back home before he took you away."

"I was found."

She would say no more about it. That had been the blackest day of her life, a day she revisited never. Even now she found herself clenching her hands, trying to ward off the power of the memories she'd locked away.

The high priest noticed her hands and made a small sound acknowledging her turmoil. "You hated your mother, then."

"I hated Kimash. I loved my mother."

The words surprised her. She wasn't sure she had ever spoken them before. But they were true. Had her mother not lived outside a shrine of Kimash, had she not served him as a cult prostitute, had she not been totally given over to the religion of her fathers, Flora would not have run from her. Her memories of her mother were only hazy. She'd been so young when she ran. But they were still warm with the simple affection and need of childhood.

The question burst from her quite apart from her intentions. "What happened to her?" she asked. "Surely you know. You are her . . ."

"Her brother, yes," the high priest said. "You do know that she is dead?"

"Many years ago, yes," Flora said. "But no one ever told me what happened."

 RACHEL STARR THOMSON

Izevel stirred on her throne on the dais. Her voice was still petulant. "She died of a wasting disease," she said. "I was with her the whole time. She held my hand at the last, and looked for the last time on me and on our uncle."

"Where were you?" Flora asked. Again the question had slipped out unbidden. Inwardly she berated herself: this was not the direction this meeting was supposed to take. "I don't remember you. I was the only child in our mother's house . . . and yet we must have been born together."

"Indeed," Izevel said, "we shared our mother's womb, you and I. But I was taken to the temple of Kimash as an infant, and you remained with her."

There—unmistakable in Izevel's eye was a flash of enmity, even of hatred. Flora's stomach turned to think of what her sister might have endured as a child. Flora's abhorrence of Kimash was birthed in the shrine behind her mother's house. Izevel had lived in the shrine of all shrines, raised by men and demons. Men like their uncle, the man who sat before them, and like Mashi, the man Flora had tried to set free from the control of evil spirits. She could not imagine that life. Or would not imagine it.

Something in Izevel's eyes was speaking to her, taunting her, provoking her. But Flora did not speak the language of that gaze, and she could not decipher it.

What she did know of a surety was that her sister was every bit as much a servant of Kimash as the high priest. She had not come out of the temple of the Hill People unscathed or with her loyalties divided. As much as Flora had run from Kimash, Izevel had embraced him.

To her own surprise, Flora's heart wept for her. The woman before her was a serpent, a cold-hearted and beautiful creature of deadly power. But once she had only been a child, just as Flora was once only a child.

Something snapped, cold, in Izevel's eyes, and she hissed, "Cease your pity. I don't need it. I am the queen of this land where you are little more than a pariah. That is how the 'Great God' of these people has repaid you for betraying Kimash."

The high priest put out his hand and gave Izevel a warning look. "Peace, my niece," he said. "Flora is not our enemy. Forgive her, Flora. Her zeal for the honor of Kimash carries her away."

Izevel glared at her uncle but did not answer back. Flora marveled at the strangeness of the moment. Her sister, the queen of the Sacred Land, speaking words that should have stung deeply—not that Flora would be counted an enemy of Kimash; that much she took as an honor; but that she was indeed still an outcast in this land where her twin now sat on the throne. Flora, loyal to the death to the Great God, had come here a prisoner, while under the spires of the Great God's temple, endless revelry celebrated the ascension of Izevel.

It *did* sting, a little. But not with near the power Izevel had meant in the barb. For the voice still echoed in Flora's heart, giving her courage, giving her hope. *Beloved.*

"You still have not told me why I am here," Flora said.

The high priest stood. He extended his hand to her. She did not take it—just stared at him. After a moment he opened his palm in a gesture of acceptance, of welcome. "You accuse us unfairly," he said. "Our friend Amon may have brought you here expecting us to mistreat you, but you are family. We do not hold you here, Flora. We welcome you here. You will remain here in the palace, where we have prepared the way for you with the king, because there are threats to you outside. And when it is time for you to go, you will be free to go."

She still stared, trying hard to comprehend.

And the voice in her soul—the voice she was beginning to realize belonged to the Great God, though she had no time to process the real-

 RACHEL STARR THOMSON

ity of that or meditate upon how she came to hear it so clearly—said, *They have brought you here to sway your heart. They have brought you to change your loyalties.*

"But that won't happen," she blurted out loud.

I know, the voice answered her.

Izevel and the high priest exchanged confused looks, and he hurried to assure her, "But it will. We are looking into the threats against you, and as soon as our sources assure us you are safe, we *will* release you."

She shook her head and smiled. "Not that. I don't believe you will ever release me, no. But I meant the part you didn't say. I will never change my heart. I will never become a servant of Kimash. I will never be one of you."

She stood and turned. "If that is all, I will return to my chambers. It's the middle of the night, and I am tired."

The high priest shook his head. "You are a beautiful woman, Flora, and a wise and well-spoken one. A woman of many talents. You could amount to so much here."

Flora smiled again. "My only talent, Uncle, is being widowed astonishingly often and early. Though lately I have also achieved a knack for making dangerous enemies. Good night to you."

And she left.

The chamber was silent in her wake. The guards and servants did not dare reenter without a summons. Whether Amon still waited outside or not, Izevel and the high priest did not know and did not care. They had paid him handsomely for bringing Flora here. That was all the reward he would get.

Izevel turned cold eyes on her uncle. "She is a blot on our people's success. An affront to everything we stand for."

The high priest smiled sardonically. "And she reads your mind,

Izevel. Don't think I can't see the real reasons you are so eager to do away with her."

"It affronts me to know we share blood. Shared a mother. A womb."

"You have taken your own path," the high priest answered. "Hers need not blight yours."

"I will not see her live. Her blood will stain these palace floors."

"Better the temple floors," the high priest said. "Let her die in the sanctuary of the Great God. But not yet, Izevel. Bide your time. She's already been canny in her dealings here. Cause her death and Beniah will ask questions, even of you. Don't make his heart doubt you. Let her set her own trap."

"You are very confident she will."

"I know her history. She always does." He placed his fingertips together again, resting his elbows lightly on the arms of the chair. "Fear not, Izevel. Your sister will pave the way to her own death, and we will reap the benefits when Kimash is shown to be supreme."

 RACHEL STARR THOMSON

In their villa on the outskirts of Shalem, above the noise and stench of the city on the cleaner slopes of the Holy Mountain, the household of Aurelius Florus Laurentinus welcomed guests and feasted them.

Ezra ben Malchi, an aged and wealthy landowner from the northern parts of the Sacred Land, had come to Shalem to participate in the wedding festivities of the king. Those festivities had gone on far too long for his liking. Nor was much else that he saw or heard agreeable to his ears. The snake-like priest of Kimash had grown too powerful through the ascension of his equally snake-like niece, and Ezra, who had never found serpents beautiful, watched it all with weighted eyes and an increasingly heavy heart.

One small bright spot in the feasting was meeting and talking with Aurelius, governor of Bethabara, and finding him to be a man of an equally troubled countenance. So when the message came from Marah, Aurelius's wife and a distant cousin of Ezra's, he did not think long or too hard about it.

Yes, he would help them escape their veiled house arrest, even knowing he chanced making dangerous enemies. There were times it was better to have enemies than to remain neutral. This was one of those times.

The feast carried on long into the night. Tall stands held torches high in the gardens, casting dancing, flickering shadows through the palm fronds and lilac branches. Tables had been laid out in the courtyard. Ezra's entire entourage from the north, some forty people, ate, drank, and made merry, as did Aurelius's house.

Guards lingered around the edges, watching the feast enviously. Those in Aurelius's employ were invited to partake, and did. The others were offered food and drink, and denied it . . . one more sign that the "protectors" around Aurelius and Marah were in fact their jailers.

By the end of the feasting, sometime around two o'clock in the morning, only four among the revelers were still stone sober, though at least two of them had pretended to be otherwise: Ezra, Aurelius, Marah, and Shem.

Shem did not revel. He sat apart from the crowd with his arms folded over his chest, watching the party with a sullen frown. Disapproving and arrogant. Fingering the amulet he was constantly wearing. Aurelius wanted to smack him. So he didn't want to drink . . . fine. At least he could play along.

On the bright side, Shem had been acting like this since they arrived in the Holy City, so the guards watching them were unlikely to grow suspicious over his behavior. Aurelius caught Marah frowning at the boy, but she said nothing to him. Better not to make a scene.

In the deepest part of the night, the torches began to wink out. Servants, wavering a little on their feet from too much wine, started to clean up. Ezra and his household packed up, said their good-byes boisterously, and left.

Aurelius, Marah, and Shem, all dressed in homespun and carry

     Rachel Starr Thomson

ing bundles of what looked to be Ezra's household goods, walked out with them.

Aurelius stood at the head of a street that twisted around the edge of Shalem and looked down on the city, gloomily lit with a few lights here and there, shadows under the starlight. A low buzz of noise rose from the streets as it always did, day and night. He breathed free air and let out a long breath of relief.

Marah touched his arm. Her voice spoke low in his ear. "I think we did it."

"We can only hope the deception holds," Aurelius replied. He took her hand and squeezed it. "We are fools."

"Better a fool on the right side of history than a coward on the wrong side of it."

Aurelius smiled faintly. The temple rose above every other building in the city, built at the top of a rise, its spires reaching out of the darkness to touch the heavens.

"And who determines right and wrong?" he asked.

"Perhaps the Great God does," Marah answered.

Ezra's entourage was moving around them like a sluggish stream splitting around a rock. Still holding Marah's hand, Aurelius picked up the bundle he had set down and reentered the flow. Ezra had had enough of the city, so they would take the street around it and not go through. That suited Aurelius well. By morning they would be well on their way down the mountain, only an hour or two from Bethabara.

What he would find there, Aurelius did not know. He could not resume his duties as governor while he was supposed to be imprisoned in his villa. But his people were vulnerable, and he could not leave them that way. If there was any way he could help them, he would do it.

After that, the future was an open guess.

Shem hung near the back of Ezra's slow-moving train. He ignored a giggling servant girl who batted her eyelashes at him and put one foot after another with increasing difficulty. He felt as though a leaden weight were tied to each foot.

Ever since the garden, something inside him had been growing. He felt it just beneath his breastbone, a heavy pressure that had begun to expand outward until it was difficult to breathe. As the pressure grew it consumed his attention, drawing all his thoughts inward, to his lungs and the temple of his spirit where light never penetrated.

He knew Aurelius watched him—more and more, it seemed, since the night in the garden. Sometimes he worried that the master had found the remains of his sacrifice, but nothing was ever said. He did not know why he feared that discovery so much anyway: Aurelius might have a faith in the Great God, but it was newborn and weak.

Not like his own faith in Amon-Heth. A faith he would kill and die for.

Besides, he still had Marah's favor. Aurelius might frown on him, but he would not lift a hand against him while his wife objected. Marah had all but raised Shem. He had always been a golden child in her eyes.

He didn't admit to himself how much he had changed—how much the eager-to-please boy who genuinely cared for Marah and her household and wanted to serve her well—had been overshadowed by the cavern he was becoming. A cavern in whose depths something grew.

Something that wanted out.

This was what it meant to become a man, he told himself. And more than a man. A chosen one of Amon-Heth in an age of change, when the gods battled amongst themselves for supremacy.

     RACHEL STARR THOMSON

His lip curled as he walked alongside a wagon, keeping slow pace with it. He did not understand why Marah and Aurelius would choose the Great God—a deity so clearly on the decline. Amon had called the Great God an old god, one in his dotage. Rising were other gods. Kimash. And Amon-Heth.

The pressure inside him grew even stronger at the thought of Kimash. Now he was the real enemy. With his high priest installed in the royal court and the new queen a devotee, the degenerate god of the Hill People was set to become the supreme deity of the People. Amon-Heth, so far his superior; Amon-Heth, stately and silent in his grandeur; Amon-Heth, the jackal-headed shape in the shadows around Shem, would be ignored.

But not if his prophet had anything to say about it.

The weight in Shem's feet, the pressure in his chest, told him he was going the wrong way. He was not intended to leave the Holy City. His destiny was here.

And so he drifted back, toward the end of the train, beyond the eyes of the servant girl, beyond all their eyes. When they passed through the shadows of a copse of trees, Shem disappeared.

CHAPTER 10

When Flora awoke the next morning, she went to the balcony and leaned over, drinking in the early morning sunlight as it filtered through the palms and sparked off the water of the fountains. The air was still cool, and heavily scented by the lavender that grew profusely below. She closed her eyes for a few moments and drank it in.

While she did, she listened for the presence of guards in her vicinity. There were no more than the usual palace guard, keeping a watch not on her especially but on the royal family and their home.

Back inside, she washed up and dressed, still listening carefully. Unless she missed her guess, Amon's guards had been removed.

She stepped into the marble hall and greeted the two men stationed there with a cheerful good morning. They stuttered their replies. She'd been right. They were palace guards, and they were alone.

"What happened to the others?" she asked. The guards seemed too surprised to answer. "The others," she repeated, "the other guards. There were a small army of you last night."

"Ordered away, ma'am," the taller of the two said.

By whom? she wanted to ask. *And for what reason?* But she didn't.

She'd learned painfully not to involve servants too closely in her affairs. She looked these two up and down: big men, both, built like warriors, but they seemed honest enough. "I'll count on you to watch over me, then," she said. "Keep a sharp eye. I have enemies at court."

With a sweet smile, she swept away, leaving them to follow her with hurried steps. If the high priest was going to allow her a measure of freedom, she would make the most of it.

Dressed in simple white, Flora descended into the garden and let the sun wash over her in warm, welcoming delight. It took her a moment to reconcile this view of the garden with the one she'd enjoyed from above, but a turn or two oriented her, and she headed for the quiet bench she had noticed beneath a lilac arbor not far from her balcony. A fountain on the other side of the profuse flowers filled the air with a soothing sound, and the scent of the lilacs perfumed the morning.

She noted with appreciation the careful pruning and manicuring of the gardens, the clean-swept white stone pathways and deliberate creation of small, private alcoves and spots like the arbor, where someone could retreat in peace. Beniah had created these gardens for his first wife, whose recent death had been so quickly and completely overshadowed by Izevel's arrival and the quick marriage that ensued. Flora remembered the story: the one-time queen had been lonely for her home in the north, where water and greenery were abundant. Beniah had recreated her favorite places for her here.

Judging from the care still taken to keep the gardens, she suspected his wife was not as forgotten as it seemed.

Flora, too, had come here to remember. She reached the place she'd spotted and noted with pleasure that the sun slanted its way in, the trees around not yet fully shading the spot. She raised her face and smiled.

Yes, the golden spires of the temple were a clear view from here. They rose from beyond the palace wall and shone in the rising sun.

     RACHEL STARR THOMSON

In days long past they had spoken of the temple shining with the light of heaven, with the glory of the Great God himself. Now it relied on the sun to shine upon it, for the temple had no more light in itself. Essea taught that the Great God had completely departed the temple many years ago.

But Flora could choose to remember the ancient days. She could kneel here, gaze up at the spires, and remember when the God's glory shone here.

She wondered if he ever really departed a place, or if he only went into waiting. After all, the Teacher had also taught her that the Great God was creator of the world, and everything and everyone in it belonged entirely to him. That meant places in rebellion as well as places at peace with him; places unholy as well as places sacred. Ruined lives and ruined temples: they must be his as much as gardens and faithful priests.

From her youth Flora had taken up praying three times daily to the Great God. In all those years she had rarely, if ever, felt that he heard her.

But she knew now that he did. Heard her, and even answered her back. The voice was quiet now. Quiet, but still there.

As she carefully got to her knees beside the bench, she realized with a start that the voice had always been there.

She just had not recognized it until now.

She folded her hands and lifted her eyes to the spire. "I'm sorry," she whispered. "I didn't know it was you, or I might have . . . I would have . . . listened."

Covering her eyes and bowing her head, she recited the morning prayer of Essea and felt the warmth of the sun as though it were the glory of the Great God shining down on her from the temple.

When she finished, she stayed on her knees, elbows resting on the stone bench, hands still covering her eyes. Her shoulder ached, and kneeling made it worse, but she did not want to leave quite yet.

A man's voice startled her so badly that she jumped.

"It has been a long time since I heard that prayer."

She pulled her hands away from her face and gazed, startled, into the eyes of a man who stood on the other side of the hanging lilac branches. He was dressed simply, in linen, and his beard was neatly trimmed. He did not wear a crown. It took her far too long to recognize him as Beniah.

"Your majesty," she said, getting to her feet as quickly as possible in order to drop a bow. He waved dismissively. "No need, no need," he said. "Have my physicians looked at that shoulder?"

She touched the bandages self-consciously. Her white dress exposed her shoulders and showed the bandaging plainly. "No," she said. "Not since my arrival."

He frowned. "I will send for them. Please, sit."

She did, for once at a loss for words. She'd intended to interact with the king again, and to be as charming as possible. His favor was her protection, more than he knew. But she'd not had time to prepare for the meeting, and certainly not for a meeting like this.

To her continued alarm, he circled the arbor and took a seat on the bench beside her. He chuckled, and she realized that he was sober. When she'd met him upon arrival he had not been drunk, but certainly overfeasted. Rumor had him constantly intoxicated since the day of the wedding.

But he was not so now, nor did it seem as though he was suffering the aftereffects of such indulgence.

"You seem surprised to see me," he said.

"I confess I am."

    Rachel Starr Thomson

"You need not stand on ceremony with me, you know," he said. "I suppose you should call me brother."

She allowed herself a smile. "I am not sure I can manage that. Not quite so quickly. I have only just found out that I have a sister."

"My Izevel," he said with a beaming smile . . . yet she saw something under it. Something . . . sad?

"You said you had heard the words of my prayer before?" she asked. "How do you know a prayer of Essea?"

"Is that what it is?" he asked, raising his eyebrows. "Perhaps now it is, but the prayer is older than Essea. My grandmother used to recite it some mornings. I know you do not think much of my family, Flora the Famous, but we did have some faith once."

"And now?"

This time it was his turn to look uncomfortable. "I don't think I should discuss that with the likes of you. My in-laws would not look kindly on the king unveiling his heart to an Essean pilgrim."

She heard the teasing in his voice and this time smiled openly. "But I am, as you said, your sister. And surely you've heard of my excessive virtue. Any secret you might reveal would be more than safe with me."

Beniah smiled, and Flora found that all sorts of unexpected things happened inside of her as a response. She found that her heart went out to him. She found that she did not loathe or despise this man who was responsible for continuing to lead his people away from the Great God and who had so foolishly brought the evil of Izevel here. She found that in fact she liked him, and even respected him. There was a boyishness in his face that drew her to him, and at the same time the grey in his hair and beard and the telling wrinkles around his eyes spoke of a life that had known sorrow and trouble. Perhaps, after all, sorrow and trouble were the reasons for his foolish behavior of late. She faulted him for it. But she could not condemn.

So she just waited for him to continue. And he did.

"Faith?" he said with a sigh, looking into the distance as though he were an actor reciting a part for which he'd prepared for months. "Do I even know what faith is anymore? Faith long ago became a matter of expedience and alliance in this city. It became so when my grandfather five generations back defied law and married a daughter of the Southern Plains, even built her an altar where she could worship her moon god, all to facilitate peace between our peoples. And there was peace. The Great God's temple still shone, my great-grandmother sacrificed to the moon, and for that generation no one died in war on our southern borders."

Flora stayed quiet, giving him room to talk. He was trusting her with a great deal. She would honor that.

"And me? As a young man maybe I dreamed of doing things a little differently than my fathers had done. Maybe I thought the temple spires had grown a little tarnished, and I would be the author of revival for the Holy People." He looked at her then, with what was meant to be a twinkle in his eye, but instead it was sad . . . very sad. She nodded, encouraging him.

"I had a friend in those days. A man ten years my senior. A priest's son. I looked up to him. As boys we played together. When he became a man, he fell in love, and I dreamed of falling in love. He had children, and I dreamed of the day I would be a father. And he worshiped at the temple like no priest had done in generations, with such passion and fervor and belief. And I dreamed of the day I would set him up on high as an example to all our people and together we would change things here."

He gave her a sidelong glance. "You didn't expect to hear any of this, did you?"

"I . . . no."

"We are equally famous, you and I," the king said. "But for quite different reasons, no? Well, my friend became an example to the Sacred Land. But it wasn't my doing. No, I didn't help him at all. Instead I caused him to lose everything. His wife, his children, maybe his sanity. Everything."

Flora swallowed hard. The king's grief was so old it had gone hollow and dry, and he spoke the words without any sign of emotion. But she knew what such a hollow would do to a man over a lifetime.

"It was my desire for alliances that ruined it after all," Beniah said. "Some of the priests were plotting behind my back, you see, to overthrow the crown. The old loyalty between the royal house and the priesthood had worn so thin as to be seen right through, I fear. So I rounded up their leaders and sent them off by ship as envoys to the mariners on the coast."

"You sent disloyal men as envoys?"

"I intended to ambush them. But I sent my friend—and, to my everlasting regret and shame, his family—to keep an eye on them. He didn't know. I didn't tell him; he wouldn't have supported my treachery any more than he would have supported theirs. That is why I sent his family with him. So he would not know."

Flora's heart sank. "The ambush went wrong?"

Beniah shook his head. "It never happened. A storm sank the ship. They all drowned. All but my friend. But his family was gone forever. He came back here seeking some kind of justice, but what could I do? What could I possibly do to repay his loss? I tried to give him money, tried to give him power. He threw it all back in my face and went into the wilderness, where he became an example to us all after all. But not the kind I hoped for once."

The truth hit her at once, and suddenly so much fell into place. "Kol Abaddon," she said.

He nodded miserably. "The same."

The memory of a conversation with the wild man of the wilderness came back to her. She had asked for his name, and he'd told her it was lost. "Then you know his name?"

"Of course," Beniah answered. "His name is Kohan."

"Kohan," she repeated, wonderingly.

Beniah wasn't finished. "And me?" he went on. "Me, I have lost all contact with that boy who wanted to lead a revival. The spires are more tarnished than ever, and I only help tarnish them more."

"But you care," Flora said, leaning forward. She wanted to take his hands but resisted. "You care. You don't have to continue down this path. Show the People where your heart lies."

He barked a laugh. "Now? Now, my heart lies with Izevel. They all know that."

"With Kimash," Flora said, unable to keep the reproach out of her voice.

The king hung his head like a dog ashamed of itself. "I know I have made a mistake," he whispered. "I know I have made the worst mistake of my life. I have known it almost from the wedding night. People cluck their tongues and bemoan that their king is always drunk, and never stop to ask why I cannot face myself, my wife, or my thoughts sober. But I do love her, Flora. She's bloodthirsty and poisonous, and I know it, but I love her." He looked over at her with an expression that begged for pity. "I should have married you," he said. "But Izevel needs me. She needs someone to save her. You could never need someone like me."

"Now you're talking like a drunk," Flora said softly.

Beniah reached over and patted her hand. "You are good to indulge me."

"The Great God would receive you again," Flora said. "It's not too late to turn back to him."

"After all these years of warning? Of Kol Abaddon calling fiery judgment and slaughter down on all our heads? Oh, people think I ignore what he says. I don't ignore it. I know every warning, every prophecy by heart. A great army will come from the west, swarming the ground like locusts. They will destroy all before them and overrun our walls, and we will die in a great conflagration of the Great God's wrath." He grew pensive again. "We will deserve it."

"But what if that future can be changed?" Flora pressed. "What if repentance would change it? Is that not what Kol Abaddon has called for, all these years?"

"Words," Beniah said. "They are just words. If the judgment is coming, it is certain. The Holy People were holy once. We were wedded to the Great God. But it has been a long time since the divorce."

He stood. Flora stood as well, unwilling to let him go on that note. "What will you do now?" she asked.

"Return to my wife," he said with a smile, "and to my wine. Did not one of our ancient prophets write it? 'Eat, drink, and be merry, for tomorrow you may die.'"

Flora watched him go with a pounding heart. She had a sense that with this conversation, everything had changed. But she did not yet know what that meant.

Her relative freedom continued throughout the day. She was free to come and go as she pleased, to eat where and when she wanted to, to interact with the royal household instead of just watch it. She met the king's younger wife late in the morning and was invited to dine with her for lunch, and so she passed the day peacefully, building bridges and seeking out the heart of the royal family. She had been brought here on Kimash's terms, but she knew now that it was for the Great God's purposes.

Late that afternoon the wives and their children went to the Great God's temple for a ritual observance. They invited Flora to go with them, but she refused. She knew the Great God's laws. No one of Hill People blood was ever to enter the temple. She would not desecrate the place she still held in honor.

Wandering the palace after their departure, she dared talk to a few of the servants and make use of the rumor mill—careful not to ingratiate any too much or make them seem closely connected to her in any way. But she had to know what was happening in the world outside. Beniah's words about judgment troubled her deeply.

Rumors did not disappoint. But they did bring dismay. Essea, rumors said, was no more. Its people had scattered, leaving the walled community abandoned. No one knew why or if they ever intended to return—but other rumors, more whispered ones, said they had fled the wrath of Izevel, who had intended to wipe them out.

She heard rumors of Bethabara also: that a great murder had been committed there, the slaughter of an entire household, and the king refused to do anything about it. She heard the name "Nadab the Trader" and knew it all had something to do with her and with Rechab, but no one here knew enough to discover the truth.

But the worst news of all was the one that buzzed most on the lips of the servants and was repeated in the most hushed and fearful tones. A small army had left Shalem three days ago under the king's trusted commander, Callum. They had marched north to crush a rebellion—a rebellion led by someone calling herself Flora Laurentii.

Rechab.

Flora's knees went weak, and she did not even make it back to her chambers before she dropped to the marble of the palace floor and prayed.

———— ·◆· ————

 RACHEL STARR THOMSON

Aaron watched the rising sun with his jaw set and his feet firmly planted on the dusty earth of the valley. Behind him the small city waited, walled by the night barricade. He heard the soft mewling of a baby somewhere behind the walls. The city was a womb, pregnant with life and hope for tomorrow, depending on him to protect it.

The sun rose perceptibly higher. The force on the hill tightened its ranks, becoming a dark mass, making the sides of the mountains heave as though it were covered with insects.

His mouth went dry, and his stomach turned. He must have made a sound or visibly blanched, because his captains on either side turned and looked a question at him. They did not dare speak. He had been a flare all night and all morning, blazing at anyone who would open their mouths to question him.

A fool, he thought. *I am a fool. Great God, forgive me. Rechab, forgive me.*

He turned to the captain on his right. "Raise a flag," he said. "A white flag."

"We are surrendering?" the captain asked, confused.

"That is not an option. We are getting the women and children out. The flag will tell the army that we just need a little more time."

The words rushed out one after another. He didn't have time to explain. The captains looked at one another and nodded, and the one to his right peeled off, shouting for a flag to be raised.

Aaron turned to the man on his left. "Get messengers. Tell them to go to every house, every hiding place and tell the women and children that they have safe passage if they will leave. We cannot go along to guard them. I am sorry for that. But they do not have to stay here."

He paused, wrestling with what he was about to say. He decided he would say it, then that he would not. But the words won out. "And tell the men that if they choose to surrender, now before the battle starts, the commander of that army will escort them to Shalem to stand trial. There is a chance some may be acquitted."

He knew his face was pale; he felt as though his blood was pooling in his feet. Thirty feet down the wall, his men were hoisting the flag. His captain took off running to gather messengers and send out the messages. Aaron stood alone at his post, staring at the armies in dread. He wondered if any would be left to fight alongside him, or if he would die today completely alone.

An hour later, Rechab sat in Callum's tent and wept through the battle. Its sounds rose up the hillside and through the tent walls, the sound of a world coming to an end. Of Aaron's dreams, over. Of her own sins come to their final consequence. Of men losing their lives, one by one.

Aaron did not die alone that day. Of the men, only a handful surrendered themselves—all villagers who had lived in Nachush before the takeover and hoped for a way out of the hell that others had created around them. The others fought bravely alongside the mule driver who had dared try to bring a new day to the Sacred Land. The women and children mostly left Nachush before the attack began, scampering over the dusty ground to the pass out of the valley, dragging each other by the hand and carrying whatever of their belongings they had managed to snatch up and roll into their bedding in the bare minutes before they had to flee.

But some had refused to leave. Some had holed up in their hiding places or their homes and died before they ever faced the fight. Callum's men carried out their orders. None survived.

 RACHEL STARR THOMSON

The Great God did not arrive in power, as in the ancient days, to deliver them by mighty hand or outstretched arm. Beniah's army did not fall dead of a scourge or burn up in fire from heaven. They marched, they killed, and they returned to their place.

———◆———

A stillness followed the battle. It was not a mere quiet, not a mere calm. It was a heavy, sorrowful silence like a fog as the spirits of men sank into the earth. Rechab looked up from her weeping, dried her tears, and left Callum's tent. No one stopped her. She wrapped her shawl tightly around herself, as though to keep out the chill although the day was already hot and dry, and wandered into the valley to see the wreckage that remained.

Smoke rose from the houses. The barricades were little more than rubble, with a few rock piles still standing. The flag Aaron had hoisted to alert Callum's armies that the women and children were fleeing still blew, tattered, in a whispering breeze. It was the only sound.

Rechab drifted over the bloody ground. She stopped where men lay to close their eyes and say a prayer over them.

That was how she found Aaron.

He was still alive. One look at him and she knew it would only be minutes, but she went to his side, took his hand, and ran her hand through his hair.

He looked at her with his eyes unseeing. "Aaron," she said.

His eyes focused. He looked confused a moment, then tried to smile. Instead he coughed, and blood ran from his mouth over his chin and onto his tunic.

He gripped her hand tightly with his bloody one. "Did you love me?" he asked.

She closed her eyes and sobbed. How many times had she asked herself that question in the last few weeks?

But she knew the answer now.

So she told him.

"I did . . . I do."

He reached up and brushed her hair away from her eyes. She felt blood streak her face where he touched her. He did not smile, but she saw a smile in his green eyes. The old, boyish Aaron looked up at her for that last moment before he died.

And she wept, full-heartedly, for the loss of that boy whom she had indeed loved.

He cleared his throat, three times, while she shook her head. She wanted to tell him not to talk, but she could not get the words out. The stillness that hung over this place pressed on her soul.

"You saved them," he finally managed to say. "They got out."

"The Great God will look after them now," she answered, trying to smile but failing.

CHAPTER 11

When Rechab returned to Callum's tent, he was already there. Captains and horses and foot soldiers in an organized swarm were taking their orders, preparing to return to the Holy City. A small group of prisoners huddled near the tent, watched over by sharp-eyed warriors. Shaul looked askance at her return, but Callum simply nodded. He didn't have to say anything. Somehow they understood each other, this commander and the girl from Bethabara. He knew she had not run away, and she knew he did not mind that she had left the oversight of her guards in order to say good-bye. Strange and unexpected though it was, she had found a friend in him.

The sight of Shaul reminded her of the scroll. From the look he was giving her, she guessed he had found it. What he'd done with it, she didn't know, and there wouldn't be any opportunity to ask now. She would have to trust that to the Great God.

The army's efficiency was breathtaking. They gathered the bodies of their fallen to return home in wagons, to be buried as heroes. They buried their enemies, much to Rechab's gratitude. They did not rest other than to eat quickly. There was no mood of celebration at their victory, no feasting or congratulations. This had not been a glorious fight but a grim execution.

By late afternoon, the tents were down, the horses were rested, and the army was ready to begin its march back to Shalem. Rechab drew a deep breath and fell into line where she was told between two squadrons of soldiers. They left her hands and feet unbound, allowing her to march with dignity. The other prisoners were behind her and overseen by two other squadrons.

Before they stepped off, Callum himself appeared through the ranks and handed Rechab a bundle. "A bedroll," he announced, "and an extra cloak, with a water skin and some rations. You will need them."

But there was something else there, too. Something heavy and long, wrapped in the cloak and hidden in the midst of the bundle. She knew it at once.

The scroll.

⸺◆⸺

Alack, the shepherd boy-turned prophet-turned lackey to a blood-thirsty butcher, stood at the prow of the ship as it cut through the waters of the Great Sea. He could see the Sacred Land lying across the horizon, its coast stretching in either direction as far as could be seen. The sight of home. Never had he wished so much to be looking at some other place. Any other land but his own. Any other coast but that of the country he loved.

Not for the first time he wondered what people would say to him. How they would look at him. What he would say to them. He knew he was not recognizable as Alack the shepherd boy. He was clean-shaven, dressed in a Westland toga, a warm wool cloak with the emperor's scarlet, and sandals laced to his knees. His hair was short, curling up just beneath his ears. And for the first time in his life, he did not smell like sheep.

     Rachel Starr Thomson

Even on board this ship, he'd been instructed to bathe every day. It was an imperial ship, a luxury craft that slid smoothly through the waves and included elegant lodgings, complete with bathing tubs, for the wealthy and important on board.

Alack did not have a shekel to his name, but he was important. He was the prophet to the Sacred Land. The one who had come to tell his own people to prepare to be overrun. Sabrus Caelius, the Sword of Heaven, once general of the Westland and now emperor of the nations, was coming.

The ship's captain, standing at Alack's elbow, gazed at the coast while the salt wind blew back his hair. "It's a fine day," he said. "We'll be in port before supper hour." He glanced over at Alack, who didn't answer. "You all right, boy?"

Alack just nodded. Of course he wasn't all right. Everything about this was wrong. But he was grateful for the captain's concern. Everyone else on board this ship ducked and dodged around him, treating him like explosive tinder while simultaneously talking behind his back. He was Sabrus Caelius's pet, a mockery of what a prophet was meant to be. Anyone who crossed him risked losing their heads, but he did not have the respect of one of them. Except the captain. The captain, perhaps because he was a father to several sons near Alack's age, seemed to see him as a human being. He called him "boy" and talked to him about the weather, the sea, the best places to find good grub at ports all along the coast. He comforted Alack's heart and made him miss his own father, Naam, so badly his chest hurt.

Would his father even know him to see him now?

Even more—did he want his father to know him? Better that Naam think his son lost in the desert, still following the mad prophet around in search of visions and daydreams, than know that he had come back as the mouthpiece of a foreigner to pronounce doom on his own people.

When the captain went to attend to something, Alack sank down on the deck in his misery and watched the waves as the ship cut through the brine toward home.

True to the captain's prediction, it was smooth and fast sailing all the way, and with the crew's deft handling, they had put into port before the sun had much sunk from its height in the late afternoon hours. Kasarea. The city where Alack's journey to the Westland, with its unimaginable ending, had begun. He felt keenly the lack of his mentor as he descended the gangplank and reeled on the dry, familiar ground, desperate to get his land legs back. They had been here together. Kol Abaddon had explained little to nothing of why they were going oversea. And then off they'd gone, paying for passage with money Alack didn't know his mentor had, across the sea to encounter a sea serpent, be attacked by pirates and taken into slavery by Westland merchants, work miracles and prophesy and finally end up here: with Kol Abaddon rotting away in a Westland jail and Alack employed as the personal seer of the man who was arguably the greatest threat to the Sacred Land alive.

But only arguably. For Alack had seen and heard things with the eyes of his spirit that told him the real threat to his people was not a man with a sword and an army, but the darkness they had welcomed into their heart when they opened themselves to the occult practices and evil spirits worshiped by the nations. He had seen it in the very stars: Isha, the beloved, running into the mouth of the Dragon. He had seen it in the depths of the sea: a ruined world, sunk down through the darkness of ages, with a serpent coiled at its heart.

Everything evil comes from the sea, Kol Abaddon had told him.

In his mind's eye he imagined the sea rising up at night and flooding the whole Sacred Land, rising and rising until it covered the mountains and overflowed the heights of the temple. Their world would drown and the noise of its people be forever cast into stillness and

     RACHEL STARR THOMSON

silence, darkness and death beneath the waves. Welcome chaos, and it will overflow you. Embrace injustice and greed, and they will destroy you. Run to the Dragon, and you will be devoured.

He shivered and blinked. His thoughts had carried him away further than he intended. The last of them, he wasn't sure if they were his own thoughts or something given to him. They sounded like Kol Abaddon's prophecies, after all. Perhaps the Great God was whispering the dire threats into his mind.

Alack took a deep breath of the salty, fishy air of the harbor town. The sharp fermented smell of beer and wine floated along on the breeze; laughter and the shouts of dock workers floated along with it. A girl standing in a dark corner beckoned to him, and he blushed deep red and turned away.

Last time he was here, he and Kol Abaddon had slept in the street near the dock, wrapped in their cloaks. This time he was a man of means, or at least the representative of one, so it would be different. He and the Westlanders would stay in the best lodging in Kasarea, in an upper floor away from the noise. He was glad. He did not want to stand in this street and face any of his people.

The captain waved him over where some of the imperial bodyguard stood. "There you are," he said when Alack joined them. "The inn is straight up that road; the lieutenant here knows the way. Follow him and they'll look after you."

Alack nodded glumly. The captain would stay behind with the ship, so he would soon be in the company of Sabrus's men only. They would keep him safe, present him in state, and ensure he was well dressed, well fed, and well babysat. He had little hope of escaping their eyesight even for a moment.

The military men formed ranks so that Alack was surrounded, along with the few other emissaries accompanying them. Of these, the leader was a deceptively portly man named Croesius. In Alack's estimation he looked like an overfed pig, but their short acquaintance on the ship had convinced the young shepherd that Croesius was as cunning, as ruthless, and as sharp-toothed as a wolf.

As they stepped off, Alack noticed Croesius eyeing the girl on the corner. "A good journey, was it not?" Alack asked.

Croesius turned to him with a smile that expressed bare tolerance. "Uneventful, which at sea is good. Only your second sea journey, was it not? Before then I'm given to understand you never left this ash pit of a country."

Croesius's eyes wandered back to find the girl again, but she had disappeared. Alack breathed a little easier.

"I was a shepherd," Alack said. "I had little use for the sea. Never even came so close to it as this."

Croesius didn't bother to answer. His lip curled slightly, and he engaged one of the other emissaries with a question about the weather being so blamed hot.

Alack allowed himself half a second as they marched to close his eyes and soak up the sun. As they ascended the street, away from the water, he could feel the dry desert air beckoning him. The scents—what he could catch beneath the general stink of the city—were familiar, welcoming. The tongue spoken around him was not strange to his ears. He had become tolerably good at the pidgin spoken by sailors and traders while at sea—as well as the more refined version the emissaries used—and could even get by a little in Westlander, but to hear his own tongue being spoken all around him made him feel like no one here was a stranger. Like they were all family, all friends.

That spell was rudely broken when he heard chanting and turned to see a small coterie of his people bowing to their faces before a shrine of Kimash. One of them was weirdly wavering on his knees, as though he could not find his balance anywhere, and the smell of narcotics hung in heavy clouds around their heads.

Croesius's lip curled again.

When they reached the inn, Alack was only too happy to bury himself away.

<hr>

Ezra ben Malchi and his train of attendees and relatives reached Bethabara in the middle of the night. Common stopover on the way to and from Shalem that it was, no one paid them much attention as they set up camp on the open, level ground near the village well on the outskirts of town.

Marah came to Aurelius as he was helping to erect a tent. Her tone was short, worried. "Have you seen Shem?"

He strained to hold up a pole while other men arranged the fabric and lines around it. "No," he said. "I haven't been watching for him."

"I'm worried, Aurelius," she said. "He left the villa with us, but he's gone."

"Gone?" The pressure of the pole went slack as everything came into place, and Aurelius released it and slapped his hands together, dusting them off. "Are you sure? This is an expansive train."

"He's not here. I've looked. And asked. I thought he might be with that girl, but . . ." She shook her head. "He must have left us, husband, sometime on the way. But why?"

Aurelius chose his words carefully. "You don't think we lost him? He might have twisted an ankle, gotten distracted, fallen behind."

The look she gave him said she would have none of that game. "I know you warned me. I know you didn't want me to trust him. But I did, and he's betrayed that trust."

Aurelius reached out and put his arm around his wife. She stiffened but didn't push him off, and he steered her away from the crowd setting up camp, slightly out to the edges of the train. He could see the well silhouetted in the moonlight—an old, familiar, homey shape. How often had he come here to address the people of the village? To gather with friends? To drive off Kol Abaddon?

He sighed. "I'm sorry he let you down, my dear. I have not wanted to distrust him, but he's changed. Still, we need not think the worst. We have no reason to believe he would betray our escape. More likely than not he was simply dazzled by the city and decided to take his own freedom. He must know we would not punish him for it."

"But he hates the city," Marah said. "I saw it on his face the whole time we were there. He looked at it with . . . with loathing."

Aurelius frowned. "I've never seen a boy get so above his fellows so quickly. Before I sent him out in search of Rechab, he was just one of our household. When he came back he seemed to think he was some kind of elite. I'm not in favor of the goings-on in Shalem either, but his response was strange. And that amulet he's always wearing. It bothers me more than it should. I don't know why."

Marah was quiet . . . too quiet. Aurelius recognized the silence as deliberation. When she offered nothing, he finally asked. "What is it?"

"I found something . . . in the garden. At the villa."

"Something? What do you mean?"

"The burned remains of an animal," Marah said. "And rocks scattered around, but not randomly enough to cover up that they'd been gathered and arranged before then. Some kind of altar, I think."

"A sacrifice?"

"That's my guess. A few nights before we left."

 Rachel Starr Thomson

"This troubles you."

"And it doesn't you?"

Aurelius held her closer. "It does me too. I have never been comfortable with anything of the kind. But I sense something more behind your words."

"Shem had already been changing, as you said, since you sent him away. But after I found the sacrifice—I caught him looking at me once or twice as though he knew. But it wasn't him looking at me. It was something else. I don't know how else to explain it."

"Once things are settled here, I'll send someone back to the city to look for him," Aurelius said. It was an empty promise, and he knew it. Things might never be settled here again. They had just left the custody of the king, and depending on what they found here in Bethabara, their only option might be to leave the country completely.

Marah sniffed. "I want to go home," she said. "We're so close."

He knew how she felt. Here, in this place that was so familiar, so safe, it felt as though they should be able to go into the town, return to the house and the servants they had left behind, and resume life as usual. They should be able to be the governor and his wife.

But it could not be. The blood of Nadab's murdered household was still unanswered, and the high priest of Kimash had sent his own people here to "explain" things to the people. Who knew but the governorship had been usurped entirely. They themselves were fugitives.

He would return to their house the following night, under cover of darkness, without Marah. He would ask questions and find out what he could about the state of things here. But neither of them could go home again.

Dawn was appearing on the horizon by the time Ezra's camp was set. Marah had long since disappeared into a tent. Reluctantly, Aurelius went to join her. They would catch a few hours of sleep in the early morning hours and be sure to stay out of sight during the day. They would be recognized immediately by any inhabitant of Bethabara who caught sight of them and could not risk it. When darkness fell again, it would be time to make his way into the town, meet with his servants, and determine what had happened in their absence and what, if anything, he could do for his people now.

———◆———

Shem stood at the servants' gate of the palace and waited for a steward to answer his summons. His face was placid, calm as water in a cistern. He meant to give no cause for question or alarm.

The steward appeared, red-faced and harried. Every muscle in his body spoke of a man overworked. "Well, what is your business here? The gatekeeper has told me nothing useful."

"As I told him, I have been sent here to give my service to you," Shem said.

"Sent by whom?"

"Governor Aurelius of Bethabara. He made arrangements with the king to lend me to your kitchens in this time of feasting."

"I was told nothing of it."

"I apologize for that," Shem said, "but I have my orders, and it seems you need the help."

The steward relaxed a little as he looked Shem over. "Governor Aurelius is a good man."

"And a generous one," Shem said, "good to servants as well as to nobles. He saw how taxed your household is and felt he could not

 RACHEL STARR THOMSON

contribute to the king's celebrations in any better way."

"Well, come in," the steward said. "You have experience in the kitchen?"

"In the kitchen, and at waiting tables. I am a trusted member of Aurelius's household in every area."

"And you'd better be a hardworking one. There is work enough to be done for fifty men like you."

Shem smiled as guards shut the gate behind him, welcoming him into the inner life of the king's palace. "I trust I will not disappoint you," he said.

CHAPTER 12

Callum's army returned to the Holy City three days after marching from Nachush. The gates opened to them, and a few people, spotting the parade, gave feeble cheers.

But this army had not gone forth in pomp and did not return in glory. Few even knew why Callum had led an armed force out. Those who heard some explanation simply said they had gone to put down a rebellion that might have threatened the Sacred Land.

Everyone knew that meant Callum had marched on some of their own. On the Holy People. Even in a land without much in the way of loyalty, that was not a cause for joy.

Limping their footsore way into the city in the midst of the army were Rechab and the other captives. Some of the villagers of Nachush looked around, wide-eyed, at the great city. Others hung their heads in shame.

Rechab didn't know how to feel. This was the one place on earth she had never wanted to come back to. The place she had fled what seemed like another lifetime ago. And why? She could hardly remember.

But yes, she knew. She had run away because her father had sold her into the household of Kimash in some way. By marriage, no doubt. She had not stayed long enough to find out. With Flora's help, she had run to the Great God.

How far the journey had taken her since then! How far, and how unexpected the twists in the road. Her flight from the same streets she now walked down as a criminal about to stand trial had led her to make the greatest mistakes of her life, and she felt regret now that was sharper and deeper than she could have imagined possible. Aaron would never again be far from her thoughts, never again far from her heart. She didn't know whether he had led her into trouble or whether she had done it to him, or whether they had both been equally complicit. But she did know, even now with grief still heavy and the trial looming before her, that what had happened had changed her. She was no longer afraid. She was no longer the mouse of a girl who had hidden beneath Flora's skirts and scurried away in search of a dark corner to hide in.

The weight of the lost scroll in her arms reminded her why she was no longer afraid. The eye she had felt upon her in Essea—the gaze of the Great God—was still on her. She knew in the depths of her being that it would always be on her, that she would always live in his sight. And that—being seen—gave her courage.

Rechab walked unveiled. She knew it was shocking, but it felt right. To walk open to the eyes of her people even as she walked open to the eyes of her God.

Even so, her stomach knotted as they passed by the high walls and beneath the soaring spires of the temple. Crowds parted. The smell of sacrifices and incense hung in the air. The hum of chants and prayers mingled with it. Outside the walls, shrines and grottos lined the streets, honoring small gods and spirits. Statues of Kimash, Amon-Heth, and their lesser attendant deities glowered from within many of them.

     RACHEL STARR THOMSON

Rechab shuddered. She knew their idols even desecrated the courts of the temple itself. Wrongful and hateful, their presence here. She longed for the purity of ancient days, when the Great God alone was worshiped and the air here felt clean. She did not remember those days, but felt as though she did.

The Great God's priests would soon act as her judges. She wondered what to expect from them.

They passed the temple and soon came to the palace: a lesser spectacle, but still grand and imposing. The army arranged itself on the paved plaza within the palace gates and arrayed out into the streets, some thousand men in orderly columns with their prisoners in the center close to the gates and their leader on horseback at their head.

The king appeared, along with a handful of senators and other important-looking people . . . and a woman.

Rechab's heart jumped into her throat. Flora!

But it was not Flora. The dread she felt at the sight of the woman told her that even before her eyes managed to make the distinctions between this woman and her friend. Her mind spun, trying to understand who this was and why she was here. She stood at Beniah's right hand like a queen. She was a queen.

The soldiers said nothing, silent and grim like the statues guarding a tomb. She wished they would tell her what was going on.

Thankfully, Callum did. He dismounted, bowed, and said loudly enough for her to hear, "Your Majesty. Queen Izevel. Our work is done."

"But it seems not," the queen said. Her voice was high and almost brittle, though it carried across the pavement like a dry, sweeping wind. "You were sent to wipe out the rebels. Who are these I see before me?"

Rechab stopped herself from shaking her head in wonder. This woman spoke as though she herself were sovereign of the army, not her husband.

"There was some question of innocence," Callum said. "I have brought back those who would surrender themselves to stand trial so that all your people, King Beniah, may know you to be a just man and may hear for themselves the dangers of rebellion against you. Should they be judged guilty, a public execution will do more to deter would-be rebels in this city than a distant battle none of them were there to see."

"I trust the smoke of Nachush still rises," Izevel said, "and you have left the bodies to rot in the sun where all may see them and fear us."

Callum did not answer. Rechab closed her eyes and pictured the neat burial rows where the commander's men had spent hours burying their enemies. She blessed them again.

And trembled within. There was no question of *her* innocence. Whatever happened to the men of Nachush, Rechab would become the public example of which Callum spoke. She had known it was inevitable from the moment she gave herself up in the commander's camp. And now, under the withering stare of her enemy, she surrendered herself to that fate once again.

Beniah spared Callum the need to give a response. "You have done well," he said, though his tone did not entirely agree with his words. "You show yourself an honorable man once again, and you show your king an honorable man as well. We will take the prisoners into our custody and call on the priests for trial. You may dismiss your men, Callum; your work is finished. You have all done well."

Callum nodded and spun around, his short cloak whirling around him. He gazed over his troops with dark, troubled eyes, and Rechab met his gaze as it fell on her and rested there a moment. She smiled at

     RACHEL STARR THOMSON

him. He had done right by her. She could ask for nothing more.

Callum raised his voice to carry across the ranks of his men. "Dismissed with honor!" he said. He saluted, and his army responded in kind. One by one, in order of rank, the troops turned and marched away, dispersing in the streets once they had left the pavement.

The prisoners stayed where they were, and the men guarding them did not move until a small troop of palace guards emerged to take their place. They exchanged a few words and glances while the prisoners shuffled nervously on their feet. Rechab alone did not show fear. She clutched her precious bundle and kept her head high, drinking in the sight of the beautiful palace with its gleaming marble pillars, garden gates, and inlaid balconies. The royals had already gone, to her great relief. She had no desire to remain under Izevel's bloodthirsty notice.

The soldiers changed places with palace guards, and the man Rechab judged to be captain of that guard looked the prisoners over with cool efficiency. He nodded to six of his men. "Take the men to the dungeons to await trial there. You two, escort the woman to the servants' quarters. She is to be kept under watch there."

Surrounded by guards, Rechab felt some relief, mingled with guilt. She had not expected any special honor but had felt some dread at the thought of the dungeons—both at their squalor and at being locked up alone with men who by now had good cause to hate her. Besides, a brief stay in the servants' quarters might give her some opportunity to take care of the scroll. She didn't yet know how she would separate its fate from her own, but she had to find a way. The words of God could not be lost again.

Briefly, she thought of Micah. She had not found him among the dead, but then, she'd not had an opportunity to visit them all. He had given no sign that he intended to leave before the battle. Having come to Nachush as a servant of God, it seemed he would die with them.

Rechab drank in all she could of the palace as the guards hurried her along. Their heads and broad shoulders blocked much of the view, but she lifted her eyes to arching, soaring ceilings, to light, to white marble. Bronze urns, fountains, and statues lined the wide halls.

But the sight that made her breath catch in her throat and stopped her heart for a moment with its poignant beauty was that of three children running across the hall in front of the guards, laughing, chasing each other in a game of tag.

These were clearly noble children, perhaps the king's own. They showed no awareness that these grand surroundings were not a place for children's games, or that a prisoner was being marched off to await her death in front of them. They laughed, and their giggles bounced off the marble. The sound made Rechab want to laugh and cry at the same time.

Behind them came a harried nurse, and behind her, much more slowly and in conversation, two women.

One of them looked up. Her eyes widened, and she rushed at them. For a moment Rechab thought Izevel was charging at her. An instant before the woman reached her, her mind caught up:

This time it was Flora.

Flora all but pushed the guards aside, and in an instant Rechab was in her arms. Flora held her tightly, pressed Rechab's head to her shoulder, and kissed it.

Rechab trembled. With the scroll in her arms, she could not embrace Flora in return. She had never felt so much like a child, long lost and weary, suddenly and unexpectedly folded in her mother's arms.

"Where are you taking this girl?" Flora demanded of the guards, who seemed not to know what to do. The other woman had drawn closer and extended her hand in an unspoken command for them to wait for her permission before acting. Instinctively Rechab knew

 RACHEL STARR THOMSON

this was also a queen, probably the mother of the children who had stopped racing around and laughing and now stood in a little cluster beside the golden statue of a gazelle, watching with their curious eyes wide.

"To the servants' quarters, my lady," the captain of the guard said stiffly. "King's orders. She is a criminal awaiting trial."

"A criminal? On what charges?"

Flora was holding Rechab so tightly she couldn't pull away to explain.

"Not my business to know, my lady," the captain said. He looked apologetically at the other woman. "Your highness."

The queen just said, "Wait a moment."

Flora released Rechab a little and looked into her eyes, searching them as though a gaze alone could tell the whole story. "I can't tell you how glad I am to find you safe," she said.

Rechab nodded, too choked up to speak. She shoved the bundle forward and managed to get out, "Take this, please. Open it in private. You'll understand when you see."

Flora nodded, but she didn't take it, still holding Rechab's shoulders and looking intently into her face. Finally she let go, took the bundle carefully, and turned on her heel. "Will you release her to my custody? I will see that she remains in my quarters until there is some call for her."

The soldiers grew more visibly uncomfortable. "We have orders," the captain said. He sounded apologetic. "The others were sent to the dungeon. The servants' quarters will be safe."

"Others?" Flora asked.

"Rebels."

Rechab's face burned. She longed to sit with her friend and tell the tale from beginning to end. To explain everything. To confess. And to share her last few hours on earth with someone she could simply call friend.

Flora stepped back and nodded. "Take gentle care of her," she said.

"We will, ma'am," the captain said. They started off again, but at a slower, less brisk pace this time. Flora's eyes promised she would not leave Rechab alone long.

She kept the promise. Rechab had not been in her prison cell—a small but clean room with a cot and a basin to wash—an hour before Flora arrived.

Flora held her while Rechab wept and confessed how badly she had failed everything. Rechab expected that Flora would chide her, rebuke her, say wise words of reproach and lecture her on the lessons that could be learned from it all.

She never did.

CHAPTER 13

Ezra remained camped outside Bethabara all day on the pretense of having business with some in the town. To keep from raising suspicion in a town where everyone knew everyone's business, he spent the day talking to shepherds about acquiring new breeding rams for his own flocks in the north. Bethabara's shepherds were a proud lot with fine sheep. The ruse worked.

Aurelius and Marah spent the entire day sweltering inside a tent. They kept the door flap open just enough to let in any breeze that might blow, but of that there was precious little. Marah visibly fretted but never once opened her mouth to express her unhappiness again. Aurelius paced.

At last the long shadows of evening arrived, and Ezra reappeared to take his meal with his guests and apprise them of the situation in the city. He smelled of his day's enterprise. It fit the rugged, sun-darkened northerner better than the finery of Shalem. Aurelius, who had always respected the shepherds of Bethabara and frequently dealt with them, found the smell oddly comforting. Marah wrinkled her nose at Ezra's arrival and cast an amused glance at her husband, but she said not a word about it.

Ezra ate spiced chickpeas by the handful as he spoke. "The high priest's emissaries arrived three days ago. They called the people to the city square and publicly announced Nadab's 'sins.'"

"How did they take it?"

"Not well. Of course word had leaked about the murders—soon after you left, as you feared."

"In a place like this, such a thing cannot be left secret."

"From what I hear, it led to an outbreak of other crimes among the people. Whether they took the chance to carry out old vendettas without fear of retribution or whether they simply reacted in fear I cannot say."

"A little of both, I would wager. There are always some who hate each other, who would jump at the chance for revenge. And others who will spook at their own shadows."

Aurelius grew reflective. Nadab's household weighed heavily on his mind. Nadab himself had been one of the former class—a man with enemies and rivals he would gladly dispense with if he could do it without fearing that justice would be enacted against him. His youngest daughter, Rechab, had been one of the latter. A slip of a girl, beautiful, capable, but always cowering and afraid. Never in a thousand years would Aurelius have guessed that these two would bring such calamity on their community.

As Ezra moved on to a haunch of lamb, Aurelius remembered a shepherd boy who had grown up with Rechab and loved her. Alack. He'd never had a chance, of course, but Aurelius had sometimes entertained the thought of urging Nadab to allow the match. It wouldn't have been expedient on his part. Governorships were not best handled with sentiment. But maybe, if he had done so, if he had interceded on the boy's behalf, everything would be different now.

"Go on," Aurelius said. "The emissaries from the high priest?"

"They stayed here," Ezra said. "As you also feared. Carried out a few executions to punish the outbreak, though perhaps not with the kind of thorough investigation a man like yourself would hope for."

Aurelius blanched. Marah's warm hand on his back brought a measure of comfort. Though the dinner laid out before them was substantial, neither of them ate. The sight of food was making Aurelius sick.

Ezra had no such trouble, though he paused intermittently to continue his news. "They are staying in your house and functioning as governors. The people don't like it. I heard whispers when I was out and about. There is sedition abroad."

"What else?" Aurelius muttered. "They aren't sheep, these people."

He'd spent twenty years learning to govern wisely and keep peace in the town where he was law. He knew Bethabara. Besides the shepherds and the usual clusters of lower-class rebels, the little city's position on the ascent to Shalem gave it unusual influence in the Holy City. It attracted merchants like Nadab and the regular visits of powerful traders. Those who wished to conduct business a little further from the eye of the king and the priests of various gods did it here. Aurelius had a reputation for being fair, being just, and not asking too many questions. None of them would be happy to have Kimash ruling them with an iron fist.

When the high priest's assassins had slaughtered the household of Nadab the Trader as retaliation for the loss of Rechab, who had been promised to him in marriage, Aurelius had feared that the twin responses of fear and aggression would bring the town to a point much like Ezra described—and things could, and would, get much worse. Beniah could have stopped it by responding with quick justice, reassuring everyone in the town that he was on their side and no such mercenary rule would be tolerated. Instead, in his drunken stupor the king had shown his people that Kimash now came first. Aurelius feared for his people, and he feared for the peace of the Sacred Land.

Outside, the lowering sun was covering the land with darkness. Inside, Ezra's servants discreetly lit oil lamps.

"I'm grateful for your report," Aurelius said, still unable to touch the food that lay before him. "I will go into the town after dark, as planned, and seek out my steward."

"Is that wise?" asked Ezra. "The high priest's men are living there."

"If anyone in this town deserves to see my face and know that I haven't abandoned them to the mercies of Kimash, it is my own steward and servants. And they can tell me all I need to know. They have served as my ears and eyes in Bethabara for years. I need them now, and it may be they need me."

"Be careful," Ezra said.

Aurelius took his leave of the camp after nightfall and slipped through the shadows to the gates of the town. Night guards were out, patrolling the perimeter of Bethabara—most likely hired by some of the wealthier men in town to keep an eye on things in these volatile conditions. In the past Aurelius himself had posted a watchman or two, but never a full patrol.

A voice called out for him to stop where he was. He did so, waiting quietly.

The guard came near with a torch and hoisted it threateningly in Aurelius's direction, casting light over his face and figure.

"Your lordship!" the man said, hushing his voice almost instantly. Aurelius knew him at once: one of the merchants' private guards, a slave of good character and good breeding. The man had many times stood in Aurelius's house, guarding over meetings with his master. "What are—"

Aurelius raised a finger to his lips and smiled. "I am here to seek peace for my people. I trust you will let me pass?"

The guard stood aside instantly. "Precious little of peace these days."

Aurelius nodded. "So I hear. I want to speak with my steward and learn more. Listen, friend . . . I forget your name."

"Brunai."

"Listen, Brunai, it is better if no one knows I came."

"My master ordered me to keep out threats and alert him if any tried to enter. You are no threat."

Aurelius found himself unexpectedly moved. "I'm grateful for your trust."

"You have earned it," the guard said. Even in the darkness, Aurelius could see a shade of trouble pass over the man's face. "Forgive me for asking. You went to Shalem to intervene for us."

"It did not go as I had hoped," Aurelius said.

Brunai's hand tightened around the torch. "Then the king will not stand with us against these—"

"Hush," Aurelius said. "Let nothing that might sound treasonous pass your lips."

The man nodded, and Aurelius passed on, troubled. This was what he had feared. For many years Beniah's people-pleasing ways had kowtowed to the demands of some at the expense of those less able to make their voices heard. It had fostered unrest, not just here, but in many places across the land. What Essea was to the religious world, many a would-be king or pocket of rebels was to the political one. Bethabara, with its disproportionate influence, was not immune to that spirit. And its position on the mountain, so close to the Holy City itself, made it an especially dangerous expression of it.

Aurelius did not fear that anyone would actually succeed in rising up against the king and overthrowing the royal house. What he feared was the inevitable response to any attempt. Rebels could not be appeased or reasoned with; by their very nature they forced a king's hand. Uprisings would only ever have to be put down.

With the guards all patrolling the edges of town, the streets themselves were dark and silent. Aurelius could have found the way with his eyes closed. He made his way up the familiar streets toward his home with a special pain in his heart. For years he'd thought of Bethabara as his validation, his proof of worth and his position at the royal table. Only recently had he realized that he cared for the little city for its own sake. Years of shepherding the flock for the sake of wealth and power had resulted in care for the sheep.

The governor's house loomed before him. He hesitated a moment outside the high brass wall that encircled it. This was home, but it was also the place where danger was most present. His enemies had taken up residence here.

The courtyard was dark as the rest of the city, not a torch blazing or lamp glowing from inside the house. Slowly, Aurelius trailed along the edge of the property, sharp eye out, till he reached the servants' door at the corner of the wall. He unlatched the gate, stepped inside, and then softly and immediately called out, "Jerish! Stay your hand!'

He let out a soft sigh of relief at the sound that responded—the barely perceptible hesitation of a man about to accost him. Then a low, burly voice spoke out of the shadows to the left, just behind a stone pillar.

"Your lordship?"

"I've come home," Aurelius said, still speaking just loudly enough to be heard. "I am relieved to find you still at your post."

"I would not leave it," Jerish said, but Aurelius knew they both understood. Jerish had been guarding this door at night for twelve years. Nothing got past him. He would accost any intruder verbally and follow up quickly with a pounding if the stranger was too slow to answer. Aurelius knew him well enough to catch him before he could bellow a demand for his name and business. But there had been no way to know for certain if Jerish still guarded the gate or if Kimash's men had replaced him.

Jerish's enormous bulk stepped out of the shadows. "It is good to see you, sir," he said.

"And it is good to see you," Aurelius said. He yearned to enter the house but forced his feet to stay where they were. "Is Reuel within? I must speak with him."

Jerish nodded. "Shall I fetch him for you?"

"I think I can manage to keep the door while you do," Aurelius said.

The hulking guard disappeared. Minutes later he returned with a smaller, balding man hurrying along in his footsteps.

"Reuel," Aurelius said.

"Governor!" All propriety aside, the men embraced and kissed each other on the cheeks. Reuel had been a servant in Aurelius's household since the governor of Bethabara was little more than a boy.

"My heart is glad to see you," Reuel said. "I feared I would not see you again alive."

"I confess I feared the same about you," Aurelius said. In the pale moonlight, the expression on Reuel's face told him his fears had not been misplaced. "They gave us to know we had no choice about serving them as we did you," Reuel said, his voice low. "But every one of us would throw them off in a moment if you commanded it."

"I don't," Aurelius said, shaking his head. "I don't. I can't. The king would not support it, and I would only bring more trouble on your heads. Tell me, Reuel. Tell me everything that has happened here."

The steward's story matched Ezra's news point for point. The high priest's men had convened a town meeting immediately upon arriving. When the people of Bethabara came, the men announced that the murder of Nadab's household had been due justice—deserved for the crime of opposing and insulting the high priest of Kimash. There would be no reparations for it. Moreover, they had declared that Aurelius was tied up in the Holy City and that they would fill his role until his return. Aided by their considerable muscle—they had come with a full armed guard—they had moved into Aurelius's household immediately and begun taking on the duties of the governorship to themselves, including the work of judging local problems and collecting taxes.

Reuel and Aurelius's other servants kept the house running, but not without threatening under their breath to poison the newcomers' wine one of these evenings. Resentment and fear ran high in the town, along with opportunism. The high priest's actions had created exactly the destabilization Aurelius had feared.

"We hoped you would return with the king's backing and free us from their presence," Reuel said. "But the fact that we are speaking outside in the middle of the night tells me things did not go as you hoped."

"Beniah will not counter the high priest," Aurelius said. "It's his new wife, Izevel. She is niece to Kimash's high priest. Beniah is not often sober, and even if he was, he would not go against his relatives now without severe provocation."

He winced even as he said it. There could be no provocation more severe than the murder of an entire household for no other reason than personal insult. If that would not galvanize Beniah to do what was right, nothing would.

"Izevel," Reuel said. "Rumor of her has reached us as well. It seems to me that dark times are upon this nation. Times that call for change."

Aurelius had never heard this particular tone in Reuel's voice before. "Change?" he asked.

"Beniah has gone too far this time." Reuel's voice was so low that

 RACHEL STARR THOMSON

Aurelius could hardly make out the words—yet he understood them, every one clearly. "I care little for the gods; if the king of the Sacred Land wants to throw open the doors of the temple, let him. But to throw open the doors of judgment, of our own towns, our own households . . ."

"Maybe there isn't as much difference as we thought," Aurelius said. "Maybe to throw open the temple to the gods is to throw open our lives to the likes of Izevel and the high priest of Kimash."

Reuel looked curiously at him. "Spoken like your sister, if you don't mind my saying so, my lord."

Aurelius laid a hand on his steward's shoulder. "Reuel, you are my oldest friend. You may say anything you like. But yes . . . events of late have caused me to rethink. What do the gods have to do with us? I have always wondered. But now I think they may have a great deal to do with us, if only because the people become like what they worship. If I had to choose a god to reign in my house, over this town, I would choose the Great God above Kimash any day."

Something was stirring in Aurelius's head, in his heart, as he spoke. An idea. A doorway . . . a way out. He could not yet put it into words. But faces were passing through his mind. Beniah, worshiper of every god and none, unstable as wine. Flora, stalwart devotee of the Great God, honest, scrupulous, faithful to the death. Shem—so strangely changed since he had taken up wearing an amulet of Amon-Heth, grown distant and cold and severe. And the priests of Kimash, blood-thirsty and licentious.

If you want to change a man, he thought, *change his god.*

He himself had only rediscovered his courage and resolve when he and Marah decided they would, if not exactly follow the Great God, at least begin to look to him.

"Sir?" Reuel asked.

"I'm having a thought, Reuel," Aurelius said. "An epiphany."

Aurelius returned to Ezra's camp hours later and woke Marah from a fitful sleep. Kneeling beside her cot, he whispered, "I know what to do."

Marah blinked, clearing away cobwebs and dreams. "Your talk with Reuel went well?"

"No. Yes. But that's not how I know what to do. I think the Great God gave me an answer."

Marah swung her legs around and sat up. Her thick hair stuck out in all directions, and her face was saggy from sleep. Aurelius wanted to kiss her. She'd never looked so beautiful to him.

"What is wrong with you?" she asked.

"Ask me what is right."

She shook her head and laughed. "Have you had a revelation, Aurelius? An ecstatic vision?"

"I only know that the way forward has become clear to me. The people can be free of Kimash's chains, Marah. We can set them free."

"Tell me, my husband. Tell me how you are going to work this miracle."

"I won't do it alone. Ezra will help us. You will help me. We will find Flora, and she will help us."

"You still have not told me."

"It is simple," Aurelius said. "Absurdly so. We can change everything. We only need to turn these people back to the Great God."

CHAPTER 14

Jonah Bar Kebna sat cross-legged on the floor of a miller's house in a small valley near the Great Sea. To his left sat one of Essea's brethren, a man named Seriah who had refused to let Jonah travel alone even though most of the brethren had gone their separate ways. To his right sat Nadab the Trader, who listened more intently than anyone to his words, although his mind would wander and he seemed not to understand all that he heard. Even so he would burst into tears from time to time, whether from joy or contrition Jonah could not always be sure.

The weakness of Nadab's mind had grown by the day, as though the effects of the attack he had suffered were slow in coming. Yet even as he grew more childlike in his mind, his spirit seemed to brighten.

Packed in around Jonah like mice in a nest were the miller and his family and his nearest neighbors and their families. All listened to the words of the scroll that Jonah read. The Teacher would pause to explain the words as well, and to add history and detail to what he read. But it was when the words of the Great God himself were intoned that the people listened most closely.

They were reading about care for one's neighbor. The Great God's scrolls spent an inordinate amount of time on the subject—nearly as much as they did on the proper way to worship the God. This particular passage detailed the fair treatment and prompt payment of servants, along with the requirement to free slaves on a yearly basis at the Gathering in Shalem.

The Gathering had not happened in many generations. Reading of it now taught the People what their lives might have been.

Of the miller's neighbors, only one man was wealthy enough to employ servants. The others in the room had sons and daughters in slavery or servitude. They commented loudly as Jonah read—completely lacking the proper comportment of students, much to Seriah's evident amusement—shouting agreement and occasionally outrage that the laws had not been followed. The wealthier man shifted uncomfortably in his seat, but he said nothing. From the look on his face, Jonah knew he was receiving the words, not resisting them. He suspected change would ensue when the man returned home, and every family in the room would be glad for it.

When the meeting broke up, the wealthy man remained behind to speak with Jonah. Seriah took Nadab's arm and led him outside with the others.

"We have to ask why," the wealthy man said, shaking his head. "Why we never heard. I was always told the Great God's laws were oppressive, but what you read . . . this is not oppressive. This is good. I say so as a man who must go home and make reparation for wrongs done. But I will do it."

Jonah bowed his head. "The Great God will honor you for it, as do I. If only all would listen the way you do."

"But why?" the man asked again. "Many never have the chance. I have never in my life heard these words until today. How could I respond to them?"

"Much of the fault lies with us," Jonah said. "We have had the scrolls for years and chose to protect them and keep them within our walls. We knew, and we did not tell you. I fear we preferred to judge you and wait for the Great God to bring judgment upon you."

"Will he do it?" the man asked. There were tears in his eyes. "Will Kol Abaddon's words come to pass? I know already that we have been faithless to the Great God. Will he be angry with us?"

"He is angry with you," Jonah said. "How can it be otherwise? And yet he was angry with me, for I sinned grievously. And he sent his grace—a way out. Another chance. I believe he is doing the same for you. Why else send out the word? Why else allow you to change course?"

"That is not the word Kol Abaddon preached," the man said. "When I heard him in the past, I quaked in my boots. But I did not know there was any chance to change the future."

"I don't know if Kol Abaddon himself knew," Jonah said. Slowly, he stood. "We will read again this evening. Bring your whole household."

"Indeed, I will. And they will come. For when they hear how much the Great God is on their side against me, they will flock to him." The man smiled. "In this case I am glad for his enmity, for it has changed me more than a friendship could have done. I feel like a new man before I have even acted."

"See that you don't lose your new man on your way out the door," Jonah said, chuckling. "Resolve is only as good as its follow-through."

"No fear of that," the wealthy man said. His expression sobered. "No fear at all."

Jonah stepped outside, into the milling group of villagers who still talked with Seriah and Nadab. No one had left. In fact, the crowd had grown as others came to join them and hear what was going on. The wealthy man put on a mock frown. "Is there no work being done in this village? We'll all starve!"

"Not a chance," another man rejoined. "We'll raid your stores and feast ourselves gladly!"

The wealthy man batted at his neighbor. "Get on with you."

Seriah left his conversation and returned to Jonah's side. "Are you weary, Teacher?" he asked.

"Some," Jonah said. He had read the word for over an hour, and they had only arrived yesterday from a tiring journey. He was indeed weary, down to his bones. Yet he felt as though life was springing up inside of him, feeding his limbs, feeding his spirit, feeding these people. "But I am not undone. A little rest and we will be ready to read again."

"They responded well," Seriah said.

"Better than I could have imagined. What fools we have been, keeping the word to ourselves all this time!"

"I cannot imagine that everyone will respond like this. Before I went to Essea, I shared what I knew of the word with my family. They beat me and threw me out."

"But some *will* respond. Some will. And those few will make it all worth it."

All. Jonah wondered, even as he said the words, what that meant. What price they would pay for this. What the end of it would be.

"What will you read them next?"

"The commands for worship," Jonah said. "They are twins, worship of the Great God and love for one's neighbor. When a heart opens to one, it opens to the other. It is time the Great God's beloved learn to love him again."

"Aurelius is coming," Nadab said abruptly. He looked at them expectantly. They exchanged a glance.

 RACHEL STARR THOMSON

"Aurelius is coming, and he will help you," Nadab said. He sounded satisfied.

"How do . . . where did you hear that?" Seriah asked.

"They told me," Nadab said. He didn't define "they," and the brethren didn't push him. No sense upsetting his addled brain. But Jonah was curious. "Aurelius, the governor of Bethabara?"

"Yes," Nadab said, nodding enthusiastically.

Jonah smiled and nodded back. He didn't ask the questions running through his head. Had Nadab heard something from the Great God? Stranger things had happened. More likely he was just imagining it. He'd had many close dealings with the governor in Bethabara. He was just importing memories to this new setting. Why would a man like Aurelius help with their cause—a foreigner with no place in their heritage, no place in their ancient covenant with the Great God?

But then, Aurelius's half-sister, twice the foreigner because she was Hill Woman as well as Westlander, and the Hill People were anathema in the temple of the Great God—her devotion to the Great God was legend.

In many ways, she was the reason Jonah was here now.

He found himself smiling. Feeble-minded men hearing from God. Foreigners calling the People back to their God. Yes, stranger things had happened. Stranger things were happening even now.

He meant to go lie down and snatch some sleep before the next reading, but villagers were waiting for him with questions. He sat down by a cistern to answer them, and while Nadab looked beamingly on, the afternoon disappeared in conversation.

———— •◆• ————

Flora sat with the lost scroll cradled in her arms for an hour in her lonely chamber, listening to the birds in the garden and asking the Great God to have mercy on Rechab. It killed her that she had not been able to do more for her friend.

Slowly, wonderingly, she unfurled the scroll again. The ancient parchment, the carefully written words: it hardly seemed believable that this was one of the original scrolls, written at the Great God's own behest by the prophets of the covenant. But it had to be.

She let her eyes wander over the words. They struck her with irony and pathos. *You shall not kill. You shall not make to yourself any graven image. You shall worship the Lord your God, and him only shall you serve.*

The People had made a mockery of these laws in every possible way. Laws that, had they been followed, would have made them free and strong. Instead they were enslaved to greed and the likes of Izevel.

She read deeply into the scroll, into the laws surrounding trials and the processes for judging rightly.

Halfway through, she sat up straighter.

You shall not kill.

The idea came to her in a rush, in a whirlwind of possibilities, of accusations and consequences and the terrible damage she could do if she acted on it.

More to the point, if *Rechab* acted on it.

She stood. Rechab would have to make her own choices, but as usual, it would be Flora who kicked the door open for them.

———◆———

 Rachel Starr Thomson

Flora followed a posse of servants through the palace, trailing far enough behind them that they didn't know she was doing it. Her sandals squeaked on the marble floor, the sound echoing off the high walls. It was unlikely they would expect that the queen's twin sister was following them anyway. Nobility usually ignored the goings-on of servants.

Flora, against usual practice, paid attention to everything and so knew where these servants were going. She passed little clusters of important people in the palace, but no one stopped her. She'd long ago mastered the art of looking unstoppable.

She hung back and waited while the servants passed through a door into an airy chamber overlooking the gardens. No one molested them. Perfect.

Looking around to make sure no one was watching, she slipped across the floor and waited unobtrusively behind the door. The servants emerged, and before the door could close behind them, she slipped inside.

The king sat on a couch, being fanned by a slave, listening to a scribe read accounts off a scroll. A few bodyguards stood about the room, but no one was looking at the door. Flora had perhaps a minute before she was stopped.

Without hesitation, she strode across the floor and dropped to her knees beside the king before anyone could leap at her.

His eyes widened. "Ize—Flora! To what do I owe this visit?" He put out his hand, stopping the bodyguards in their tracks. She let out a breath she hadn't known she was holding and smiled weakly at him. Now was not the time to look competent or assured. "I need your help," she said.

The king sat up from his reclining position and waved the scribe away. "Leave us," he said.

"But your majesty—"

"We shall come back to the books at a later date. I have more charming things to attend to."

He smiled at her, and to her relief, she could see that he wasn't drunk. That explained the accounts. No king deep in his wine would choose to spend an afternoon listening to sums.

She let tears form in her eyes. "I am in trouble," she said. "I rely on your goodness to help me."

"Trouble?" he frowned. "Who dares trouble you here? The high priest told me you had enemies, but . . ."

"More accurately," she rushed to say, "I want to intercede for a friend. Her troubles are mine."

Now Beniah looked a little less certain, like an animal starting to suspect it had been cornered. Even so, his expression invited her to go on.

"The king knows a rebellion was recently put down in a valley to the north," Flora said.

"Of course," the king said. "I ordered the attack myself."

More to the point, Flora knew, Izevel had ordered the attack and Beniah had lent his support because he felt he had no other choice. She'd been listening to palace gossip for days and knew the story well. Rumor said Izevel's real wrath was for Essea, but the religious community had disbanded before she could vent her fury against them. "A sad business," Flora said.

"I had no choice," Beniah said. "Rebellion cannot be allowed to foment in a nation. The damage it does goes far beyond insult to this house."

"I understand," Flora said. "But you know some of those involved were brought back here to be tried by the priests? They say they surrendered because they have no true guilt. That the rebels were outsiders who took over their town, and these men were only innocent bystanders."

Beniah's face clouded. "Flora, I know you have a compassionate heart. But I doubt their story. Innocent men are not as common as you might think."

"I know about sin," Flora said. "I'm a religious fanatic, if you recall. I expect that you will try them fairly and see justice done."

"Yes," Beniah said slowly. He gazed sidelong at her, trying to figure out what she was trying to do.

"Among the captives is a woman," Flora went on. "My friend."

Beniah's face turned a little ashen. "I am told she confessed to her guilt already."

"Perhaps she did," Flora rushed to say. She rose a little on her knees and laid her hand on the couch beside Beniah. "I do not know where her guilt lies, or doesn't. I have not come to ask you to release her."

He breathed a little easier. The bodyguards were leaning in to hear the conversation better, and birds in the garden outside chirped merrily. "Then, Flora, it's not that I'm not happy to see you, but I don't understand why you are here."

"Because there are plots afoot, and I rely on you to be better than they are," Flora said. She took a deep breath. Every word was true, even if she was spinning them a little and taking advantage of Beniah's desire to please a beautiful woman. She hoped there was something deeper there too—that their conversation about the Great God had led him to truly regard her as she truly regarded him. But she could not count on that.

"My friend has enemies in Shalem, as do I," Flora said. "If the priests are allowed to try her privately, I fear the result will be condemnation whether deserved or not. You know they are too easily influenced—too easily bribed. I pray that you will insist on a public trial. Let it be held in the temple, and let all the people be invited to see. Insist on it because this rebellion was a public affront to your rule and to your honor. The People should see it tried and learn that you will not tolerate treachery."

She held her breath and studied his face. He looked confused.

"That is all?" he said.

"Yes. I believe that if the trial is public, it will be fair. The People will hold the priests accountable. If it happens behind closed doors, they may simply be bought off."

Beniah narrowed his eyes. "You are playing an angle, my sister," he said, "but I cannot tell what it is."

She shook her head even as her cheeks flamed red. Oh, what was the use in trying to lie? She'd never not been honest.

"I am trying to ensure that truth prevails," she said. "Whatever the outcome, I believe that will be best for my friend. And for you. And for the People. That is the only angle I am playing."

He stared at her for another minute and then nodded his head. "I will have my servants call for the high priest of the Great God," he said. "I will ensure that the trial is held publicly and the people are invited. But I cannot promise you it won't be painful for you. If she is guilty as all accounts say she is, she will be executed, and the trial will bare her guilt before all."

"I understand," Flora said. Slowly, she stood. Her legs ached from the cramped position on the marble. "I thank you."

He looked up at her and slowly shook his head. "You are a puzzling woman, Flora Laurentii."

She smiled. "Puzzling?"

"I am not used to honesty or forthrightness in one like yourself. Or in many at all."

    RACHEL STARR THOMSON

Her smile faltered. "There may be more of an angle in what I've just said than I have told you."

"I know that."

"I'm not going to tell you what it is."

"I know that too." He stood and took her hand, then unexpectedly kissed it. "But I also know you will not lie to me, nor cheat me, nor do me harm. So I will leave you with your secrets."

She left him with a heavy heart. She hoped he was right—that she would not do him harm. But she knew what she had accomplished in the meeting and what its consequences could be. She had spent the night since Rechab praying, and she'd heard the voice in her spirit telling her what had to be done. Her audience with Beniah had put everything in place. All that was left was to convince Rechab to loose the arrow in her grasp.

⸻ ◆ ⸻

Shem worked harder in the kitchen than most servants ever worked, comported himself with all the charm and well-spoken courtesy Marah had endued him with, and prayed that Amon-Heth would smile on him. He did, and Shem was promoted to server within days of arriving. No one asked further after the circumstances of his coming. It was not terribly unusual that a wealthy man would lend a servant to another at such a busy time, and as far as Shem could tell, no one had yet caught on that Aurelius and Marah were no longer in the villa. Their plan had worked exactly as they hoped.

Although the king's sudden spate of soberness had caused a slight lull in the festivities, it was not much. Izevel kept the feasting going on her own, inviting all of the local and visiting nobles and politicians daily to the palace. Shem wondered if her dissolution was draining the king's coffers dry. Not that it mattered to him.

What mattered was the glory of Amon-Heth. Kimash was a swaggering, sickening usurper of honor that rightly belonged to others. He was embodied in his servants, just as Amon-Heth was embodied in his. The tall, cold priests of the Southern Plains, clean and disciplined and ascetic. And Shem himself.

Shem, his prophet.

Nightly, when the festivities had at last ended in the drunken swaggering away of the guests, Shem prostrated himself in the garden before a tiny shrine. He had not put it there. Someone else had built it and then abandoned it. Other shrines in the streets brought more public glory to the god of the South, but Shem did not wish to leave the palace until his task was done. He lit incense and breathed in the intoxicating presence of his jackal-headed god until daylight.

The nights were lost to him in the scents and the darkness. He could never remember them in the morning, but he knew he had not slept. Sometimes he opened his eyes flat on his back as in Aurelius's garden, but still he knew sleep had not taken him. Something else had.

His night vigils were the only relief from the pressure still building in his chest. As he breathed in incense, he could breathe truly. All through the day, especially in the king's presence, the pressure grew. Only at night could he release it.

With the pressure came violent swings of emotion that he fought to keep under control as befitted a servant of Amon-Heth. Not for the god of the South were the wild displays and cavorting furies of the Kimashians. He expressed nothing, but he felt it nonetheless. He felt anger and disgust at the revelers. He felt deep contempt for the servants of Kimash and the king. And he felt hatred for his old master's sister, whom he sometimes came across wandering the halls or the gardens,

     Rachel Starr Thomson

talking with the king's wives—all except Izevel—or listening to the servants. He felt hatred, too, for Amon, the Southern trader who had brought Flora here. The man was still hanging around the king's courts, waiting to be thrown a bone. He was pathetic. Shem had once thought him an impressive man, a servant of the gods. Now he thought of him as a dog or less than a dog . . . a flea. A man who refused to choose a side and instead jumped from one host to another, sucking blood wherever he could find it.

But for all his depth of feeling, no matter how wildly the emotions of anger and contempt and hatred shook his spirit, he would not act. He would not lift a hand against Flora, nor against the others.

He knew his mission, and he would carry it out at the appointed time.

Darkness had fallen hours ago as Shem finished clearing away serving dishes in one of Izevel's feasting halls. The king had not appeared today—he must be still sober. Shem carried the platters to the kitchen and scraped them off without being told. His hands shook as he did. He needed to go. He needed relief.

He pocketed a flint as he ducked out of the chores. The other servants would handle the rest of the kitchen and not even miss him— much. If he was questioned for his absence, he would say he'd been called away by one of the nobles. It was hours later even than usual, and he could not wait anymore.

He descended the servants' steps to the garden and lost himself quickly amidst the fragrant trees. His shrine was hidden in a copse of orange trees. He hurried there and slowed as voices drifted his way. Someone else was playing hooky from their duties.

The voices were female—two of the house slaves, he thought.

"They say the trial is to be public," one of them said. "The king is insisting that the People must attend. But I've heard it was Flora the Unlucky who put him up to it. What game do you think she's playing?"

"Who knows?" the other answered. "Maybe she just wants the People gathering to the temple to worship the Great God."

The other one snorted, and they both laughed. "As if the temple were anything more than a brothel for the gods."

"How would she know? She's never been in there. Hill Woman."

"Her sister doesn't let that stop her. Izevel has been in the temple every day, sacrificing to Kimash in the outer courts. The Great God hasn't struck her with lightning yet."

"Maybe that's what Flora's up to. Maybe she hopes if Izevel will stay in the temple long enough, the Great God will notice and express his offense."

They both laughed outright at that. Shem stood still on the path, his whole body quivering. They were blocking the way to his shrine. But he needed to get there. He needed release.

The first woman dropped her voice lower. "Have you heard the other rumors? They say Kol Abaddon's been seen again."

"After all these months? I figured he'd dropped dead in the wilderness somewhere."

"So did we all. But word has it he's crossing the desert with slabs of stone strapped to his back. Slow as a crippled mule. And saying *nothing*—just nothing. No warnings, no judgments. Just carrying the stones."

"Carrying them where?"

"Nobody knows. Can't be here. He hasn't set foot in this city since my father was a boy. They say he hates this place."

The second woman dropped her voice low. "They say the king killed his family."

They say, they say. Shem thought he would burst where he stood if these women did not get out of his way. For a moment he considered setting upon them, beating them to a pulp to teach them not to gossip and not to get in the way of a man who worships.

He took a staggered step forward and then regained himself. It bothered him that he'd had such a thought. But the images of violence would not leave his mind.

Then a voice from behind startled him. "Shem, isn't it?"

A woman again—but not one of the servants. He knew her before he turned to face her. The voice was familiar from his years of service in Aurelius's house. Flora Laurentii. The master's ill-fated sister and the one person in this palace whose presence made him feel truly murderous.

With both his fists clenched so tightly that his nails dug into his palms, he turned to face her. The soft lighting of garden torches lit her face, striped with shadows. She was looking at him curiously, head tilted to the side, but when he faced her, her eyes narrowed.

"Shem? What's wrong?"

He was shaking. He could hardly contain himself. He wanted to fly at her, tear out her throat. He wanted to make her suffer.

The pressure in his chest was going to make him burst open like a seed pod and release whatever life force wanted out.

Flora's eyes widened, and a voice in Shem's head screamed, *She knows! She sees!*

Overwhelmed by sudden terror, he turned and fled.

<h1 style="text-align:center">CHAPTER 15</h1>

Alack spent the first three days in Kasarea hiding out in the inn. The captain of the guard was busy convening a caravan to take them across the desert to Shalem. Croesius and the other emissaries spent time in the more upscale taverns. But Alack did not want to see or be seen. Ruefully, he considered that all the time spent hiding away was lightening his skin and making him look more and more like a Westlander with each passing day. No one outside would even recognize him as one of them. But no—he would open his mouth and speak, and they would know he was a native-born son, here to betray them. No one could pay him enough to emerge.

Besides, the overland trek lay ahead of them, and it would be painfully public. Everywhere they went they would go grandly, dropping money, parading, making a show. They wanted to start tongues wagging, such that every nomad and passing merchant would begin to carry the word ahead of them that emissaries from the Westland were coming with a message for the king.

And when they arrived, Alack would have no choice but to give the message.

He played the scene over in his mind a thousand times. Perhaps he could escape it after all. He could run away before they reached Shalem. Or *when* they reached Shalem, he could change sides, claiming asylum with his king and revealing the whole plan of their enemies.

And then what? What good would that do? The Sacred Land would still be at the mercy of Sabrus Caelius. The only difference would be that Alack would have broken his word to the emperor of the Westland and endangered the life of Kol Abaddon, who was imprisoned in a Westland dungeon and would most certainly take retaliation if Alack jumped ship.

Besides, there was the Great God. Alack was a prophet, and the Great God's message was one of coming judgment. It had been so for years. Sabrus Caelius had simply put a face on that judgment. A face, a sword, and ten thousand mercenary troops.

Alack leaned back in a chair and sighed. His head nodded . . . alone in the inn as usual, he thought boredom might kill him before he had to deliver any messages at all. It was better than the shame of revealing himself. But still miserable.

The inn had a window looking out over the harbor, and Alack rose from the chair and drifted over to it. He rested his arms on the wide adobe wall and leaned out a little for a better view. Late afternoon sunlight sparkled off the water of the Great Sea, which was calm as far as the eye could see. A knot of camels and camel-drivers argued in the street just below him, the beasts laden with bundles of cloth. Their voices drifted up. In former days he would have laughed at the passion with which the drivers insulted one another. But today it was hard to laugh.

Overwhelmed suddenly with a desire to be outside, Alack did the next best thing and climbed into the window, settling himself on the thick adobe sill. He let one leg hang down, bathed in the warm sunlight, and steadied himself with a hand against the wall. He perched like a gull above the harbor and prayed to be released.

But he knew the Great God would not answer that prayer.

The Holy City was his destiny. He was meant to give this message. He hated it, but he knew to his bones it was true.

This land that he loved was primed for judgment.

He noticed an unusual bustle below, near the shipyards. Someone was standing on a pile of crates and shouting over a crowd that was gathering quickly. A herald? He leaned forward a little, curious, careful to keep his balance.

Not a herald, he realized. A preacher.

The man on the crate was dressed in white linen, and he held a scroll. He was not tall or striking in appearance, yet Alack's eyes were riveted to him. At first he thought he might be a king's messenger, but no: his clothing was too simple, too plain, and he had none of the usual trappings of a royal servant. No bodyguard, no trumpets, no horse.

He did have a magnificent voice, and it carried over the crowd and stilled it.

"This is the word of the Great God!" he said. "Hear the words of the lost scrolls!"

Goosebumps rose on Alack's skin. The lost scrolls? Could it be possible? Why here? Shouldn't this man be in the temple in Shalem?

"You shall have no other gods before me," the man read. "You shall make for yourself no graven image. You shall love the Lord your God, and him only shall you serve."

The words fell through the crowd like silver. They were silent. Alack held his breath, caught up in the spell.

"You are the holy people," the man read, "my own special possession in the earth. Let your light so shine before men that they may see your good works and glorify your Father in heaven."

Father, Alack thought. Immediately upon thinking the word, something quickened in his spirit. Yes, this was right. The Great God was more than just a deity to him, to all of them. The Great God was Father.

"You shall not do as the nations around you, worshiping demons as gods. You shall not make images of anything on earth or in the heaven and say of it, 'This is our God,' for your God is invisible in the heavens. You shall not cheat one another, sell one another, or falsify your weights and scales. You shall be holy, as I am holy, says your God."

The crowd was growing. Workers in the shipyard had ceased repairs to come and hear. Sailors were gathering around the edges.

Alack waited for someone to disrupt the meeting. To scoff, to throw things, as they had always done to Kol Abaddon. But no one did. The words fell on ears that were listening.

You shall not enslave one another. Alack thought of the slaves who came through Bethabara with their masters, so many of them Holy People enslaved all their lives to Holy People.

You shall not cheat. He thought of the merchants in the Holy City who had to be watched and their weights tested, whose words you could not rely on any more than you could expect water to hold you up.

You shall not worship other gods or make any graven image to bow down and worship it. He thought of the temple. The temple, where he had never been, but where Rechab feared to go, where Kol Abaddon refused to go, and where it was said that the pagan gods were arrayed in an open marketplace of wicked unfaithfulness to everything the Holy People were meant to be.

But then the man in the shipyards paused, and his voice broke a little as he read, "My faithfulness is higher than the mountains, and my loving-kindness deeper than the seas. Though I am angry with you for a moment, I will turn and have compassion on you as a mother has

     RACHEL STARR THOMSON

compassion on the child of her heart. I will deliver you and be merciful to you, for I have loved you with an everlasting love."

Alack found himself struggling to breathe as the window seemed to tilt. For a moment he thought he would fall. This was not the message Kol Abaddon had preached. Not the message he had seen in the stars. Not the message of the Dragon in the darkness of the sea, coming to flood the Sacred Land and destroy it.

I may be angry with you for a night.

But I will have compassion.

He found himself suddenly back inside a vision—one of his first. He had been standing in a wadi, holding a lamb tightly to his chest as he stared at the threatening forms of jackals circling around the canyon mouth. A lamb who had also been Rechab, who had also been the Sacred Land; jackals that had also been the Dragon, the Adversary, Leviathan in the waters.

And he had stood between them. The lamb's protector.

He had seen the danger, looked it in the face. But his job had not been to throw the lamb to the Dragon's teeth.

His job had been to save it.

The vision had ended there, but the calling had not.

He clung to the sides of the window as the Great God's voice reverberated through his heart more powerfully than he had ever heard it, shaking the foundations of his soul and of everything he had ever known or believed.

Save my people, the Great God said. *Save my Beloved.*

CHAPTER 16

Beniah didn't waste time acting on Flora's request. He decreed a public trial and invited the entire city to attend. Immediately, Izevel put a stop to the wedding feasts. Her wrath echoed through the halls. But the king's decree was unchangeable.

Rechab, locked away in the servants' quarters, nodded slowly as Flora told her about it.

"Rechab, you must take this opportunity," Flora said. "There may never be another chance."

"But I am guilty," Rechab said. She looked over her shoulder at Flora, who was standing in the far corner of the room. Rechab had been pacing since her friend arrived, the news making her too nervous to be still. "I am worthy of death. How can I deflect that without increasing my sin? I must walk openly before the Great God."

"But their sin is greater," Flora said.

"And if we expose it? If I do what you want me to, and the priests are pitted against one another? What will happen? How much more bloodshed and strife may come of my actions? There is no guarantee the king will side against his wife and her family. Our interference could make things so much worse for worshipers of the Great God."

Flora nodded and looked away, clearly frustrated. "I think he would do what was right. There is a good man inside Beniah. He has just been locked away a very long time."

"I fear he won't come out of that prison soon enough or completely enough," Rechab said. "But I can't do it anyway, Flora." She stopped pacing and held out her hands. "I am guilty."

Flora sighed and took Rechab's hands. They were friends. Equals. Flora had fallen from power since their first meeting, and Rechab, somehow, had risen. A prisoner, a criminal on the eve of being condemned, a fugitive—yet she was a higher, better soul than the mousy, fearful girl Flora had tried to rescue. The Great God's eye had transformed her.

"I understand," Flora said finally. "I even respect you for it. But I wish you would reconsider. Yours is not the only guilt, nor even the greater guilt. You forget that I knew Aaron. Almost all his life, he served me. I know that what happened was not all your fault."

"He did not force me to anything."

"And I respect you for saying so. Still, Rechab . . ." Flora bit her lip. "Please, don't honor the dead at the cost of your own life. Take the blame that belongs to you, not the blame that doesn't. Tell the judges the truth. Let them decide how deep your guilt goes, not your own heart. Your heart is grieving and vulnerable."

Rechab's eyes filled with tears. "I'm glad you're here," she said. "I have needed a friend."

"So have I," Flora said. She stepped back and dropped Rechab's hands as though she were shaking something off. "I am going to be there, at the trial," she said. "I fully intend to interfere."

Rechab bit her lip. "I wish you wouldn't."

"I won't let you die if I can stop it. I know you have some guilt,

 Rachel Starr Thomson

Rechab, but I do not believe there is blood on your head. It was Aaron who killed the elders in Nachush and Izevel who ordered the rebellion stamped out. Not you."

"There wouldn't have been a rebellion without me."

"And what were your intentions?" Flora asked sharply. "Did you really intend to throw off Beniah's rule? To rise up against the king?"

"I . . . I don't know what Aaron planned."

"There," Flora said, triumphant. "My point exactly. The plans were Aaron's. The treason, if there was any, was Aaron's. Not yours. You led people in worship, Rechab, and you tried to free them from unjust judges. Those are not crimes worthy of death."

Rechab shook her head and sat down on the stool next to the whitewashed wall. "But I lied, and I helped Aaron lead. Without me it wouldn't have happened."

"I'm going to interfere," Flora said again, and this time her tone made it clear she would brook no argument. "If I can possibly save your life, I'll do it."

Rechab sighed. "Save it for what? I am not even sure what I have left to live for." Her father was likely dead. Her household slaughtered. Alack, the boy she had once loved, was gone; and Aaron . . .

"Live for the Great God," Flora said resolutely. "Live for the sake of hope. There is a wise saying, something I learned in Essea: 'Precious in the eyes of the Lord is the death of his holy ones.' But their lives are more precious still."

Rechab looked up and regarded Flora with interest. "You have changed," she said.

"Oh?"

"In Essea, you were different. You were . . . ashamed."

Flora smiled. "Me? But I've always had too much confidence."

Rechab shook her head. She was sure of what she saw. "Just to survive," she said. "You were always just surviving. This is different. You've changed."

Flora sat down on the floor and suddenly broke into a smile—the most free, genuine, joyful smile Rechab had ever seen on her face. To her surprise, there were tears in Flora's eyes as well.

"I heard something," Flora said. "After I came here, the Great God spoke a word to my heart. A name. And you're right. It has changed me. I can't explain it. But I am not ashamed any longer."

Rechab grabbed her friend's hands again. "Flora, be careful. Be careful at the trial. You're in danger here, I can feel it. Please, don't take any chances."

"My whole life has been one long chance," Flora said, "but I believe now the Great God has always had his hand on it. I am not going to leave you alone tomorrow. If the Great God can save you, he can save us both. That is my promise."

Rechab shook her head and laughed. "He couldn't have changed your stubbornness while he was at it?"

"Maybe," Flora said, "that is one thing he didn't think needed to be changed."

Flora remained in the little room for another hour before finally dismissing herself. Rechab watched her go, her heart a tangle of joy and worry. She did fear for her headstrong friend, a fear made sharper by the joy Flora's presence brought her. When they were together she felt as though she was truly not alone. And it wasn't just Flora: it was as though Flora represented something more. The Great God himself, perhaps, or the sum total of his people all across the Sacred Land. Everyone who would still stand for faithfulness and goodness and light in this tainted place. Somehow, Rechab knew Flora wasn't the only one.

She could not be. What the Great God had done in her heart, he must have done in others.

The trial would be held tomorrow. Rechab bowed her head and prayed.

———◆———

After he returned from visiting with Reuel, Aurelius and Marah had spent a long night in conference with Ezra. They expected to be faced with the need to convince him of the wisdom of their plan. To their surprise, he was already convinced.

"I have long believed the land's fortunes would return if the People would turn their hearts back to the Great God," Ezra said. "My fathers believed this and sought to live faithfully. But it is time we do more than live faithfully. The enemy is not quiet, and so we cannot be quiet anymore."

"Do you think the People will listen?" Marah asked.

Ezra spread his hands wide. "Who knows? All we can do is talk. They can open their ears or not."

"But what do we tell them?" Aurelius said. "It won't be enough just to tell them to turn back to the god of their ancestors. They don't know how to turn back. I don't know how to tell them."

Ezra looked thoughtful. Marah said, "It has been so long since most of the old families worshiped that our traditions are gone. The priests don't teach them. We could send messengers to the priests and beg them to take up their mantle again, but who knows if they would listen? And we would betray ourselves if they refused to keep our confidence."

"Better if the people themselves press them," Ezra said. "If the

People were to come to Shalem, to the temple, and ask to be taught. That would change a thing or two."

"A dream," Aurelius said. "It would change things indeed, but how to make it happen? Sheep do not show up all at the same watering hole just because you want them to. You have to lead them there. We would have to find a way to rouse people across the nation, move them all to drop their business and come at the same time to a place that has long meant little to any of them. I fear it is impossible."

Ezra sat back and slapped his knees. "The Gathering."

"Ah," Marah said, nodding. Her face lit up.

Aurelius looked between them, impatient.

"The Gathering is an ancient ceremony," Marah said. "In the earliest days of the covenant, every family would come to Shalem to dedicate their firstborn son to the Great God. In place of actually sending the child to live in the temple, a sacrifice would be offered. The Gathering took place every year. It was a time also of feasting and celebration. It connected the old families from across the country, keeping our ties strong. My grandmother often mourned its demise."

"Why did the People stop celebrating it?" Aurelius asked.

Ezra shrugged. "Who knows? They were busy. The priests were lax in teaching. The feasting lacked its old joys, and feuding among the families kept some apart. But the memory of the Gathering will not be far lost for any of the old families, or for the villagers, I would guess."

"The law of the firstborn applied to all," Marah explained, "rich and poor, landowner and tenant. The Gathering was a great leveler, for no one was above another. I have heard our own servants speak of it—when they thought no one was listening. Slaves were released there as well. For most of the People, talk of the Gathering recalls the golden age."

     Rachel Starr Thomson

Aurelius was beginning to understand. "And when would this Gathering be held?" he asked.

"A week from now," Ezra said triumphantly. "After the first harvest."

"If we can only send messengers out, I believe the People would respond to a call," Marah said.

"They would come, Aurelius. Those with grievances would see it as a way to make their voices heard. Those in need would see it as a way to renew old alliances. And all would come to the temple and present themselves before the priests."

Aurelius nodded slowly. It made sense. Draw on the People's oldest instincts, the nearly-but-not-quite lost markers of their identity. Bring them to the temple, and press the priests to finish the task of awakening worship of the Great God.

It could work.

It all depended on whether the People would respond.

He thought of Kol Abaddon near the well in Bethabara, preaching his message of impending judgment. Aurelius himself had chased the mad prophet away half a dozen times if not more. Other times, his men had cleared the rabble rouser out. But the people . . .

Had they listened?

Did they believe the wild man of the wilderness?

Slowly Aurelius said, "I begin to see my own guilt more and more. If I had not interfered, I think some of the People would have listened to the voice of Kol Abaddon and returned to the Great God long before now."

"In that case," Ezra said, "if you use your influence to the contrary now, they will listen. Ground does not go hard overnight. And even if it does, you can always plough it again."

"I fear we don't have time to plough," Aurelius said.

"In that case," Ezra answered, "You had better hope the ground is ready for the seeds you plant now. But you cannot know that except in one way: that you go out and plant them. Leave the harvest to the Great God. Go and plant your seed."

Aurelius nodded. He knew what to do.

"Where will we find messengers enough?" Marah wondered aloud.

"I have some I can lend you," Ezra said.

"There are others in Bethabara," Aurelius said, "and still more who can be called into action from the towns around the mountain base."

"Will they go?" Marah asked.

"They will for gold enough," Aurelius said.

For the first time Marah looked alarmed. "Whose gold, Aurelius?"

He met her eyes straight on. "Ours."

She stared back at him for a moment before nodding her head. "So be it. Let the message go forth. The Gathering will convene in a week's time."

Ezra had left Bethabara that very night—after Aurelius returned to Reuel and began the work of sowing seed. His steward would spread the word in Bethabara and stir the hearts of the people toward the temple. Aurelius and Marah themselves left Ezra to go north and headed west toward the Great Sea. So they came across Essean pilgrims preaching the word. So they came across a band of refugees from Nachush and helped them.

And so the work of calling the Holy People home began.

CHAPTER 17

In days long past, the outer court of the Great God's temple had served as the nation's high court. In the beginning, tradition said, it was the Great God himself who set it up so. His priests were to be the arbiters of justice for the People, and his house was to be the place where the wronged and oppressed found their grievances put to rights. The power of judgment and justice was vested in the priests, not in the royal house, so that even kings would be accountable and the People remember that their True King reigned on high.

It was a responsibility that waned as the decades and then centuries wore on. The temple lost its place as the center of communal festivity in the land, and the priests became corrupt. Rather than accountability, the priesthood and the kingly line became enmeshed in private alliances and the power of the bribe. The priests continued to serve as judges, but few of the People trusted them as arbiters anymore, so they did not come. When the priests *were* placed over a trial, rarely now did they ever hold it in the courts of the temple. That place had become a marketplace of nations anyway. Trials were held privately, away from prying eyes.

For all these reasons, Beniah's declaration that the rebels would be tried in the temple raised the interest of the entire city and the ire of many. But for every one whose world was shaken by it, there were five others who eagerly anticipated watching the trial.

Making the show even more intriguing was the undisguised anger of Izevel. It was an open secret that she had ordered the attack on the rebels in the first place. Why she was now angered by a public trial of some of them was anyone's guess. Perhaps the queen felt that her own judgment was being questioned, that some would believe she had ordered the annihilation of innocents. Perhaps suggesting that any of the prisoners *could* be innocent was an affront to her. Or perhaps she was simply angry at the honor and attention paid to the Great God's priests. Everyone knew that the enmity between the gods was personal to this woman. Many said that she would never be content for Kimash to be worshiped even in the inner court. She would move him into the Holy Place and displace the Great God completely if she could.

Other, darker rumors said it had already happened: that anyone who could enter the Holy Place would find Kimash installed there.

The arrival of Flora Laurentii in the palace had caused many to draw comparisons between the two, and many judged them not altogether different. Both were fanatic worshipers of their deities. Both were beautiful, powerful women. And both, or so the gawkers hoped, would be on display at the trial.

By contrast, few knew who Rechab was or much cared. They'd heard that a young woman would be tried, and certainly that raised their interest. But the rebellion in Nachush had not really impacted Shalem in any tangible way, and to most, Rechab was nothing but a curiosity. Some of the merchant class took interest in her for her father's sake. But even among these, few had any real sense of the machinations that lay behind Rechab's precarious position now.

Flora knew. She knew the story from beginning to end and cared deeply about the girl who would soon be on display before the whole

     RACHEL STARR THOMSON

Sacred Land, by Flora's own doing. She hadn't said as much to Rechab, but she felt the weight of her own guilt in the whole matter. In a sense, it was her money and her name that had trapped Rechab in the position of power that had led her to make the mistakes she now so deeply regretted. Aaron had been Flora's servant, sent by her to Rechab's aid. True, she never would have imagined he would abuse his position the way he had done. She'd known Aaron was passionate and that he harbored a sense of grievance against the world, but if she'd realized how deep that ran—or had picked up on his attraction to Rechab—she might have thought twice about sending him to her.

Regardless, she hadn't realized it, hadn't seen it, and had sent him. At least a little of the blame belonged to her.

Farther back, of course, it was her fault Rechab had run away from home to begin with. But that she refused to feel sorry for. Had Rechab not run off with her, she would be married to the high priest of Kimash by now. Instead, Flora hoped Rechab would find the conviction and clarity to become the high priest's worst nightmare. She prayed she would do so.

But even if she didn't, Flora thought as she stood outside the gates of the temple and fought down a lifetime of instinct that told her not to step inside, she would be by Rechab's side today whatever came.

The crowds pushed around her on every side, surging like a sea through the open gates. Flora's mouth went dry as she gazed up at them—high gates of gold, ancient gates, the gateway to the presence of God. For centuries the gates had been there to open to the Holy People and to keep women like her out.

A thousand old, accusing voices rang in her ears.

Hill Woman, said one. *Half-blood.*

Outcast, said another.

Illegitimate. Unwanted. Run off.

One voice, sounding much like her mother's, said *Forgotten*.

Another said *Betrayer*.

All together they shouted *Unworthy*.

Unlucky.

Unloved.

Unwanted.

Unworthy.

The voices converged from a lifetime. Her mother. Her father. Her half-brother. The priests of Kimash. The Teacher and the brethren of Essea. The families of her dead husbands. And her own. Her own, always in agreement with the others; her own, nevertheless shouting defiantly into the wind; her own, stubborn and strong-willed against the world and bowed and broken before the Great God.

This was the one place in the entire world that Flora feared.

She'd never been in doubt as to why. Yes, the Great God had allowed her to run to him. He had allowed her to use his name and to hang around the fringes of his garment. He had allowed her to attach herself to his people and to pray and to act as much as possible like one of them.

But she was not. The blood in her veins was tainted. And she had always feared that if she passed through these gates, even in spite of the Holy People's adulteration of this place, she would encounter the undiluted presence of the Great God and he would repel her from himself. She would face the one she wanted more than life, and he would reject her.

And so Flora had sworn she would never enter these gates. Out of respect for the Great God, the ancient laws, and the holiness these people were called to, yes. But also out of fear.

 Rachel Starr Thomson

That fear shook her now. It made her weak even as the voices in her head shouted, naming her, condemning her, telling her to turn and run.

She shook her head. Sought the other voice. The one she had only recently come to recognize for what—for who—it was.

She couldn't hear it. The press of the crowd was too close. The voices in her head were too strong.

So she took a deep breath and stepped through the gates anyway.

On the other side, she entered a wide court around another set of walls and gates. The inner court was past there, she knew, and beyond even that the Holy Place.

She looked around. The high, sweeping exterior walls cut this place off from the world. The sandy floor was packed down and glistening in the sun. Golden washbasins, fountains, and incense altars dotted the way toward the inner court. Just outside of the second wall, a large altar overlaid with gold stood, just visible through the milling crowds. Flora's eyes went dark with anger at the sight of other altars and idols, and of the merchants and vendors set up all around the perimeter of the court. Sheep baaed; cattle lowed. Sacrifices for sale. Merchants hawked idols, amulets, and offerings not only for the Great God but for any god of choice.

Flora had to physically resist the urge to attack the nearest idol hawker and overturn his tables. She tore her eyes away and turned them toward the inner court, where she was going. Where the trial would be.

And then she heard the voice.

Peace, Beloved, it said.

The other voices were not quieted. They did not go away. As she took one step after another toward the inner court of the temple, clenching her hands to steady herself, she still heard all the accusations.

But she chose to cling to that one name alone. *Beloved.* And the clinging gave her the strength to walk through the second set of gates.

She closed her eyes for a second immediately after entering. It was here that she was not allowed; here that all the ancient laws forbade her and her kind. The Teacher of Essea had told her so a hundred times, warning her strictly never to dare enter this place. She repeated "Beloved" to herself, but she was not sure the Great God wouldn't strike her dead if she took another step.

So she took one, just to see.

She lived.

She breathed a sigh of relief and looked around for a seat.

In the center of the inner court stood the Holy Place, a tall, narrow building, rectangular in shape, with an enormous curtain across its door. Before this, up a flight of seventy steps, was a broad dais with an altar. It was here that the trial would take place.

On the ground before the structure, crowds amassed. To either side stands had been set up where the king, his family, and other nobility could be seated above the crowds, perched on a level with the proceedings and privileged to hear and see more clearly. Flora headed toward these. Peasants moved instinctively out of her way. She wore a white linen dress with a cloak of deep red. Bangles circled her arms and earrings adorned her ears. Her face was veiled—for propriety and so that no one would see how much she resembled Izevel—but everything about her bearing spoke of wealth, power, and position. No one tried to stop her.

And yet, she was deeply aware as she started up the steps to a seat near the king that she was alone. No one stood with her. No one guarded her. There were no Esseans here to call her one of their own, nor members of her entourage to serve and protect her. Here in this

 RACHEL STARR THOMSON

place she was one and one only. Her enemies surrounded her. The girl about to be placed on trial was her only friend.

The crowds grew, filling the inner court of the temple till it overflowed. Flora watched them nervously. They packed themselves tightly, leaving little room to stand, little room to breathe. The crowds were the great unknown in the trial. Their reaction could sway decisions, change justice. The priests, polished politicians, were skilled at reading response.

Why so many had come, Flora couldn't say. It was unlikely word of Nachush had even reached half these people. Perhaps it was morbid curiosity, or simply a matter of boredom. Flora said a prayer for them. Rechab had given her little reason to expect that she would do as Flora had asked her to do, but if she surprised her, a riot could break out. The more people who kept packing in here, the more dangerously things could escalate.

Flora drew her veil closer around herself and trained her gaze on the dais in front of the Holy Place. She frowned slightly as she wondered where the priests and Rechab were now. Surely they wouldn't be so blasphemous as to use the Holy Place as a waiting room. Tradition said the presence of the Great God dwelt behind that curtain, a fire that never went out.

A stirring from the gates, followed by a blast of trumpets, turned her attention away from the Holy Place. They were entering from the back. Good. But now the huge crowds presented a problem as the people crushed backwards, trying to open a narrow passage through their midst. Somehow the room was found, and the procession began, led by soldiers on horseback. Behind them, surrounded by bodyguards, came an impressive line of personages: the king and Izevel, the high priest of Kimash with a small band of his underlings, and twelve of the Great God's priests, including Jeshiel, the high priest.

The twelve were men Flora should have honored, almost revered, for their position, but could not respect. She bowed her head as they passed by.

Behind them all came Rechab, on foot, followed by the other prisoners from Nachush. The last were men who looked terrified. They shrank away from the crowds and the fanfare and the very grandeur of the temple as though they wished to crawl their way beneath the sand to the dais.

Rechab, on the other hand, walked tall. Flora was proud of her. The change in her young friend was a wonder to behold. But Flora understood it. Was not she also changing? Rechab had told her about the Great God's eye upon her and how she had found courage in him. Just as Flora was finding new courage and new life in the Great God's voice.

Suddenly it felt appropriate—despite everything else, all the idols and the history and the adulteration of this place—that both women were here, in the Great God's temple, where he who was so real to them both dwelt.

Even though Flora should not be here. Even though the Great God should have struck her dead when she entered.

So it was a day to upset expectations. So be it.

The royals and the priests climbed the stairs to the dais, and the accused arrayed themselves at the bottom, surrounded by soldiers and temple guards. Flora almost scoffed. The show of might would lead one to believe these people were dangerous warriors instead of cowering country criminals who were on trial for listening to the wrong man. Rechab was the only really dangerous one, and few here would ever guess why.

A blare of trumpets stilled the noise of the crowds as the trial began. Drummers beat out a slow pace as the first of the accused was marched up the stairs to stand before his judges and accusers.

It was Izevel who read the charges. Flora bristled. As though this has been a wrong against her. It should be Beniah, whose authority had been challenged by the uprising, doing the accusing. One more sign of the inordinate position and power held by her sister. The high priest of Kimash listened with a smug expression behind his heavy makeup. Flora wondered if anyone here was actually fooled into thinking the king was in charge.

The crowd learned eagerly forward as Izevel read the charges. Flora heard a few voices call for the man's head. The tone was cheerful. These weren't an offended people interested in justice or passionate for the defense of their kingdom; they were vagrants out for a lark.

The man cowered even more at the catcalls. Izevel finished her charges with a flourish, and he trained his eyes on the priests, who stepped forward. Flora bristled to see three of the priests of Kimash step forward with them. Would they take part in the judgment? Might it never be!

One of the younger priests of the Great God acted as spokesman. "You have heard the charges," he said to the man. "What have you to say for yourself?"

The man's stammering voice was barely able to be heard, but Flora was sitting close enough to catch most of the words. "Please, my lords, I am an innocent man. I did nothing but live in the town and work the mines." He swung around and pointed a trembling finger at Rechab, who waited at the base of the stairs behind the other men. "It was her! It was her what came and stirred everything up! Other men came to be part of her sedition, but I tell you, I had nothing to do with it all."

The priest frowned. The crowds began to buzz, and he held up his hands for silence. Flora was tense, every muscle straining. She restrained herself. It was not yet the time to come to Rechab's defense.

"Yet you were taken by our soldiers when you surrendered," the priest said, drawing the eyes of the man and attention of the crowds back to himself. He looked up. "Commander Callum! Tell us what this man was doing when you took him prisoner."

A tall, heavy-browed soldier stepped forward. Flora hadn't recognized him before as an officer of special rank—his bearing and clothing were unostentatious. But his men cleared the way for him with obvious deference. He was a Hill Man, Flora realized from his features. Standing in this place, as she was, without retaliation from the Great God. Interesting.

"The men of the village were building a defensive wall," Callum said, "and preparing to fight against us."

"Taking up arms against the king's men! An act of clear rebellion!" one of the Kimashian priests shrilled. The crowd responded with loud agreement. But Callum held up both burly arms and shouted with a voice like a deep horn, "If I may speak, your honors!"

The priest who acted as spokesman nodded, and with gestures and threats from the soldiers, the crowd was quieted. "Speak as you will, Commander."

"Defending one's home when attacked is not usually considered rebellion," Callum said. "This same woman who stands accused came to me in the night and claimed that some of the men of the village were not part of the sedition but were only hapless bystanders pulled in by circumstance. For their sake, and at her urging, I offered terms of surrender to any willing to stand trial. I do not think any true rebel took me up on those terms. The men here are either innocent or bigger cowards even than they appear."

Laughter and calls of approbation or agreement rose with a clamor, and once again the priests and soldiers quieted the crowd.

"Your opinion is noted, Commander, but noted too to be your

 RACHEL STARR THOMSON

opinion only." The spokesman narrowed his eyes. "If I understand correctly, you were sent to wipe out the rebellion without mercy. This trial might be considered a consequence of your disobedience."

"Come, Esan," Beniah burst out, his first comment in the trial, "that's a bit strong. Callum is a good man, and he made his decision to bring these men here with my honor in mind. I approve of it. Let there be no more talk of accusation in his direction."

Flora sat back a little. She hadn't realized she had moved to the edge of her seat.

Esan nodded. The crowd seemed slightly subdued by the king's intervention and waited now with quieter but more intense interest.

"It seems to me you're wasting your time trying this man first," Beniah continued. "If you want to get to the bottom of things, ask the woman. She's clearly at the center of it all."

"Why did you bring *her* here, Callum, if your only desire was to spare innocents in the name of the king? Her guilt is clear," spewed the Kimashian priest who had been vocal before.

Flora smiled to herself. Maybe it was not as clear as they wanted to believe.

Callum simply bowed his head. "I did it for the honor of the king," he said. "I felt a public trial would be more effective in reminding us all of the consequences of rebellion. For yes, it is as you say. Her guilt is clear."

"And Callum cannot stomach killing a woman," someone near Flora muttered. A pair of women next to him twittered in response. She rolled her eyes. God spare me from the upper classes, she thought. Not that the crowds were much better.

"Enough of that," Beniah said. "I already said I want to hear no more accusation toward Callum. Put the girl on trial, Esan. That is where the real answers lie."

The priest nodded and gestured to the soldiers, who pulled the hapless villager away from the center of attention and prodded Rechab up in his place. She walked up the steps unhurriedly despite their poking and gazed up at her accusers without fear. The crowd hushed as she came to a stop.

"Your name?" one of the high priests asked.

Flora tensed. No. They could ruin everything in a moment if she answered.

But she didn't, because the man who was being herded off the steps did. Wildly he shouted, "That's Flora Laurentii! She came to Nachush and took us over through treachery and force of arms!"

Flora let out the breath she'd been holding as the crowd started shouting. Though they had no room to move, motion surged through their ranks, the cumulative effect of hundreds of men and women reacting together.

In the confusion, Esan was beckoning to the soldiers to bring the man forward again. They did, positioning him on the steps directly next to Rechab. She hung her head rather than looking him in the eye as he pointed at her, and everyone quieted to hear his words.

"This woman, Flora Laurentii, came to our village and struck up a deal with our elders because of her gold," he said. "She was to trade with us, see, and have some part ownership in our mines. But she betrayed the elders and murdered them, and then she coerced our people into following her. She started gathering rebels, mercenaries. They was the trouble, not us. We never wanted her there."

Rechab's head still hung, and Flora said aloud, "It wasn't you. It was Aaron."

The priests whispered to each other, but someone saw Rechab

slowly shaking her head.

"You express disagreement," Esan said. "Tell us, woman—are this man's words true?"

Rechab looked up tearfully. "They are true and not true," she said. "I did come to the village and try to strike up a deal with the elders. They were corrupt, and I wanted to help the people. But I didn't murder them or order their deaths. That was . . . that was someone else."

The shouts from the crowd were almost deafening. The soldiers went to work quieting them, and this time even Beniah got into the action, waving his arms in agitation. "Silence!" he bellowed when all could hear him. "I want to hear!"

Suddenly self-conscious as relative quiet fell, the king took a deferent step back and nodded to the priests of the Great God. "More important, our judges need to hear."

"Proceed," Esan said. "Who was it who murdered the elders?"

"His name was . . ." Rechab began, but she faltered. "His name does not matter. He is dead. I would honor his family by allowing his name to die with him."

Flora was holding her breath again. But Rechab had acknowledged that the guilt was not all hers. That was enough. It was what she needed to set her own heart free. Perhaps free enough to take the next step . . .

"The rest is true," Rechab went on. "I did lead the people in Nachush, and I . . . we . . . gathered rebels to ourselves. I never meant to rebel against you, good king, nor to oppose your forces or this temple. Yet I fear that is what happened. I am guilty."

Once again there was a stir, and this time the priests conferred with one another and waited for it to die down naturally. Rechab lifted her eyes to heaven, and Flora knew she prayed to the Great God.

Esan walked forward and raised his hands. The last of the crowd's noise died off. Flora readied herself. The moment had almost certainly come.

"By your own admission, we find you guilty of—"

"You can't!" Flora cried out. She stood and began to stride down the steps of the stands, pushing past anyone in her way. Her voice rang out over the court. "I call a miscarriage of justice! You cannot find this woman guilty!"

It seemed everyone was too stunned to stop her. She strode up the steps toward the dais and stopped next to Rechab, who looked at her with wide, almost panicked eyes. "What are you doing?" she whispered.

"I told you I would not leave you alone," Flora answered. She cast her veil aside, relishing the universal gasps when she appeared. She made a point of meeting Beniah's eyes and nodding slightly to him before turning to Esan and the other priests. Izevel and the high priest she pointedly ignored.

"You cannot find this woman guilty," she said confidently, though her pulse was racing and she knew that any moment she might be dragged away. Yet she did not expect that. She had the fleeting sense that Callum's presence over the military would benefit her as much as Beniah's on the stand of judgment. At least two men in this place were not after blood.

"The charges do not hold," Flora said. She dared the priests to respond.

"Pray tell us why," Jeshiel said even as Esan burst out, "Who are you?"

Flora smiled. "I am Flora Laurentii," she said. "And that is why the charges cannot stand."

Rechab gaped. Flora ignored her. Even the crowd seemed cowed into silence. "Tell me," she said, turning to the cowardly man who still stood on the step next to her. "Who did you say came to your village? Who led the rebellion?"

"F-Flora Laurentii," he stammered.

"Yet I can produce witnesses who will swear I was not there," Flora said, "and not a single one who can put me on the scene. So I cannot be guilty."

"But it was her!" the man said, pointing at Rechab again.

Flora smiled sweetly at him. "You are mistaken, my good man," she said. "Even the king can tell you that I am Flora Laurentii, and you say it was Flora Laurentii who wronged you. I'll wager every man below will say the same. The charges of sedition are against me. And I can be proven to have had nothing to do with the events in Nachush. You cannot hold the charge."

The lower buzz of the crowd erupted, but the Kimashian priest shrieked out again, cutting through the noise. "Nonsense! All you've done is charge her with impersonation as well!"

"But I have not charged her with that," Flora said. She sought Esan's gaze and held it. "Tell me: according to your law, who must bring a charge of impersonation?"

"The one wronged," Esan said.

"That is me," Flora said. "But I do not bring any such charge. So you cannot inflict this woman with the charge of impersonating me, nor can you place me on the scene of the crime. It seems to me you must dismiss the charges."

She felt a hand on her arm—Rechab. Reaching out . . . to stop her? To strengthen her? She didn't break her gaze. The crowd was shouting again, and Flora heard laughter and cheers in the midst of the shouts. They were taking her side.

"I will bring another charge before you, however," Flora said, "one pertinent to this matter." She met Beniah's eyes, and he nodded. She knew the priests saw. They would let her speak.

"Go on," Esan said.

"One of my servants, Aaron by name, murdered the elders of Nachush and began a rebellion against this house and this throne. He did it without my knowledge or my approval. I will make reparations as I can from my wealth. I would deliver him to you, but he is already dead. Your fine commander has brought him to justice. I charge Aaron with rebellion."

The high priest of Kimash stepped forward, and his gaze bored into Flora like an iron spear. "This is ridiculous," he said. "You allow this woman to make a mockery of your courts."

Flora wanted to speak out again. With all her heart she wanted to put the final piece in place herself. But she could not. Rechab had to do it.

And then, against all odds, Rechab did.

Her fingers tightened around Flora's arm and then let go, and Rechab took a step closer to the judges.

"No," she said. Her eyes fixed on the priests of the Great God and especially on Jeshiel. "No, it is this man, the high priest of Kimash, who makes a mockery of your courts. I throw myself on your mercy, for you are the ancient keepers of justice for the Holy People, and I trust you to keep your charge in the presence of all these whom you represent. You asked my name. I am Rechab, Nadab's daughter of Bethabara, and I have an accusation of murder to bring against this man."

This time the reaction of the crowd was palpable. The tables had suddenly turned on the priests of Kimash, and even they knew it. The high priest took a step backward, his eyes flashing.

"Speak, daughter," Jeshiel said. "But know your words are grave."

     RACHEL STARR THOMSON

"Grave as the crime that prompts them," Rechab said. "I speak as a daughter of the Holy People, one who has lost everything. Some time ago, fearing for my life, I fled my father's house. In retaliation, as I have only recently learned, the high priest of Kimash sent assassins to my father's house and slaughtered our entire household, leaving only my father alive. In clear violation of all our laws he took the lives of men, women, and children who were guilty of no crime. My father is missing, and I fear he is also dead, for he went to seek me and has not been seen again. I own my fault in running away—but that is no capital crime. And the actions of this man are an affront and a danger to all of us."

Flora let out a breath she hadn't known she was holding. Rechab had done it. She had brought the charge. They both knew the possible consequences if they tried this. But they also knew that before the eyes of their people, they had the chance to challenge their king and their priests to reclaim their rightful authority and oust the enemy from their midst. Rechab reached over and took Flora's hand. They stood together and waited.

"This charade," the high priest sputtered, "this . . . debacle . . ."

"Peace," Jeshiel said. "These are serious charges. I think we must hear them out. Have you proof of what you say, Rechab?"

Rechab's grip tightened till Flora thought she would break her hand. "I have only what I have been told, and what is whispered in all your streets. People say the priests of the Great God and the king will not enact justice, but I know you have not been given a chance to deal with the matter. I ask you now to launch an investigation. Send messengers to Bethabara and learn the truth from those who were present. There are witnesses."

"This is outrageous!" the high priest shrieked. "How dare they bring charges against me? Against the queen?"

"I did not hear charges against the queen," Jeshiel said. The high priest's voice was like ice. "Are there any?"

"Husband!" Izevel said. "Will you rise to my defense?"

Beniah put out his hand to his wife but said nothing. For a moment the whole scene on the dais froze. The tensions and conflicted loyalties afflicting the royal house and its attachment to the temple had been dragged into the open by Rechab and Flora, and they lay exposed and raw before the eyes of the people. Callum seemed tensed and ready to spring to action—but on whose side? The high priest of Kimash had murder in his eyes, but anything he did or said now would incriminate him before a hostile crowd. And the priests of the Great God, who had for decades dropped the mantle of true judgment, were being challenged to pick it back up. There was no way to buy their way out of this position, no way to hush everything back into subdued remission. Even the crowd seemed like a tight-stretched line on the verge of snapping.

For a moment Flora wondered what she had done.

And then Beniah spoke. Fumbling his words, red-faced, sounding nearly like the drunk he'd been for weeks, he said, "This—this isn't the place. These matters need privacy. We must discuss this elsewhere. You are all dismissed."

That was when the riot broke out.

Flora could never quite put all the events of that afternoon back together in her mind. It was as though something had shattered, and its pieces went out in every direction, shards that pierced and destroyed. The crowd rising up in anger. The soldiers fighting back. The nobility panicking, trying to make it out of the court. Callum, commanding his best forces to surround the Holy Place. Flora remembered the high priest of Kimash flying at her with lethal venom in his eyes, and she remembered the stone that struck him in the head and the way he crumpled to the ground like a bird of prey brought down in midflight.

She remembered Izevel's scream.

Callum's shouts, his orders, formed a protective wall around Rechab and Flora both. They were herded up the steps, toward the royals and the priests, likewise protected by Callum's men and his valor. Everywhere was noise and blood, trampling feet and screams, men fighting one another and voices accusing.

And then Rechab's eyes widening as she pointed ahead and said, "Flora!"

Flora's eyes widened as well as she realized where the soldiers were taking them: to the nearest shelter, the nearest walls.

The Holy Place.

"NO!" she cried, and tried to break loose from their protection. "We cannot . . . we must not . . ."

But the soldiers, determined to save her life, physically hauled her through the curtain and the doors, and then all was deathly still.

The Holy Place was lit by the bright flicker of candles in a silver lampstand. A low fire burned, its embers glimmering on an altar.

"Oh, Flora," Rechab choked out, holding on to Flora's arm again. They both saw it at once.

The worst rumors had been true: an idol of Kimash had been erected inside the Holy Place. Just as Amon had said. The Holy People had welcomed the Dragon into their very heart.

But the idol lay on its face. Its hands, its feet, and its two heads—man and dragon—were broken off and lay smashed and shamed before the altar of the Great God.

CHAPTER 18

Stillness reigned in the palace of the king as the news spread. The doctors had tried their best, but word at last had come: there was nothing they could do. The stray blow had been fatal. The high priest of Kimash was dead.

The stillness broke at the sound of Izevel's screams of anger and of grief.

Flora and Rechab waited together in Flora's lavish quarters, where Rechab had slept on a servant's cot in the corner. Flora tried to talk her into better accommodations, but Rechab didn't want to be alone, and she said the cot was as good as anything she'd ever slept on anyway. They hardly spoke. They didn't need to. Both knew what they had done, and the weight of it was heavy on their hearts and their tongues.

Rechab had not been sent back to the servants' quarters to be held prisoner—Callum's act of treating them both like members of the royal house had been implicitly accepted by all, and they were free though under surveillance. Flora hoped Beniah would summon them, but he did not. She hoped Jeshiel would call for them, but he did not. The household had been plunged not so much into grief as into darkness as they all waited to see what would come of the trial.

A trial that word on the streets now described as one where the priests of two gods, the king himself, and perhaps even the Sacred Land had been put on the stands, accused, and found wanting.

The riot had left many dead and others maimed. Scarcely a household in the city was unaffected. It was the kind of event that usually turned into murmuring and upheaval—against the king, against the nobility, against the priesthood. Against someone. But in this case the subdued atmosphere of the palace hovered over the city as well. It was as though no one knew who to blame.

Flora and Rechab expressed to one another their desire to go out into the streets and listen—to hear what the people were saying. They couldn't, so they did the next best thing and listened to the servants, who carried in whispers from the streets.

So it was they heard that some of the People, at least, had gazed upon the broken statue of Kimash in the temple and asked whether they themselves might be to blame. Whether, after all, their unfaithfulness to the ancient covenants of the Great God might have led them to this point.

Flora's heart leaped when she heard that. She dared let her thoughts go, let them explore the possibilities if in fact those few whispers were part of a much larger whole: if in fact what was stirring in the stillness of the city after the riot was revival.

An awakening. A return.

She found the words to tell Rechab what was on her heart. Rechab listened, but her brow remained furrowed. She trailed her fingers absently along the edge of Flora's bed as she spoke.

"When I was a child," she said, "the only voice that ever spoke on behalf of the Great God was Kol Abaddon's. And he always said a terrible end was coming. That the Great God would crush us with his army of foreigners because of his anger at our unfaithfulness."

 RACHEL STARR THOMSON

"Essea taught the same," Flora said. "And I can believe the Great God has been angry. I believe Kol Abaddon truly spoke for him. But what if he didn't tell us everything?"

She hesitated. Her hands were clasped in her lap. Sunlight streamed in through the flimsy white curtains overlooking the garden. A bird flitted down to land on the balcony rail, hopped over a few steps, and sang its song at them before flitting away again.

"I have heard the Great God's voice in my own heart," Flora said, "and it is not angry. It . . . he . . . speaks to me as one he loves."

She blushed deeply. To say the words aloud made them sound ridiculous and horribly self-exalting. But Rechab smiled and said, "I understand. And I believe you."

"But then what? How do I understand that voice and also understand the prophecies of Kol Abaddon? What if the people of the city are starting to turn—to repent? Would the Great God who watches over you and speaks to me refuse their repentance?"

"He would have every right," Rechab said. "And yet, I was not condemned at the trial . . . and not just because you interfered. Your objections would never have stood if the priests had considered them a few more minutes. I was not condemned, though I deserved to be, and then Callum treated me like royalty, like he has always done. Protected us both and took us into the presence of the Great God. Where we *all* should have died for our trespass. But we did not. We lived. You, me, Callum, the king, the priests. Even Izevel. We all lived."

"But we saw the Dragon broken," Flora said. Rechab nodded. They understood each other—understood the hope just barely stirring in both their hearts. That judgment could mean an end to the darkness, to the Dragon, but bring grace to the People. Though they surely did not deserve it either.

A sudden panicked scurrying in the hall and in the garden told them Izevel was calling for attendants.

Days passed. Whispers grew. Other rumors began to insert themselves: of emissaries coming from the sea.

And then the Westlanders arrived.

CHAPTER 19

The Westlanders marched into Shalem with great pomp. Escorted by a hired caravan, they were a small but commanding group of military men, political emissaries, and one young man who didn't seem to be either—a boy who seemed uncomfortable in his own skin, walking at the front of the column alongside a fat politician with an evil eye, looking the whole time like he wanted to shrink back and disappear among the caravaneers. Rechab and Flora watched their approach from a frescoed window above the plaza, and Rechab wondered why he seemed familiar.

Flora touched Rechab's shoulder. "I'm going inside," she said. "I want to hear the king's response."

Rechab nodded as Flora disappeared. She remained where she was, watching the young man. He looked up in her direction, and her heart started to race. Their eyes didn't meet. He looked away.

Flora didn't have far to go. She nearly ran into the king, striding down the hall surrounded by courtiers, waving his arms and demanding in a voice that was just below a shout, "Why now? Why do all the blessings of heaven have to curse me at once? Of *course* the Westland is welcome, the Westland and all its gold. But NOW?"

Flora took a step back and curtsied, startling the king. She saw the fleeting expression that said he'd mistaken her for Izevel again, as everyone did for the first split second they saw her. She also realized that he had been drinking again.

"Flora," he said, and he paused in his stride to stop and extend his hand. She rose and took it questioningly. "Come with me," he said. "A welcoming committee should have a feminine presence, and I'm afraid my wife is indis—"

"Your wife is what?" asked a chilled voice from behind.

Everyone turned at once. Izevel stood in the hall, six shrinking attendants behind her, dressed in splendid queenly attire. Her face showed no sign of the clamorous weeping all had heard for days; her skin was smooth and ghostly white, her eyes darkened with kohl, her lips red.

"My wife is beautiful," Beniah said. He released Flora's hand and reached out for his wife.

She stepped to his side and trained her gaze on Flora. "You are dismissed," she said.

"My dear . . ." Beniah started to say, perhaps to admonish her for treating her own sister like a servant. But Izevel ignored him, he trailed away, and Flora simply curtsied and left.

Once Flora was out of sight she all but ran to rejoin Rechab. If she could have cursed Izevel in good conscience she would have. She'd have given her eye teeth to greet the company alongside the king, but at least she and Rechab could finagle their way into the throne room where any official news would surely be pronounced. Beniah spoke of

 RACHEL STARR THOMSON

their coming as a good thing. But she knew the prophecies. She knew Kol Abaddon's words. The army of the Great God, the swarm of judgment, would come from the west.

❖

Alack stood before his king in the chief throne room of the palace. The room was expansive and ornate, with the throne in the center, lifted off the ground on a dais with seven wide steps, a lion carved of marble resting on each one. Scarlet and purple decorated its surroundings, lush fabric and pillows and couches for the king's loyal followers.

Beniah looked uncomfortable on the throne, built for a long-gone ancestor whose glory had far exceeded his own. His family and courtiers surrounded him. The emissaries of the Westland were arrayed on the marble floor at the base of the steps, with Alack standing dead center before the king and Croesius and the military captain on either side of him.

The shepherd boy looked up at the unhappy king and felt like he understood him. He saw a man on the verge of losing the nation his fathers had governed, of watching everything they had been slip through his fingers. He saw a man weary, sorrowful, frayed. A man too beaten down by life to remain sober for more than a few days and too full of regret to move forward. They both felt like imposters here.

And yet Alack could see a wind moving slowly through the room, swirling around the king, breathing in and out. He had seen it before, and it didn't surprise him now. Such visions were becoming more and more a part of his life. And this one spoke of *more*—of more to these people than the eye could see; of more to their lives, more to their significance, more to their futures.

He had been trembling when the emissaries marched into place, awed by this place and the presence of the king and afraid to give his message. But the trembling grew stronger now, and he realized it wasn't only his surroundings affecting him: it was the heightened sense of the spirit world.

He followed the wind with his eyes from person to person while Croesius droned an introduction. So it was that he found them standing amidst Beniah's train: Flora Laurentii, the governor's sister . . . and Rechab.

Rechab was here. Here, and shining like Flora was shining. The wind gathered around them both and rested in a mist of light. His heart pounded.

And Croesius's voice yanked him back to the present. His tone was mocking. It took Alack a moment to recover himself enough to realize it was he being mocked, and along with him, the king and all the Sacred Land.

"One of your own," Croesius was saying, "to deliver the emperor's message. A prophet of yours, we are told. Who better to deliver the words of our emperor, a god among men? We cleaned him up and bathed him, for which you should be grateful. He will give you the emperor's words now. I give you Alack, the Prophet."

Croesius presented Alack with a grand flourish. The Westlanders exuded smugness; the king's entourage showed confusion and some consternation. This was not the tone they had hoped for, not the meeting of equals to discuss trade and benefit for all.

Alack's mouth was dry. He could feel Rechab's eyes riveted on him. He drew strength from her. He wished he could speak just to her, that he could explain things.

Croesius nudged him roughly in the back. "Speak, boy."

Alack's limbs were trembling so hard he could barely stand. He

     RACHEL STARR THOMSON

closed his eyes and breathed deep. But the words that came out of his mouth were not the words he meant to say, and certainly they were not the words of Sabrus Caelius.

"Come back to me, Isha," he said, "my Beloved, and I will heal you. Return to me and I will deliver you. Keep faith with me, though you have been faithless, and you will know my compassion and truth. This is the word of the Lord."

Flora Laurentii stifled a cry. Alack looked at her, and their eyes met—both filled with tears. Rechab was smiling, wiping away tears of her own.

"What is that?" Croesius boomed out, shoving Alack in the shoulder this time. "Enough speaking nonsense! Deliver the king's message, boy, or I will break your neck."

Alack straightened himself, blinked away his tears, and faced Beniah. "I have been sent by the emperor of the Westland, Sabrus Caelius, the Sword of Heaven," he said. After weeks of worrying over what he would say, at last he knew. He knew just what to do. The word of the Great God had come into his mouth, and it was everything he needed to understand at last.

"Sabrus is a great general, a terrible warrior. He has gathered himself an army from the nations and become their liege. He killed the king of the Westland and took his throne by force. And he sends you a message, by me, a shepherd of the Sacred Land, so that he may shame us all and so that he may try to shame the Great God. He calls for your unconditional surrender, for he is coming. If you will meet him at the ports of Kasarea with peace offerings, he will accept your surrender and march through the land without bloodshed to assert his overlordship here in Shalem. If you do not, he will destroy the land, its people, the temple, and this house, and when Shalem is overrun and its people slaughtered, every stone of the city will be pulled down and Sabrus will be lord. That is his message."

There were gasps and even sobs of terror amid Beniah's household. The king himself looked stunned. But Alack was not finished. He looked around at them all and then bowed his head.

"He sent me to give that message, and I have done it. But I am not just a messenger for the Westland. I am a prophet of the Great God. I trained under Kol Abaddon. And I have already spoken his word to you: the judgment Kol Abaddon foretold is at the door. But it is not too late for you. You have run to the Dragon, but you may yet turn, and your God will save you. Return to him, and he will return to you. Cleanse the temple of idols and the priests of corruption, and his presence will again come to this place and deliver you."

"Enough," a voice snapped. A woman stepped forward from behind the king. Somehow, Alack had not noticed her until now—as though she'd been shrouded. Her hand rested on Beniah's shoulder. She was dressed as a queen, and she looked exactly like Flora.

And yet, Alack thought, not like Flora at all.

"We have heard enough," the woman said. Her voice rose like a serpent's warning hiss before a strike. "This boy mocks you, my lord, and these foreigners insult us. The boy is a traitor: why should you listen to a word he says? The Sacred Land's greatness rests on its ties to the nations, its alliances with the gods. Should we destroy those ties at a stroke by turning the temple into a house of fanatical separation? Have we learned nothing from the recent rebellions, the murder of my uncle? You urge us on a course of destruction!"

The woman stepped forward and began to descend the steps. She pointed at Alack, and her eyes fixed on him. The king did not move or speak. It was as though he and all the others with him were in a trance.

"Cast this traitor in the pit where he belongs," the queen declared, "and send these men back to their emperor with their backs flogged and their tongues cloven. We will not meet him with peace offerings;

we will meet him with an army!"

The spell broke. Everyone in the room began to shout and surge forward—soldiers to do the queen's bidding, others to stop them. It was Beniah who put a stop to it, rising and bellowing over the cacophony, "Enough! Peace! We will do as the queen says. She speaks wisdom. We will not bow down like dogs before the Westland, nor will we cut off our allies when we need them most. Do as she says!"

<hr>

The clamor in the throne room lasted hours. Soldiers guarded the doors while others carried out the king's orders. The moment she could break away from the tumult, Flora rushed to the king's meeting chambers, where he was already conferring with his officials and contingents of priests. She forced her way through the press of people outside the doors and entered before anyone could stop her. Bodyguards grabbed her immediately, but not before Beniah had looked up from a close conference and heaved a heavy sigh at her interruption. He waved a hand. "Let her go."

The bodyguards did. Flora arranged her rumpled clothes and stepped forward, ignoring the pain in her shoulder that had flared at their rough handling. She went to her knees beside the king. "Please, my lord," she said, "the boy. Tell me you did not cast him into the pit."

Beniah's jaw jutted out. "I did as Izevel said. She sets the course for us now."

"Izevel will drown us in blood," Flora said. She bit her words off and forced herself to be calm. "Please, tell me where the boy is. Let me get him out. He is not a traitor. He is a loyal servant of yours and does not deserve to die this way."

Beniah's face softened almost imperceptibly. "He will not die. I will order food lowered down to him. But he stays in the pit. I cannot afford to be lenient toward those who would take sides against me. He came here as a messenger against his own people."

"It is a wise saying," Flora said, "that sometimes a faithful messenger is the one who brings bad news."

He shook his head and turned his eyes back to his officials. "I have spoken, Flora. Go and do not return here unless I summon you. There are many who question your loyalty. I do not want my hand forced against you."

Nodding, Flora rose slowly. Waves of anger and helplessness washed through her. Only days ago she had hoped for change in this house, that the Great God would return to honor before the king and his priests and their hearts would stand for justice once more. How had Izevel managed such a complete takeover in such a short time?

Worry for Alack dogged her as she departed, shrugging off the bodyguards who tried to escort her out. She did not meet the eyes of any who waited outside the chambers, instead following her feet on a straight line toward the kitchens. The entire palace still buzzed with energy and conflict. Statesmen and courtiers argued in every corner. She ignored them all.

She burst into the kitchens unannounced, startling the servants. "It's Flora," she said, "not Izevel. I need food . . . bread, figs, hard cheese, and a flagon of wine. Quickly."

Two of the servants nodded and scurried off to find what she'd called for. The kitchen steward hesitated, clearly wanting to know what this was about.

"It's for the boy, Alack," Flora said. "Don't fear; the king ordered it. Sooner or later I'm sure he'll send you word. I don't want to wait for him to do so." She met the steward's eyes and smiled. "Thank you."

To her surprise, the steward smiled back. "For you, Lady Laurentii, I would dare the king's displeasure. You are the one light in all of this awful business."

"And you?" Flora asked. "What do the servants think of all this?"

The steward laughed outright, though the laugh was tinged with bitterness and sorrow. "You are the only one of the nobility who asks what servants think. Oh, we know you listen to us—that you eavesdrop, more like. We don't mind you knowing. But we cannot say, lady. Not this time."

Flora nodded. She understood. With Izevel so completely in control, no one dared express an opinion contrary to her lest a stray bird carry it to the queen's ears. The servants returned and handed her a cloth bag filled with food, along with a skin of wine. The bag was heavy. Good. She turned to go.

"Lady Laurentii?" one of the servants called out. She turned. "Yes?"

"Be careful."

She nodded.

CHAPTER 20

Alack stirred from the lethargy of unconsciousness. He did not want to awake. The stink, the slime, the darkness . . . all of it encroached on his senses, promising a nightmare when he came to. He wanted to sink back into sleep and remain there forever.

But he couldn't. He awoke.

He sat in mire, a mix of mud and waste that reeked and chilled him. The air was stagnant and cold. He did not have enough room to stretch out his limbs: the pit, a mostly dried-up well, was narrow and round. He fought down panic at the sense of being buried alive. There was no light trickling down from above; they had replaced the cover over the pit after lowering him in. He wasn't sure when or why he had lost consciousness—if he'd hit his head or simply been over-whelmed by fear.

At least he had escaped flogging. No one seemed eager to carry out more punishment than Izevel ordered.

Drawing his knees up to his chest, Alack wondered how long it would take him to starve to death down here. He could feel objects in the mud beneath him and wondered if they were the bones of some other prophet, banished here and forgotten.

Deliberately, he shoved away the morbid thought and the fear that spiked up with it. He would not survive here by giving way to fear.

And he wanted to survive. Rechab's face was etched in his mind—new, fresh, no longer just an image of the life he'd left behind. She'd been there in the court of the king, she'd been shining with courage and the light of the Great God, and he loved her more than he ever had. More than anything in the world he wanted to sit with her, his best friend from childhood, the girl he wanted to love as a man loves a woman. He wanted to hear everything that had happened to her in the intervening months since he'd seen her last. He wanted to tell her everything that had happened to him. He wanted to touch her face and kiss her lips.

He wanted to live.

A shout welled up from within him, and he let it out—a roar in the deep darkness of the pit, a cry against the evil that cloaked the Holy City and had sent him here. Let the spirits that dwelt in this murk hear his voice. Let them know his desire to rise again. Alack wanted to come back from the dead. Oh God, his thoughts rushed out after the sound died away, leaving his throat raw. *Oh God, oh God, I don't want to die here. Don't let this be the end. Don't let this be the final act. I am just a boy. I want to live.*

Every ounce of stoic resignation he'd managed to drum up over the voyage here, and in the desert days with Kol Abaddon before even going west, left him. He was a prophet of the Great God, yes. Prophets of the Great God were usually persecuted and sometimes killed. They roamed wildernesses and had visions. But Alack wanted to be a prophet who lived and got married and actually saved somebody for once.

Unexpectedly, a memory came to him. Kol Abaddon's reaction after his vision in the wadi. He'd told Alack that his way of entering into a vision, truly experiencing it, might mean he had a role to play in the way the events he saw unfolded—that perhaps he was not merely a seer but a savior. And he remembered the call he'd heard so clearly in the window in Kasarea: *Save my Beloved.*

Not much chance of that while he was trapped down here.

A sound from above startled him, and as he jumped to his feet—hit with a wave of dizziness as he did—a beam of light streamed down, widening as the cover was pulled away from the well.

And then a familiar voice called down. "Alack!"

"Flora?" he called back. After his roar his voice sounded raspy and weak.

"Oh, thank the Great God," she answered back. He squinted up at the light, trying to make out her features, but she was too far away. The bottom of the pit was a fifty-foot drop. She darted away, letting in more light, but a moment later something blocked it again.

Not something, Alack realized; someone. Someone else was being lowered into the pit.

He recognized Rechab when she was halfway down. His heart jumped into his throat and choked him even as alarm overwhelmed him. "It's not . . . you shouldn't . . ." The mire around his ankles sucked at him; the stink was overwhelming. What did she think she was doing?

"Hush," Rechab said. "Here—catch."

There was enough light to see the bag she threw at him. He caught it and clutched it to his chest. Even through the stench of the pit, he could make out the smell of bread. Of life. His heart pounded as Rechab continued her descent.

Her feet touched the bottom, and she let go of the rope and yelled up, "I'm down!" A moment later she had flung herself on Alack and wrapped her arms tightly around him. His chin rested on the top of her head. He kept clutching the bag of food to his chest like a fool. He wanted to take her in his arms, but there was nowhere to put the bag down.

She said into him, "I am so glad to see you. I'm so glad you're alive. I've missed you so much."

"I . . . I've missed you too."

She looked up at him, and in the muddy light he made out her smile. It was an older smile than he remembered. Wiser. Still Rechab, but a Rechab transformed. "So much has happened," she said. "And look at you . . . shaved clean as an egg. I didn't even recognize you until you spoke. You seemed so familiar, but I couldn't put you together with my shepherd boy."

Alack blushed and hugged the bread bag tighter. "It's the Westlanders. They all shave their beards like this."

"It will grow back," Rechab said.

He swallowed hard, and then before she could say another word he kissed her. She didn't pull away. She clutched his arms and rose into the kiss.

"I'm sorry," he said.

"Don't be."

"That wasn't appropriate."

"Then don't do it again until our wedding day," Rechab said.

"Our wedding . . ."

"My father is gone. There is no one to deny you permission."

Her eyes were filled with tears. His mind raced but couldn't seem to land anywhere, couldn't make sense of what she was saying. "I'm sorry for your loss."

She shook her head and laughed. "Oh, Alack. So much has changed. And I'm . . . I'm just happy to have you back."

"Does this count?" he asked, nodding to the darkness around them. There was barely enough room in the pit for them both to stand. "This

 RACHEL STARR THOMSON

place is having me back?"

"We'll get you out, Flora and I, or we'll die trying," Rechab said. "I promise you."

Alarm rose in him. "I don't want you to die trying." The energy went out of him in a sudden rush, and he leaned back against the stone wall of the pit and nearly dropped the bag. "Rechab, if Sabrus comes here we are all going to die. He is the one Kol Abaddon prophesied. I saw him in visions before I ever saw him in life. Beniah will never stand against him, not even if the Hill People and the Southern Plains together were to come to his aid."

Rechab reached up and touched his cheek. The gesture was at once womanly and childlike: she was the best friend of his past and the bride he desperately wanted for his future. Standing here before him, in this darkest place, she was his future.

"You did all you could," she said. "You gave the Great God's message faithfully. And the message, Alack! You called the People to *hope*. You called for them to return. The Great God spoke through you his willingness to save us. Maybe he will. Maybe they will return."

She pulled him close again, and he kept hugging the food bag like the witless oaf he was. "I'm so glad you're alive," she whispered. "I never thought you would come back to me. I . . . oh, Alack, I've been a thousand times a fool. I have so much to ask your forgiveness for."

"No," he said into her hair, "no, there can't be anything that needs to be said here. It's enough for me that you're alive too. And that . . . that you're here."

He choked up. She sighed deeply, relaxing against him. They stood together for a long time, not speaking, and then slowly questions came, and stories. He told her about Kol Abaddon, the journey over the sea, the emperor. She told him about Nachush and asked his forgiveness for Aaron.

"How can I fault you for that?" he asked. "You thought I was never coming back. You weren't unfaithful. There were no promises to be broken."

"But I loved him," Rechab said. "Not the same way I love you. But I did."

Alack nodded, trying to be understanding. He felt glad Aaron was dead and immediately chastised himself for the thought. He would deal with his feelings about this later.

Finally Rechab told him about Izevel and the trial in the temple. She told him about the riot and the broken idol. "Ever since, the city has been different. It has felt like when a storm gathers but does not break. As though everything is in waiting. And then you came. Flora says you are the one we were waiting for."

Alack shook his head. "I wish Kol Abaddon were here. I am lost in all this, Rechab."

"But you're not! You spoke to the king the very words of the Great God. You are a prophet, Alack—a true prophet."

He smiled down at her. Her words heartened him. There was truth to what she said. He wasn't just the gawky, uncomfortable boy who had followed Kol Abaddon across the desert sands. Somehow he'd done it. He'd stepped into his mentor's shoes and filled them.

"I don't know if it will do any good," he said. "They threw me down here."

"Izevel threw you down here. The People may not tolerate her much longer."

"I think I have another prophecy," he said, glancing up to where Flora's shadow paced. The light that had beamed down to the bottom of the pit now hit the walls high above. It was getting late. "If you stay down here any longer you'll fall sick and die, and then I'll go too, of a broken heart."

He reached up and tugged the rope to let Flora know it was time to pull Rechab back up.

She stepped away from him and shivered. "I can't leave you down here, Alack. This place—"

"Well, you certainly can't stay here with me, and it's not worth risking yours and Flora's necks to get me out of here."

"She tried," Rechab said. "Flora did. She went to the king to plead for your release, but . . ."

"But the queen isn't in the mood. It's all right. Kol Abaddon has been delivered out of tighter places than this. Perhaps the Great God will work a miracle and pull me out himself."

He managed an encouraging smile, even though his heart had begun to sink before Rechab even started her ascent, half-walking up the walls as Flora pulled in the rope. Darkness seemed to swallow him as she rose further and further away, until at last she disappeared, the cover on the well was replaced, and Alack was alone.

But he heard a voice say, *I am here. In the darkness. In this Suffering Place, I am here.*

The voice brought a measure of comfort. The murky, watery muck around his ankles was cold, and Alack shivered violently. Suddenly faint, he pulled open the bag and reached inside. His hand closed around a loaf of bread, and he pulled it out and ate slowly. He could feel it giving life back to him, but here in this place it tasted like sawdust. He wondered if Rechab would come back again or if he had just seen her for the last time. If their conversation had been the only future still left to him.

And then he noticed the warmth.

Around his ankles, the mud had grown warm—and then hot.

It seemed to melt away, sloughing off, and he pulled up one foot after the other to keep from burning—but there was nowhere to put them back down. Pinpricks of light broke through the mud, shining straight up at him with the accompanying smell of smoke. Fire? How could—

Before he could finish thinking the question, the bottom of the well disappeared, and Alack was falling through a vast, dark, fiery cavern.

Straight toward the open maw of an enormous dragon.

◆

Izevel had barely sent the emissaries back to the coast, disfigured and beaten as threatened and breathing curses against her all the way—at which she laughed—before the first of the uprisings took place. It happened when Beniah went to the temple to sacrifice as he had always done. He'd made the decision to go very suddenly, ignoring Izevel's derisive comments, mumbling something about tradition and the king needing to put on a confident face. Not that his face was anything to inspire confidence. Beniah was ashen. He trembled like an old man.

His bodyguards surrounded him as he entered the temple court through the Dawn Gate without the accompaniment of a single Kimashian priest. He noted vacantly that some of the altars and shrines were gone, and that there were fewer devotees here of any kind. But his observations were interrupted by a man who flew toward him with drawn sword and cried out, "For all of us, the king must die!"

The guards took the man down in an instant, and Beniah just

stared in shock as his attacker bled on the sand of the outer court. His guards closed in around him. "Your majesty, we must get you out of here," one of them said.

Beniah looked around slowly, like a man in a daze. He saw shocked stares, blinking eyes, but no threat.

"Is there some further threat?" he asked.

"There might be any number of—"

"I came here to sacrifice," Beniah said. He waved his bodyguards back a little and staggered toward the great altar near the doors to the inner court.

The high priest, Jeshiel, met him there. "Your majesty," he said, "I'm so sorry . . ."

"No, no," Beniah said. He could hardly do more than whisper the words. He reached out and took the priest by the arms, shaking him a little with the earnestness of his words. "It is I who am sorry. I alone. I want to sacrifice. I have brought a ram . . ."

The sacrifice did not happen. The guards had been right: the initial attacker was not alone. A band of men rushed at them all together. After a brief fight, the attackers were dead or subdued and Beniah had been ushered out of the temple and back to the palace.

He and his guards were met by a harried Callum. The commander strode past them and straight up to Beniah, ignoring the guards who were trying to appraise him of the situation. "Sir, the city is exploding. There are uprisings on every side. They are calling for the Westland emissaries to be brought back and Izevel to be deposed as queen. You must act."

"I . . ." Beniah fought to find words, but he could not make sense of what Callum was saying, could not make sense of the man flying at him in the temple, could not make sense of anything. He'd been in his wine earlier in the day, trying to shut away the thought of the Westlanders and the sound of his wife's glee in ordering the young prophet thrown into a pit. The only thing he knew clearly now was that he wanted to sacrifice to the Great God, and his guards had pulled him away.

"Sir," Callum repeated, almost threatening in his manner and tone, "you must answer your people. You must assure them that you hear them and will act on their behalf, or I tell you, you will not retain your throne another night."

Beniah heard himself answering as though from far away. "Put the rioters down, Commander," he said. "That is your job. Make it all end."

Callum's expression hardened. "My lord, you are drunk."

Beniah patted the commander's thick-bearded cheek. "I suppose I am. Do you know, I killed Kol Abaddon's family? It was me. Or might as well have been. The responsibility is all mine. If judgment will come, let it come. It was due here long ago."

Leaving his dumbstruck commander behind, Beniah turned and wandered toward the palace. He wanted his rooms. He wanted his wine. He did not want his wife . . . he would divorce her, he decided. Later.

Callum turned to his men, who waited behind him with grief-stricken faces. "Do whatever you can to make peace," he said.

"But sir—"

"I know." Callum looked after the king and shook his head. "I know. But try. Use force if you must. Or tell them the king is reconsidering. Tell them a new plan is underway. Get them all onto one side, do you hear me? As long as we're dealing with a thousand factions, we'll spend all night doing nothing but swatting flies. Get them together into one."

 RACHEL STARR THOMSON

"Sir . . ." His captain stared at him, stricken. "Sir, what you're saying . . ."

"I will not betray Beniah," Callum snapped. "But I make no promises about his wife. And right now, deposing our king might be the best thing for him too." He clapped a hand on his captain's shoulder. "I don't know what I'm doing," he said. "Only that whatever it is, I will do all I can to protect this people, this house, and this king."

"He doesn't deserve it," the captain muttered. "We would follow you."

"That is treason, Captain," Callum said. He trained his eyes on his subordinate until the captain dropped his eyes. "But I did not hear it. Serve me. We all need you now."

CHAPTER 21

Alack fell through a thousand years with the mouth of the Dragon open beneath him, but he never reached the terrible teeth, the hungry tongue. Instead he found himself at long last standing on the cavern floor with a sword in his hand and the Dragon's sinewy neck stretched out above him. Its face was Kimash's face. Its body was the sea serpent's body. Its eyes were Amon-Heth's cold, merciless stare.

Behind the Dragon and all around them were the burning spires of a city. Smoke rose and billowed until it turned everything above the city black. There was no sky, no stars, no heaven. This, Alack knew, was the past. But it was also the future that could be. The future that would be if Isha did not turn from the Dragon, if she ran into the jaws of her enemy.

"I see now," Alack said with his sword held high. "You are the cause of destruction. You are the poison that can only be cleansed by judgment. You are the liar, the thief, and the destroyer the People should hate and despise." He looked around him, around them, at the burning city. How many worlds had this creature destroyed? How many dreams had it dragged down into darkness forever, all while men and women worshiped it and sought its favor?

The Holy People had turned their backs on their ancient covenant with the Great God in order to curry the favor of this monster.

The Dragon opened its mouth, and Alack tensed to be consumed by a stream of fire from its jaws. But there was none. Instead the Dragon laughed . . . a low, cruel chuckle. A man's voice came from within its dark bulk. "I have not hidden my face from them," the Dragon said. "Man loves his enemy and chooses to be devoured. I only oblige."

Alack tightened his grip on the sword hilt. "I do not choose you," he said.

The Dragon laughed again. "You would like to stop me," it said. "But you are not enough. They have thrown you down to me that I may swallow you whole."

For a moment Alack feared it was true. The loneliness and despair of the pit washed over him again.

But then he recalled the last thing he'd heard before he descended into this fiery place. The voice of the Great God, telling him, *I am here. In the darkness.*

And Alack understood. Yes, his enemies had thrown him to the Dragon.

But he had brought the Great God with him.

It had never been about him. He was not the savior. He was not even really a prophet. It did not matter that he couldn't stand before the Dragon or defeat it. The Great God could. The Great God would. *And the Great God was with him.*

Now the Dragon opened its mouth and loosed its flame.

Alack held his sword and leaned into the blast. He felt himself picked up by a wind, thrown forward, propelled straight at the heart of the creature even as the fire burned the skin from his bones.

Beniah wandered down the hall in a haze of his own making. He heard servants running after him—more of those pesky bodyguards. Where were his stewards? His cupbearers? His harpists? Someone who could take his mind off of . . . whatever was plaguing him?

He found his private chambers and sank onto his couch. Someone was there, some servant moving around in the shadows. In his peripheral vision he could see the lad was holding a wineskin. Good.

"Come," he said, "pour me a drink, for I am a man of great sorrow, and I want to drown it."

As the servant moved to obey, Beniah put his face in his hands and sobbed. Was it remorse? Was it just the wine? He didn't know and couldn't say.

He reached up and grabbed the lad's sleeve before the servant could get away. "I'm sorry," he said. "I'm so, so sorry. I was such a fool. Such a lustful, drunken fool. We've all been fools, all of us."

"I have not," the servant said.

His words took Beniah aback. Even more so his tone. It was cold, hard, unfeeling.

He remembered the lad's name just a moment before the boy pulled a knife from beneath his tunic and stabbed the king in the side.

Shem.

The lad's name was Shem.

A servant girl found the king and alerted the palace with her screams. His guards, who should have been there, had lingered to hear Callum out. No one knew what had happened, who had done it. It threw the palace into chaos.

Flora pushed her way through the crowds of servants and courtiers around the king's chambers. Sobs, shrieks, and nonstop clamor filled her ears. They were all in her way—blocking her access to the king.

Casting aside her veil, she threw as much ice into her voice as she could and demanded, "Let me through!"

It worked. She heard Izevel's name amid the gasps as the crowds parted and the way was cleared. She rushed through the door before anyone could recognize the deception.

Beniah lay on his bed, covered with a sheet, tossing and moaning in pain. A small crowd of physicians leaned over him, but Flora could see at a glance there was nothing for them to do but wait. They had already tended and tried to dress the wound. Stains in the sheet showed the bleeding was already soaking through. Several feet away, the king's couch was soaked with blood, and blood marked the marble floor where he had fallen and tried to crawl and call for help. Six servants lurked around the edges of the room, wringing their hands and looking ready to spring into action should they be called upon. In the far corner, Beniah's youngest wife wept softly. Izevel was nowhere to be seen.

Flora rushed to the king's side and dropped to her knees beside his bed. She reached out and took his hand, surprised at the strength with which his fingers closed around hers.

An unexpected light came into his eyes as he looked at her and studied her face. "Izevel?" he croaked.

She shook her head, too sorrowful to speak.

He sighed and closed his eyes. "Flora."

"It is."

He tightened his fingers even more. "I'm . . . glad." His whole body tensed as a wave of pain went through him, and he groaned with its intensity. Flora held his hand tight and let her tears fall on his bed.

"My sister," he rasped when the wave had gone and he relaxed into the bed again. "My . . . friend and confessor. Pray. For me. For all of us."

She tried to smile, tried to shake her head, tried to say something. But no words would come. It wasn't right that he should die like this, without a chance to make things right—as he would have done. She was sure of it.

The king, her friend, would have done right in the end.

He coughed, and the cough turned into a spasm that had him choking and spitting up blood. With tears in her eyes she kept hold of his hand by just the fingertips as the physicians crowded in closer and forced her back. They did not make her let go.

When the fit subsided and they made room for her to draw close again, Beniah had gone completely white, and she knew he was dying. He looked like a man ten times his age. It was as though death had peeled back the layers over his soul and now showed in stark relief the effect of years of weariness and regret.

The king rasped, "When you see Kol Abaddon, tell him again that I am sorry. Make the high priest offer my ram. For atonement. The Great God must hear it from me here, though this room is no altar: I am sorry. I was not the king I should have been."

Flora nodded. Part of her wanted to stop him. But the better part knew the words he was saying needed to be said.

He flexed his fingers, indicating that he wanted her to let go. When she did, he raised his hand and set it on top of her head.

Then, to her utter surprise, he found the strength to raise his voice so loudly it could be heard in the far corners of the room. "My throne must not go to Izevel, nor to my sons," he announced. "They are too . . . too young and too unwise. In all your hearing I give my throne to Flora Laurentii the Unlucky, to keep for them as queen regent."

She gaped like a fish, searching for something to say. He locked his too-bright eyes on hers. "Swear to me you will keep my throne safe for my sons."

"I . . ." She looked around the room frantically. Every eye was on her. But no one moved. No one stepped forward to say this was a mistake. No one shouted out that the king could not do this.

Because of course he could. It was his right. And everyone could hear he was of sound mind.

"I swear it," she said, matching her volume to his.

At those words his entire body relaxed and sank into the bed. He removed his hand from her head and let it sink back to himself. He smiled. Then, "Leave me alone to die, all of you."

One by one the servants turned and filed toward the door. After them, more hesitantly, the physicians. "There is nothing more we can do," one said aloud, explaining to himself, to everyone.

But Flora didn't move. He had called her sister and friend.

She was by his side when he died.

<hr>

Amon the Southern Trader brooded as he awaited his audience with the queen. He was one of many—dozens if not a hundred packed into the anterooms of the palace. Izevel had locked herself inside the throne room when news came that Beniah had been stabbed.

Now the news sang its way through the palace like a dirge: Beniah was dead. The king had been murdered in his bedroom. Some said it was the Westlanders' revenge. Others that a plot had been hatched in the household.

Amon knew the truth.

He stood with his fingertips touching, still as a statue and equally implacable. Others kept their distance from him, as though something emanated from him that repelled their presence.

The knowledge was a gift, shown to him in a vision so that he might be reinstated in favor with Izevel. She had spurned him after he delivered Flora to her. She would not spurn him now.

Had Amon been the sort of man to smile, he would have smiled to himself now. If only the king had known just how far back Izevel and Amon went, and the nature of their relationship, he would likely have flayed Amon alive when he dared to show up here. But now Beniah was dead, and Izevel was queen, and there was nothing standing between them. Destiny was within his grasp.

Amon gestured to a nervous herald who waited like a guard outside the throne room door.

"I wish you would tell her again," he said. "Amon the Southern Trader is waiting with news she will be most interested to hear." He lowered his voice. "Tell her I can reveal the killer to her and give her favor with the people when she brings justice swiftly upon him."

The herald's eyes widened, and he nodded. Pale-faced, he ducked back through the door from which Izevel had sent him scurrying several times already.

She'd had time now to vent her fury and do whatever it was she did to find solid ground again. This time she would listen.

Amon was not disappointed. The herald reappeared, causing all of those waiting to stand on tiptoe in anticipation.

"Amon the Trader," the herald said, clearing his throat. "The queen will see you."

Satisfied at the grumbling that arose from the others at the announcement, Amon inclined his head in acknowledgment and followed the herald into the throne room.

Izevel sat like a storm cloud atop Beniah's throne, leaning over one arm with a harried, nail-bitten expression. The obvious turmoil of her soul did not make her any less beautiful, but it did assure Amon that for once, she would be easy to manage. The upheaval of the last few days was more than even Izevel could have prepared for.

"Speak," she barked out as he approached the throne. "Tell me what you know."

"That is not much of a greeting," he said. "The king is dead, Izevel, and your uncle too. Will you go on pretending you don't know me?"

Her eyes flashed at him. "Don't play games with me, Amon. You are nothing to me."

"Severe words."

"Tell me what you know."

"Very well. I have had a vision. Amon-Heth himself has shown me the murder and the murderer."

"Amon-Heth," she spat. "I don't care for your dog-headed god."

His fingers closed reflexively around the hilt of his ornate dagger. No one had taken it from him in the anteroom. It seemed the guards were too busy dealing with turmoil in the city to worry about protecting the rest of the royals. But he relaxed his fingers quickly and removed his hand. Izevel was not his enemy.

"Amon-Heth and Kimash are one," Amon said. "That is what the boy did not understand. That is why he despised all of you."

"What boy?"

"The one who killed Beniah."

Izevel sat up straighter, clearly interested. "Don't dance around your meaning, Amon. Tell me what you saw."

"Beniah was killed by a servant in this household, one who came here from elsewhere. His name is Shem. He serves Amon-Heth with radical devotion and does not understand that his god and your god are the same. There are only two gods, Izevel: the Great God of the People and the Adversary, the one also called the Dragon, Leviathan in the sea."

"Shem," Izevel repeated. "Can you point him out?"

"I know where he is," Amon said. "He is cowering in fear in the cellars beneath the palace even now. The spirits left him when the deed was done, and with them his courage." Amon laughed. "Poor, stupid boy."

She stood. "I will send the guards for him now. You, Amon—you have been useful to me." She strode down the steps and paused to regard him curiously. "I did not reward you properly when you brought my sister here. I honored the wishes of my uncle, but you and I would have done the same with her."

"So I believed."

"What do you want now? In return for all this?"

"For delivering your enemy to you, for revealing your husband's killer and giving you a way to be raised up in the eyes of a people who are even now revolting against you? Make me a part of your court."

"It is done," Izevel said.

"Make me a close confidant again," he said.

She met the dare in his eyes with a flirtatious smile and responded, "Perhaps. Eventually."

They were interrupted by the breathless arrival of the herald. Izevel snapped her eyes onto the man. "What?"

"Please, your majesty," the herald said. "Rumors . . ."

"Tell me."

The herald composed himself. "They are saying the king removed you from the throne before he died. They are saying he made Flora Laurentii queen regent."

Amon dared hold out his hand to stop Izevel from flying at the man. He, three times the man the king had ever been, knew how to handle this woman.

"Do not fear, my queen," he said. "We will stop the usurper."

"How?" Izevel asked. "They will side with Flora. Callum, the priests. They have never accepted me."

"They will not dare endanger the king's children," Amon said.

"What danger are they in?" Izevel asked, impatient.

"Much in every way," Amon said with a smile, "for you have taken them hostage."

Izevel's face lit, but still she looked questioningly at him. "And how will I do this, with the whole palace against me?"

"I have a guard of my own," Amon said.

She nodded. "Send them."

He strode to the doors to give the orders, but when they flung them open, a stone-faced wall of palace guards blocked their way. Next to them, her face shining triumphantly, was the girl Rechab.

 Rachel Starr Thomson

"On the authority of the queen regent," she said, "arrest them."

———◆———

Callum, rushing through the palace on his way to seek audience with the queen, heard her voice echoing—shrieking—down the halls. Shrieking his name.

He motioned for his soldiers to follow him and broke into a dead run. Around them the cry was going out all over the palace and spilling into the city: "The king is dead! The king is dead!" And now it seemed someone threatened the queen already.

He skidded around a corner to a scene of utter confusion just outside the throne room: Izevel and Amon the Trader were being manhandled by palace guards. Courtiers were shouting, some trying to interfere. Rechab stood surrounded by guards—but they were protecting her, deferring to her, not arresting her.

Izevel's eyes lit on Callum. "Commander! Command your men to arrest these usurpers!"

"Don't do it!" Rechab cried out. "Callum, the king has made Flora queen regent! Izevel has been deposed!"

Callum simply barked out, "Stop! All of you! Release the queen and stand back!"

The guards obeyed. Quiet fell over the anteroom as Callum strode into the center of the action. Izevel swept the crowd with her eyes, searching their faces, then sneered.

"How dare you turn on me?" she spat.

"Izevel . . ." Callum said warningly. For this moment he still owed this woman his loyalty—unless Rechab's claim could be substantiated.

But she seemed to take it for granted that he would not turn on her.

"Silence," Izevel snapped. She turned on her heel to go back into the throne room, motioning for him to follow. But he quickly signaled for his soldiers to block the way. Queen or not, he would not allow her to escape this moment.

"My queen, all of these people have business with you. You cannot turn your back on them. They are desperate for leadership. Treat them as nothing now and your ill-gotten throne will come down in a bloodbath."

"If blood is needed, let there be blood," Izevel said. "We will bathe the temple in it and cleanse this city of its treachery against me. This is how I will bring order back, Commander: the troublemakers will be sacrificed in a ceremony to dedicate the temple to Kimash, and you will see what real power can do."

"The troublemakers?" Callum asked, barely able to force the word out for its irony.

"Flora." She gestured at Rechab. "This girl who pretends to be something when she is nothing. The boy in the pit. Let messengers go forth to the people to remind them that all this trouble started when they dared question Kimash. Now the god has had his revenge. We must placate him and call his power back to our side."

Callum trembled with anger. Izevel meant every word. Amon, the smooth-headed trader from the Southern Plains, stood warily with his arms folded, an ornate dagger at his waist. Curse these usurpers and their gods!

"You would destroy these people," Callum said.

"Nonsense. I will rule them. Enough from you. Do as I say, or I will remove you from your position and put Amon in your place. Arrest this girl at once. Send your soldiers to bring me the other troublemakers and inform the people of what is to take place. I must prepare for the sacrifice. We will consecrate the temple at sundown tomorrow."

 RACHEL STARR THOMSON

"Madness," Callum said quietly.

Her eyes flashed. "Are you refusing to obey me?"

Deliberately, Callum turned to face Rechab. He bowed to her—a sign of honor that came not from the demands of decorum but from his heart. "Tell me," he said. "What were you saying before I interrupted?"

Izevel began to say something, but Callum held up his hand, and she went silent.

"Izevel has been deposed," Rechab said. "The king appointed Flora queen regent before he died. There were more than ten witnesses. The priests of the Great God have already accepted her ascension."

Callum fought to keep off the smile that wanted badly to rest on his face. He turned back to Izevel and Amon. The palace guards were already closing back in around them, not prevented by his soldiers. Everyone waited for him to speak.

"In that case," Callum said, "it is clear where my loyalties lie. You may continue your arrest."

But before the guards could carry out his order, more screams and shouts issued from outside the anteroom, and a breathless herald arrived, stopping short at the scene playing out before him.

"Now what?" Izevel snapped.

Clearly confused, the herald looked from Izevel to Callum and back again. "Your majesty," he finally said, the title uncertain on his tongue, "word has come from the watchmen on the walls. An army approaches. They are coming up the mountain even now."

Callum wasted no time. Without a word, he nodded to the guards to continue their arrest and then turned to run for his horse and a vantage point from which to see the approaching threat.

When he reached the gate at the top of the ascent to Shalem, it took his eyes minutes to adjust to what he was seeing. Men swarming the road, covering it like locusts. There were hundreds, lining the road for miles back. But not soldiers. There were women and children among them. He could see few swords, few spears. Instead these people carried bushels of produce, bags of incense, and the lead ropes of sheep, goats, and cattle for sacrifice. Many covered their heads and sang as they came. Before them, carrying a staff and walking with a strong stride, was a tall, white-haired man dressed all in white. These were not warriors. They were pilgrims.

Callum dismounted, left his sword sheathed, and strode into the road beyond the gates to meet the pilgrims. From behind the tall leader in white, a well-dressed man with a clean-shaven face and Westland features stepped forward to meet him.

"Commander Callum," he said.

"Have we met?" Callum asked.

"We've not had the pleasure. I know you by reputation. I am Aurelius, governor of Bethabara."

"And these?" Callum asked. "We were told an army approached. But I see pilgrims, not warriors."

"You see truly. We are not soldiers, and we have not come to shed blood. We are here for the Gathering of the Great God." Aurelius scanned Callum's face. "Is there trouble?"

"More than you can imagine," Callum said. "But I would say the sun is beginning to shine again." He clapped Aurelius on the shoulder. "My friend, you could not have come at a better time. If ever the Holy People needed to return to their god, it is now."

Callum turned toward the city and roared, "Open the gates! Let the people of the Great God in!"

As the watchmen on the walls obeyed and the gates of the city began to open to the pilgrims, a royal procession on the other side

 Rachel Starr Thomson

rode through. Callum nearly laughed with joy at the sight. How the decisions of a few minutes could change things!

Flora rode on horseback at the head of the procession with Rechab to her left and the king's oldest son, a sixteen-year-old boy, to her right. Two of the king's other wives were also riding with them. They seemed crowned with joy.

From its seat of power, the Holy City had sent out women and children to greet them.

And Callum could not have been happier about it.

CHAPTER 22

It was the sound of singing that first reached Rechab's ears as her horse cantered down the city streets at Flora's side, headed for the gates. An old, old hymn of praise to the Great God, wending its way up the road. Her heart wanted to burst at the sound. It told her that what some of the watchmen had already sent back was true: it was not an army at the gates. It was a throng of worshipers.

The gates were already opening when they reached them, and with a glance back at Jeshiel and the other priests who rode right behind them, Flora nodded and led the way through.

It was Callum who greeted them first. Rechab's heart warmed at the sight of him: the gruff warrior on whose mercy she had thrown herself and who had proven so unexpectedly to be a friend. A moment later she realized who else was here, and her heart reeled with a mix of emotions so strong she didn't know how to process them. Aurelius and his wife. The Teacher from Essea. Women and children whose faces she recognized from Nachush, clustered around Micah, who was alive. He must have gone with the refugees. She wondered if Aaron had sent him with them. Certainly Callum had turned a blind eye to his going. She was grateful for them both.

And . . .

Her father.

Rechab's eyes filled with tears as she dismounted and stumbled toward Nadab. A single glance told her he was not the same man. He was thinner, and his face was haggard and scarred from pain and the process of healing. He looked ten years older. And yet there was something in his eyes she had never seen before. Something childlike.

Nadab's own eyes were awash. With every hurried, uncertain step she took, Rechab tried to find the words she would say when she reached him. But when she did, he folded her in his arms so she could not speak and said, over and over again, "My daughter. My child. My daughter." His voice was weak and wavering like an old man's when he began to say it, but with every repetition new strength seemed to come into his voice until at last he shouted it—"My child!"—with all the strength of a man young and strong, and then he broke down and wept on Rechab's shoulder.

Behind them, Flora had dismounted and held out her hand to her brother.

Aurelius took it and bowed. "My sister," he said. "Can you explain to me what I'm seeing?"

Flora bit her lip. "Beniah is dead and made me queen regent before he breathed his last. Frankly, I think you are seeing some kind of dream."

With a loud laugh, Aurelius embraced his sister. "I have never been so glad to see you."

"And I have never been so startled to see you," Flora said, wiping tears from her eyes as she pulled away. "Leading pilgrims, Aurelius? To the Great God?"

"To the Gathering," he said. "It was time they came home. Perhaps it was time we all did."

 RACHEL STARR THOMSON

The Teacher waited silently for them to finish their greetings. Flora turned to him and opened her mouth to stammer something, but before she could, he bowed low at the waist. "Flora Laurentii," he said. "I am a man deeply humbled and broken. I can only beg your forgiveness."

"No," Flora said, shaking her head. "No . . . Essea has been lost, and I fear it is my—"

"Essea has gone into the world to spread the word of the Great God," the Teacher said. "That is no tragedy. It is a very great grace." He lifted his eyes beyond Flora to Jeshiel, the high priest, who was approaching on foot.

"Your honor," the Teacher said.

Jeshiel inclined his head. "Our friend."

An old man stepped forward from the line of pilgrims. He was a small, wizened man with heavy brows and wise eyes full of hope and full of grief. "Naam!" Rechab cried out. "Oh, Alack!"

The old shepherd clutched his staff and bowed his head low to Flora Laurentii as Rechab rushed to his side. "My lady," he said. "I hoped you could help me. At the Gathering we dedicate our firstborn sons. But my son is missing."

"I know where he is," Flora said. "We will restore him to you at once."

⎯⎯➤◆◄⎯⎯

Alack had been lowered into the pit without ceremony and without friend. On the orders of Izevel and Beniah, he'd been abandoned there by the palace guards. Now a great crowd gathered around the pit, an old well on the palace grounds near the temple walls. Flora, Beniah's family, Jeshiel and other priests, the Teacher and Aurelius. And Rechab, supporting Naam on one arm and Nadab on the other.

Naam trembled when they came within sight of the narrow, covered hole in the ground. Rechab patted his hand. "It's all right," she said. "He's had food, drink. He will be all right."

But she too shuddered at the awfulness of this place. Beneath the spires of the temple, it was as though the pit was a doorway to the netherworld where death and corruption reigned. Since her visit to its depths to be with Alack, the memory of its stench and its darkness had haunted her.

Callum gave the commands. His soldiers wrestled away the well cover and dropped a rope inside, shouting down.

There was no response.

Rechab tightened her hand around Naam's arm as the soldiers exchanged troubled glances. Further shouts still elicited no response, and they lit torches in an attempt to see into the depths. "Send me down!" Rechab heard herself shout. "I'll go after him!"

But no one listened. Callum was already giving orders for his men to descend. In a matter of minutes two soldiers had vaulted down. Rechab held her breath as stillness overtook the courtyard. She saw Flora casting a worried look her way, but neither knew what to say to each other.

In less than ten minutes the soldiers had climbed back up, this time with Alack. He hung limp, his arms tied around the shoulders of one of them while the other followed behind to make sure he didn't come loose and fall. Rechab's heart leapt into her throat as they laid him on the cobblestones. Naam staggered forward. Rechab wanted to rush to Alack, but she stayed by his father, helping him forward.

They both dropped to their knees beside Alack. A hand on Rechab's shoulder told her Flora was there with her.

 RACHEL STARR THOMSON

His face was pale from days without the sun, and his breathing was labored as though he were in distress. His eyes were open but unseeing. He was neither unconscious nor awake.

"What is this?" Naam whispered, reaching out to stroke his son's brow. Rechab took Alack's hand and willed him to grip hers, but he did not respond to her.

The Teacher knelt beside them, leaning on his staff. "The boy is in some kind of trance," he said. He seemed about to say more, but thought better of it.

"We will make him comfortable in the palace," Flora said, raising her voice enough that the words served as orders. "We will watch over him until he awakes."

If he awakes, Rechab thought. She blessed Flora for her kindness and her confidence and tried hard not to give way to fear. As they filed away from the pit, Alack being carried by Callum's soldiers, the Teacher drew near to her. "He battles for us," he whispered. "Such things have been known before. But I have never seen it."

"What can we do?" Rechab asked.

The Teacher looked grim. "Be faithful to hold the line ourselves," he said. "Fight our part, and pray for him as he fights his."

The Gathering began in the temple with the first of the dedication sacrifices: Naam the shepherd, dedicating his firstborn son. Alack lay in the palace, tended to by servants and by Flora herself. The queen regent refused to leave the boy's side, and she insisted that the Gathering begin without her presence.

"I am still a half-blood Hill Woman," she had told Jeshiel and others who protested. "I will not lead the People in honoring the Great God by ignoring his ancient laws."

"But Flora," Rechab said, "the Great God himself welcomed you there."

Flora had smiled. "He has welcomed me to his heart. That is enough for me. What is between him and the Holy People is sacred and should be treated as sacred. It is a wise saying: the heart of the Great God is jealous for his own. I only request one thing: that Jeshiel be certain to offer the king's last ram and pray that Beniah's sins be atoned for. I know his heart truly repented of his sins."

Rechab stood in the temple at Naam's side as the sacrifices began. She marveled at the beauty of the golden temple and the surreal sensation of being here, the place she had so feared and loathed, to worship the God whose eye she now knew was fixed on her. Outer and inner courts of the temple were full of worshipers, mostly the pilgrims who had come with Aurelius and the Teacher. Jeshiel and his newly consecrated priests led the ceremonies as they remembered being taught.

This place was the heart of the ancient faith, the temple where the Great God dwelt among his people and made them holy by the cleaning power of his presence. It was right that the Gathering should take place, that this newborn remnant of worshipers would come here. Yet the rest of the city looked on with a mix of fear, suspicion, and interest. With the shadow of invasion still hanging over their heads, many offered sacrifices to Kimash, Amon-Heth, and the heavenly bodies, begging for deliverance from any quarter possible. Some spoke out against the release of Alack or even called for the reascension of Izevel.

Callum, who like Flora chose to stay outside the temple walls, sent men to every quarter of the city to listen and return to him with news. His network was effective, and as he kept his finger on the city's pulse he passed on its beats to Flora and to Jeshiel. Flora listened with

 RACHEL STARR THOMSON

her eyes fixed on Alack, who stared up at the ceiling and sometimes moaned or twitched.

"It is not enough," she said when Callum finished reporting on a small group of Kimashians who were sacrificing near the temple gate, wailing and cutting themselves as they begged the dragon-headed god to arise and protect them. "What my brother and the others have done is right and good. I know the Great God smiles on the Gathering. But the rest of the city . . ."

She bowed her head, and Callum saw her shake it slightly as though someone was speaking in her ear. When she looked up at him again, her green eyes sparked with conviction.

"It is good to give medicine to a man who is sick, but you must also cut off the poison. Send out the word, Callum. The People must all be invited to join the Gathering. Whether they will or will not come must be their own choice. But the idolatry must be cut off. Every shrine is an open door to the evil that brings judgment on this city. The idols must be burned and the shrines destroyed."

"Flora . . ." Callum began. She shook her head, determined. "It must be so. If the worshipers of other gods will come and join the Gathering, they may stay. Otherwise they must leave the city under threat of punishment."

"Flora, a man in my position gives a lot of thought to legacy, to how he will be remembered," Callum said. "It is not fair, but if the judgment comes on this place after you have taken such a drastic action, you will always be remembered as the one who destroyed the Holy City. Generations will believe it was your actions that left the city without protection."

Flora nodded, but she turned her eyes to Alack again and let her hand rest on the shepherd boy's chest. "We are not without protection," she said. "The Great God fights for us through this boy and meets with his people in the Gathering. He will not abandon them, Callum. They are beloved. But we cannot let the adultery continue. The poison has to be cut off."

Callum nodded and left the room after executing a salute. He did not relish the orders Flora had commanded him to give. And yet, somehow, he knew that she was right.

The first shrine began to burn within an hour. Callum wasted no time informing his captains of their orders. "I want no more blood on our hands," he told his captains. "No unnecessary violence. You are to drive out those who will not cooperate, not kill them."

But even as he said it he knew the process would not be bloodless. Passions would run high. The worshipers of Kimash were especially volatile. He prayed the Great God would subdue the people before his army and hold them guiltless for what they had to do.

The invitation his men gave was clear. Four hours from Flora's command, every shrine and idol in the Holy City was burning, and beneath the smoke, the People filled the streets on their way to the temple.

———◆———

Aurelius felt the shift in temperature as the outer court of the temple began to fill with latecomers. He saw the glares and the suspicious, hesitant approach of many. He saw anger boiling in faces. But he also saw despair, curiosity, and in some, hope. In the very air of the temple was a growing sense of Presence and of fear: as though a reunion long overdue was about to take place, and no one knew exactly how the parties would respond to one another.

And suddenly, he knew he should not be there.

He turned to Marah. "I must leave," he said.

"What?"

"It is not my place to be here," he said. "The Great God is calling the People to deal with him face-to-face. I should have respected this place as my sister and Callum do. Forgive me."

She stared at him a moment before loosing his sleeve. "Very well," she said. "Go safely, my husband."

He nodded. The sense of Presence was growing. He almost fled the temple grounds, driven by fear. But this was not like any fear he had ever felt before. It was not crippling, not craven. It was clean. Right.

Holy.

Aurelius passed through the temple gate, looked back at the people crushing their way inside, and smiled.

"Master?" a tremulous voice beside him asked.

Aurelius turned and blinked. Shem was crouching, cowering, in the shadow of an alley. He was pale, his face raked with scratches. Had he done that to himself? His eyes were almost yellow with fear.

"Shem!" Aurelius said. Shem looked around frantically and waved for Aurelius to be quiet.

"Hush, hush," the boy said. He was shaking now, trembling so hard Aurelius thought he might come apart. "Please, don't say my name."

Aurelius ducked into the alley and took the boy by the shoulders. His shirt was soaked with sweat.

"Shem, what's wrong?" he asked quietly.

"I . . . I want . . ."

The boy broke down and began to sob. Aurelius shook him. "Shem, speak. Tell me. Pull yourself together."

Shem's voice was nearly inaudible. "I want to go to the Gathering," he said. "I want to go to the Great God."

Aurelius didn't understand. "Then go! You are only feet from the temple gate!"

Shem shook his head violently. "I have sinned. I have sinned. I . . ."

Aurelius reached out and laid a finger against the boy's cracked lips. "Shem, we have all sinned. This Gathering: it's different. It is not a gathering of the worthy or the faithful, if such celebrations ever were. It is the confession of an adulterous people that they want to come home."

Shem nodded, and Aurelius noted that the amulet of Amon-Heth was gone. The servant buried his face against Aurelius's chest, and Aurelius held him like a father. He didn't know what had happened. What sins Shem so violently regretted. But he was sure of two things. That Amon-Heth had betrayed the boy, and that the Great God would give him refuge.

"Go home," Aurelius whispered into his hair. "The temple gates are open. Go home."

━━━◆◆━━━

That night, two hundred idolaters fled the Holy City, cursing the names of Flora Laurentii and the Great God. With them went their idols, their incense, their books. Most headed toward the Southern Plains or the Hill Country. Others went to the smaller towns and villages where they were still certain to find a sympathetic ear.

Everyone else stayed.

Everyone else—ten thousand men, women, and children—packed into the temple and filled its courts.

 RACHEL STARR THOMSON

To a one, they felt something there they had never felt before. A Presence that pressed them to the ground with their faces in the sand, bowing low, trembling. Seeking. It emanated from the Holy Place and spread through the temple like a ceaseless wave.

They stayed that way all night. Esseans and priests wandered through the crowds, murmuring prayers and blessings, as the smoke of dedication sacrifices rose.

And at dawn, a man arrived. He stood in the Dawn Gate with the light of the sun behind him, silhouetting him against the new day. He and the stones he carried with him.

Kohan, priest of the Holy People, in full sight of his countrymen carried the covenant stones up the steps of the Holy Place and looked down over the inner court and the people gathered there. He knew others waited to carry his words to the further reaches of the outer courts. Many sat on the wall separating the courts, watching like birds perched high above.

As he looked out on them, many still bowed with their faces to the ground, and saw the anguish and the fear on their faces, mixed with the sense of awe and wonder at the Great God's presence, the prophet of the Sacred Land felt his heart move with something he had not felt in a long time:

Compassion.

These are my people, Kohan, said the voice he knew so well.

I know, he answered.

These are my beloved.

Yes.

Speak to them, Kol Chesed. Tell them that I love them with covenant love. Tell them that my faithfulness to them is higher than the heavens.

And so the man who had spent forty years as Kol Abaddon, Voice of Destruction, spoke out for the first time as the Voice of Grace.

"Behold the covenant stones," he called over the crowd. "The signs of your marriage to the Great God and the signs that he has come to renew his vows. Come to your God, Chosen City, Holy People. Come and be embraced, and your God will save you."

They came. Rich and poor, landowner and homeless, soldier and merchantman, they came. Surging up the seventy steps of the Holy Place to fall down before the curtain and be loved. A brightness emanating from inside began to settle on them like a mist.

Rushing ahead of the rest was a boy, his clothes torn and his face scratched. He fell before the covenant stones, kissed them, and wept.

CHAPTER 23

Kohan, Kol Abaddon, Kol Chesed. The prophet slept on a veranda overlooking the palace gardens. Flora had given him luxurious quarters, of course. But he was not comfortable sleeping inside.

In a dream, he stood on the edge of the veranda looking out. The scents of lilac and lavender washed over him like holy water. Then, through the shadows came the boy, Alack. He held out his hand.

"Come, my friend," Alack said. "There is something for us to see."

"Now? I am sleeping," Kohan said.

Alack laughed. "That has never concerned you before."

"I have not slept in twenty years. Bad manners to interrupt me now."

"I always suspected you didn't sleep," Alack said with a chuckle. But still he held out his hand. Kohan ran a hand through his tangled dream-beard and looked the boy over with a critical eye. "And where were you when I was calling the People back to the god, eh?"

"I was busy," Alack said. "We both had things to do, you and I." He turned and motioned for Kohan to follow him, impatient of waiting for him to take his hand.

Together they stepped into the air and climbed above the garden and then above the palace, flying over the wall of the city. The stars shone brilliantly above as the Sacred Land rushed by below them with every step they took.

Finally they stood on the cliffs that bordered the sea north of Kasarea. The stars over the water were supernaturally bright, telling their ancient story in light. Beneath them, covering the sea like a dark blanket, was a fleet of military ships stretching to the horizon. The Westlanders.

In the lights of heaven, Isha still rushed to the Dragon as she had done for hundreds of years. But even as they watched, the brightest star in the constellation, the Dragon's eye—Kimash's star—fell.

One by one, the Dragon's stars dimmed and winked out. Isha, the Beloved, grew brighter and brighter until her light washed over the sea and the waiting fleet and shone on something in the water: a dark, rounded, undulating shape.

The Serpent arced out of the water, rose to a great height, and fell, destroying ships with its body and tail as it slapped back down to the sea. Its sinking created a whirlpool, and as the prophets of the Sacred Land looked on, it sucked every last ship down with it.

"Well," Kohan said when the water had gone still again. "I suppose that was worth seeing."

Alack slapped him on the back. "I think it's time we both awake," he said.

<hr />

Alack blinked. The action was followed by what he thought was an inordinate uproar. A servant girl screamed, Flora leaped to her

   Rachel Starr Thomson

feet with both of Alack's hands in hers, and then there was Rechab, kissing his face.

He closed his eyes again and smiled. The uproar wasn't so bad after all.

"My son, my son," he heard a familiar voice say. Smiling up at Rechab and wishing he could steal a kiss without everyone looking on, Alack swung his legs over the side of the bed and sat up. His head immediately began to split, but it didn't matter. Naam was there in an instant, hands on both sides of his head, kissing his hair. He smelled like sheep.

Alack thought it was the best smell in the world.

Crowding around, beaming, were Flora, Aurelius and Marah, and Kol Abaddon. And one more—a man who was also beaming. Rechab's father, Nadab.

Alack tried to stutter out a greeting, but his tongue wouldn't work. Nadab fixed his eyes meaningfully on him and then looked pointedly at Rechab with a nod.

"I . . ." Alack managed to get out. Rechab grabbed his hand and sat down beside him, laying her head on his shoulder like the little girl he had always loved.

"Where were you, my son?" Naam asked.

Alack opened his mouth to say, "I was battling the Dragon." But it already seemed to him that he couldn't remember what had happened in the pit. That he had stepped into another life, and that one was quickly fading into the long-forgotten past. He wasn't sure where he had been or what he had done. Only that he was home now.

Back from the dead, and home with the ones he loved. The prophet of the Great God would live after all. And get married, and be happy, and save his people.

So he didn't answer. He just looked around the room at the Great God's unlikely collection of mouthpieces, his beloved outcasts and prodigals, and grinned.

EPILOGUE

Years later, the royals and the priests of the Holy City learned that Sabrus Caelius had indeed sent his fleet against the Sacred Land. The first of the ships had even made the harbor in Kasarea. But before the leaders of the enterprise could make landfall, messengers from home overtook them and commanded them to return to the Westland. Sabrus's quickly won empire had already begun to fracture in rebellion, and a significant uprising among the barbarians required him to call all his troops to a front far to the west. The Sword of Heaven remained a scourge to his neighbors all his life and built a powerful and wealthy empire, but it would be left to his successors to come against the Sacred Land again.

The revival that began with the Gathering lasted two generations. Its effects held on even longer, especially among the priests of the Great God, who joined with the pilgrims of Essea to recover the lost scrolls and teach the law again.

The troublers of the Sacred Land did not rise again for many years. After Alack's sudden awakening, both Izevel and Amon the Trader were found dead in the dungeon. Who had killed them, no one knew. Some suspected they had turned on each other. Others believed they had been slain by the very spirits they served.

Flora reigned ten years before turning the throne over to Beniah's oldest son. Known for a time as "the Lucky," she was remembered forever as the Loved.

The End

 RACHEL STARR THOMSON

Rachel would love to hear from you!

You can visit her and interact online:
Web: **www.rachelstarrthomson.com**
Facebook: **www.facebook.com/RachelStarrThomsonWriter**
Twitter: **@writerstarr**

THE SEVENTH WORLD TRILOGY

Worlds Unseen   Burning Light   Coming Day

For five hundred years the Seventh World has been ruled by a tyrannical empire—and the mysterious Order of the Spider that hides in its shadow. History and truth are deliberately buried, the beauty and treachery of the past remembered only by wandering Gypsies, persecuted scholars, and a few unusual seekers. But the past matters, as Maggie Sheffield soon finds out. It matters because its forces will soon return and claim lordship over her world, for good or evil.

The Seventh World Trilogy is an epic fantasy, beautiful, terrifying, pointing to the realities just beyond the world we see.

"An excellent read, solidly recommended for fantasy readers."

– Midwest Book Review

"A wonderfully realistic fantasy world. Recommended."

– Jill Williamson, Christy-Award-Winning Author
of *By Darkness Hid*

"Epic, beautiful, well-written fantasy that sings of Christian truth."

– Rael, reader

Available everywhere online or special order from your local bookstore.

THE ONENESS CYCLE

Exile   Hive   Attack   Renegade   Rise

*The supernatural entity called the Oneness holds the world together.
What happens if it falls apart?*

In a world where the Oneness exists, nothing looks the same. Dead men walk. Demons prowl the air. Old friends peel back their mundane masks and prove as supernatural as angels. But after centuries of battling demons and the corrupting powers of the world, the Oneness is under a new threat—its greatest threat. Because this time, the threat comes from within.

Fast-paced contemporary fantasy.

*"Plot twists and lots of edge-of-your-seat action,
I had a hard time putting it down!"*
—Alexis

"Finally! The kind of fiction I've been waiting for my whole life!"
—Mercy Hope, FaithTalks.com

"I sped through this short, fast-paced novel, pleased by the well-drawn characters and the surprising plot. Thomson has done a great job of portraying difficult emotional journeys . . . Read it!"
—Phyllis Wheeler, The Christian Fantasy Review

Available everywhere online or special order from your local bookstore.

TAERITH

When he rescues a young woman named Lilia from bandits, Taerith Romany is caught in a web of loyalties: Lilia is the future queen of a spoiled king, and though Taerith is not allowed to love her, neither he can bring himself to leave her without a friend. Their lives soon intertwine with the fiercely proud slave girl, Mirian, whose tragic past and wild beauty make her the target of the king's unscrupulous brother.

The king's rule is only a knife's edge from slipping—and when it does, all three will be put to the ultimate test. In a land of fog and fens, unicorns and wild men, Taerith stands at the crossroads of good and evil, where men are vanquished by their own obsessions or saved by faith in higher things.

"Devastatingly beautiful . . . I am amazed at every chapter how deeply you've caused us to care for these characters."
—Gabi

"Deeply satisfying." —Kapezia

"Rachel Starr Thomson is an artist, and every chapter of Taerith is like a painting . . . beautiful."
—Brittany Simmons

Available everywhere online or special order from your local bookstore.

ANGEL IN THE WOODS

Hawk is a would-be hero in search of a giant to kill or a maiden to save. The trouble is, when he finds them, there are forty-some maidens—and they call their giant "the Angel." Before he knows what's happening, Hawk is swept into the heart of a patchwork family and all of its mysteries, carried away by their camaraderie—and falling quickly in love.

But the outside world cannot be kept at bay forever. Suspecting the Giant of hiding a treasure, the wealthy and influential Widow Brawnlyn sets out to tear the family apart and bring the Giant to destruction any way she can. And her two principle weapons are Hawk—and the truth.

Caught between the terrible truths he discovers about the family's past and the unalterable fact that he has come to love them, Hawk must face his fears and overcome his flaws if he is to rescue the Angel in the woods.

"A beautiful tale of finding oneself, honor and heroism; a story I will not soon forget." — Szoch

"The more I think about it, the more truth and beauty I find in the story." —H. A. Titus

Available everywhere online or special order from your local bookstore.

REAP THE WHIRLWIND

Beren is a city in constant unrest: ruled by a ruthless upper class and harried by a band of rebels who want change. Its one certainty is that the two sides do not, and will not, meet.

But children know little of sides or politics, and Anna and Kyara—a princess and a peasant girl—let their chance meeting grow into a deep friendship. Until the day Kyara's family is slaughtered by Anna's people, and the friendship comes to an abrupt end.

Years later, Kyara is a rebel—bitter, hard, and violent. Anna's efforts to fight the political system she belongs to avail little. Neither is a child anymore—but neither has ever forgotten the power of their long-ago friendship. When a secret plot brings the rebellion to a fiery head, both young women know it is too late to save the land they love.

But is it too late to save each other?

Available everywhere online.

LADY MOON

When Celine meets Tomas, they are in a cavern on the moon where she has been languishing for thirty days after being banished by her evil uncle for throwing a scrub brush at his head. Tomas is a charming and eccentric Immortal, hanging out on the moon because he's procrastinating his destiny—meeting, and defeating, Celine's uncle.

A pair of magic rings send them back to earth, where Celine insists on returning home and is promptly thrown into the dungeon. Her uncle, Ignus Umbria, is up to no good, and his latest caper threatens to devour the whole countryside. He doesn't want Celine getting in the way. More than that, he wants to force Tomas into a confrontation—and Tomas, who has fallen in love with Celine, cannot procrastinate any longer.

Lady Moon is a fast-paced, humorous adventure in a world populated by mad magicians, walking rosebushes, thieving scullery maids, and other improbable things. And of course, the most improbable—and magical—thing of all: true love.

"Celine's sarcastic 'languishing' immediately put me in mind of Patricia C. Wrede's Dealing with Dragons series—a fairy tale that gently makes fun of the usual fairy tale tropes. And once again, Rachel Starr Thomson doesn't disappoint."
— H. A. Titus

"Funny and quirky fantasy."

Available everywhere online.

THE PROPHET TRILOGY

Abaddon's Eve   Comes the Dragon   Beloved

A prophet and his apprentice.
A runaway and a wealthy widow marked as an outcast.

They alone can see the terrible judgment
marching on their land.

But can they do anything to stop it?

The Prophet Trilogy is a fantasy set in
a near-historical world of deserts, temples,
and spiritual forces that vie
for the hearts of men.

Available everywhere online or special order from your local bookstore.

Short Fiction by Rachel Starr Thomson

BUTTERFLIES DANCING

FALLEN STAR

OF MEN AND BONES

OGRES IS

JOURNEY

MAGDALENE

THE CITY CAME CREEPING

WAYFARER'S DREAM

WAR WITH THE MUSE

SHIELDS OF THE EARTH

And more!

*Available as downloads for
Kindle, Kobo, Nook, iPad, and more!*